Bethlehem: The War of Jesus Paul's Plan for Peace

Ray Shortell

Copyright © 2018 Ray Shortell

All rights reserved.

ISBN: 978-0692081075
ISBN-13: 978-0692081070

DEDICATION

To two millennia of proscribed ignorance (the Dark Ages)
And the widows of Antioch whose husbands preached Paul's gospel in Jerusalem.
And Grandpa, forever memorialized as "some of the men" aboard the USS Cowpens:
Grandpa tied down bombs rolling about the deck of his aircraft carrier during a hurricane in WWII.
And similarly "some from Jacob (James)" at Antioch who showed that all is not as it seems.

…and Longinus the soldier pierced his side with a spear…And the priests and Levites said to one another: "If Jesus is remembered after fifty years, he will reign forever and create for himself a new people."…
Gospel of Nicodemus Chapter 16
Pg 361, 373-374 The Other Bible, Willis Barnstone 1984

…The Scribe - How different the one who devotes himself to the study of the law of the Most High! He seeks out the wisdom of all the ancients, and is concerned with prophesies; he preserves the sayings of the famous and penetrates the subtleties of parables; he seeks out the hidden meanings of proverbs and is at home with the obscurities of parables (Sirach 38:34 – 39:3).
New Revised Standard Catholic Edition 1989, 1993
BibleGateway.com

…Now that scripture which is laid up in the temple… Note here that the small book of the principal laws of Moses is ever said to be laid up in the holy house itself; But the larger Pentateuch, as here, somewhere in the limits of the temple and its courts only.
3.2.1 Antiquities of the Jews, Josephus
Pg 95 Josephus, the Complete Works translated by William Whiston A.M. 1998

Many of them also which used curious arts brought their books together, and burned them before all men: and they counted the price of them and found it fifty thousand pieces of silver. So mightily grew the word of G-d and prevailed.
Acts 19:19-2

COVER

Bethlehem means "the house of bread", although practically desert. Bread is life in the desert, especially for the Essenes during the famine. Essenes were pledged to poverty for the purpose of being untaxable. Acts' 23:8 Sadducees teach no resurrection (sad-you-see), while from Bethlehem, Joseph, the father of Jesus, teaches the Egyptian theology of eternal life and Hall of Judgement, signified by the Star of Bethlehem, the immovable compass of the Northern Star, pointed out by the pyramids of Egypt and Jerusalem, the graves of the Essenes, and Daniel's fingers which write upon the wall "you have been weighed and found wanting". My three book covers therefore depict three visions of heaven, the Roman Catholic, the Roman Elysian fields and the Pyramids, for the Jews only had a "record" of a good life (2 Sam 23:8-39) in my opinion misinterpreted in Revelations as "the Book of Life".

The War of Jesus was more than metaphor. Jerusalem means "the city of peace" although its founder, King David, was a warrior. Melchizedek was also the king of Salem after whom David styled Psalm 110, declaring a non-Levitical priesthood forever, for himself and his children, eating the shewbread, retrieving the ark, wearing the ephod and sacrificing. After the descent of the Spirit, paralleling Roman adult adoption (i.e. Josephus, the author), our gospels claim both Jesus' descent from David and kingship of Jerusalem: Jesus tells the story of the nobleman going away [to Rome] to receive his kingdom before returning to deal with those who would not submit (Lk 19:12-28). Jesus then triumphantly enters into Jerusalem over palms strewn in his path (37 Gaius, Philo), while on a donkey and the foal of a donkey (per a probably misinterpreted Zech 9:9), crowned with thorns, and crucified with a sign noting "The King of the Jews", gaining at least Stoic immortality (Seneca, On Tranquility of Mind). Rome then killed everyone. A hundred thousand were taken as slaves to build the canal at Corinth and twenty thousand to build the coliseum at Rome. Theologians gloated over the genocide.

Paul's Plan for Peace was probably for his Herodian brood of snakes, but the main battle was between Rome and Parthia who had previously battled back and forth over Armenia while Rome simultaneously fought England and Germany (Tacitus). After Gaius Cassius Longinus took over Antioch, Paul fled Antioch and several chapters of Tacitus were 'lost', when presumably the Cassians, who hate foreigners (like Cleopatra), made Israeli taxation intolerable. Paul struggled to keep the peace by allowing Romans (Greeks) into the temple, however in my opinion Parthia managed to secretly supply the Sadducees to encourage a proxy war. Vespasian was Rome's general, who departed upon Caesar's death to Antioch and Alexandria gathering legions for his return to Rome to be named Caesar. Meanwhile other generals were busily sacrificing legions in Italy fighting with each other. Afterwards Vespasian Caesar had a vested interest in telling the greatness of his conquests, justifying the destruction of Israel, supplanting zealot Sadducean Judaism, and silencing Parthia.

BETHLEHEM: THE WAR OF JESUS
PAUL'S PLAN FOR PEACE
CHAPTER #---CITY---YEAR---TITLE

Prelude

Paul Rejected By Jerusalem

1. Beit Horon 40 CE The Language of Rome
2. Damascus 40 CE The City of Blood
3. Gadara 42 CE Highway to Herod
4. Jerusalem 42 CE The City of Peace
5. Jerusalem 42 CE Jacob (James) Tumbles
6. Caesarea 42 CE The Samaritan Woman
7. Caesarea 42 CE Banished from Israel
8. Bethlehem 42 CE The House of Bread

Paul Rejected by Antioch

9. Antioch 42 CE Paul's Roman Amphitheaters
10. Adiabene 43-48 CE Queen Helen
11. Jerusalem 45 CE Queen Helen's Israel
12. Antioch 46 CE Cephas' (Peter's) Arrival
13. Jerusalem 48 CE The Four Evangelists
14. Caesarea 48 CE Banished Again
15. Philippi 48 CE Escape from Caesarea
16. Philippi 48 CE The Philippi of Mark Anthony

Paul's Leadership in Corinth

17. Corinth 50 CE Castaway
18. Corinth 50-58 CE The Politics of Rome
19. Corinth 58 CE The Letter of Jacob
20. Tarsus 58 CE I Cor 13 Astrology
21. Tarsus 58 The Unknown G-d

22 Antioch 58 CE Widow's Revenge

23 Jerusalem 58 CE The Book of Hebrews

Paul's Journey to Rome

24 Caesarea 58 CE Paul the Writer

25 Rome 60 CE The Egyptian

26 Rome 62 CE Jacob's Kiss of Death

27 Caesarea 62 CE Herod's Gospel of Matthew

28 Rome 63 CE The Temple Wall Affair

29 Rome 58 CE Rome Burns

30 Rome 65 CE Deaths of Paul, Seneca & Poppea

31 Galilee 66 CE The Surrender of General Josephus

32 Jerusalem 70 CE Vespasian Burns Jerusalem

33 Rome 125 CE The War is Finished

33 Epilogue: America 2017

Appendix: Rome 90 CE Editing the Talmud

Appendix: Homosexuality; Abortion; Women Preaching; Married Priests

Appendix: Snakes and Tongues

Afterword: Crucifixion 40 CE

Afterword: Herodian Paul, Roman Building Inspector; Herod writes Matthew

Afterword: Paul's Infirmity

Afterword: The Gospel of Thomas

Thesis

Index of Metaphors

Sources

Bibliography

About the Author

ACKNOWLEDGMENTS

Robert H Eisenman for releasing and interpreting the Dead Sea Scrolls.
Pierre Krijbolder for setting my mind free to work in its natural habitat, metaphor.
The widows of Antioch, graced by the presence of all the brothers of Jesus who could walk.
Mom who said: Quit studying the Bible and go to church!
Dad who said: Whatever you do, think.
Paul Jude for listening to my stories.
My men who like to tell me: Don't make anything up.

PRELUDE

When Paul was first exiled by Herod to Syrian Antioch where Christians were first so named per Acts, both Caesar and Antioch's governor were sympathetic Claudians of the family of Mark Anthony (Marcus Antonius). These attempted to hide their familial associations due to the Cassians (Mark Anthony killed Cassius at Philippi). In 48 Gaius Cassius Longinus became Antioch's governor and Paul fled to Corinth/Rome like the traitorous Jewish historian Josephus. Under the patronage of Caesar's secretary, both Paul and Josephus authored pro-Roman books while perceived by Jews as unethical traitorous lying wind-bags, spiritually empty (1), old wine-skins (sacrificed foreskins or saggy grizzled scrotums) (2), leprous or childless and full of the wrath of G-d like cups of blood or wine (the blood of grapes)(3).

Paul was probably Herodian (4). Although half-breed Maccabean with every right to rule Israel and serve as High Priest as viewed by Rome, Paul's family was hated by temple zealots (Sadducees), due to Herod's and Mark Anthony's mutual support in quelling temple uprisings and killing the first Sanhedrin long ago in 63 BCE. In 44 BCE Brutus and Cassius fled Rome after assassinating Caesar, but Cassius' family remained very much in power in Rome. By 31 BCE Mark Anthony traitorously fought the battle of Actium off Greece against Rome with Herod's support and Cleopatra's Egyptian navy. Mark Anthony lost and killed himself in Syria or Egypt as did his Egyptian ruling Greek/Macedonian lover, Cleopatra (a descendant from Alexander the Great). In times of peace Cleopatra with her son by Caesar would supply Rome with crops from the fertile Nile valley South of Israel while wheedling additional territory from Mark Anthony who governed from Syria North of Israel. After their defeat Herod declared his loyalty to Rome changing allegiances to the family of Caesar and naming a son Agrippa after Caesar's general.

As a Herodian, Paul wanted everyone to have access to the temple: Paul's hermeneutic (self-referencing theology)(5) is catholic (universal or cosmopolitan) having the support of Rome. Paul's eschatology (end of time) supports introducing everyone into non-circumcising Judaism realizing the Bible's promises of Abraham being a blessing to everyone with all hearts knowing our creator. Paul's apocalypse (unveiling) reveals only the present, opening the temple to all and giving neither Jew nor Roman the right of glorying at the expense of unity. Paul struggles to prevent a fateful war with Rome. Meanwhile in Jerusalem the Essene (pacifist) vow of poverty prevents Roman taxation, but many starve during the 46-48 famine. Sadducees (zealots) are on the verge of revolt when Herod selects the High Priest. Paul complains that no one from the East wants to listen to his spirituality (2 Tim 1:15), while the Dead Sea Scrolls refer to Paul as "Ruach", the Jewish word for "wind/spirit" (a spiritually wind-blown man full of hot air who talks too much).

Ray Shortell

1 BEIT HORON 40 CE THE LANGUAGE OF ROME
This is what the imposition of Roman control really meant – destruction.
p50 James, the Brother of Jesus, Robert Eisenman 1997

A Roman centurion leads eighty soldiers, bidden by Saul (Paul), walking up a dusty road. A road sign, merely an arrow, points up into the hills beyond a priest sitting in a tent making pottery. The centurion, saddled on his horse with no stirrups, asks the priest, "is this the way to Jerusalem?" The priest, sitting in the pass to Jerusalem at the foot of the mountain of Samaria, is mystified at the soldier's Greek and responds in Hebrew, "What language is this?"

The language of the Bible, the language of Rome, is metaphor, as here where soldier meets priest and West meets East. The first battle of the War of the Jews will be fought at this pass in 66. These soldiers, bidden by Saul to the crucifixion, trample holy ground in Samaria, soon to be explained as the remnants of the Northern Kingdom, the ten lost tribes of Israel with their own version of the books of Moses. The Bible fails to explain the origins of Samaritans or set the context of Rome's sweeping conquests.

Rome ruled the Mediterranean. In 483 BCE the "Three Hundred" of Greek Sparta faced the Media-Persian Empire bringing the dawn of Western civilization per our earliest historian, Herodotus. A hundred years later Greek Athenians were philosophizing that their yoke was not unbearable: *We are only doing to you what you would do to us were you in our position* (1). By 31 BCE Cleopatra, the Greek Macedonian descendant of Alexander the Great's general, and ruler of Egypt, flees the battle of Actium, Sampson and Delilahing Mark Anthony (Marcus Antonius) as metaphorically canonized in Shakespeare's play, Romeo and Juliette (2).

Historians and authors are always part of Rome's plan for peace: In the 100s BCE Polybius was captured from Corinth and along with a thousand Corinthian Greeks imprisoned at Rome. Polybius was released to accompany the Roman army documenting its exploits in Spain. After twenty years the remaining three hundred from Corinth were repatriated. These revolted with Corinth again. Rome razed Corinth installing Polybius as governor who spent his remaining years authoring from Corinth on the superiority of the Roman constitution.

Rome overwrote the history of Carthage, Rome and Jerusalem seeking to erase their memory. Polybius's history of Rome includes the destruction of Carthage circa 150 BCE: Carthage was a North African colony of Phoenecia (Lebanon). Rome herself claimed non-Italian origins, the mythological Greek twins Remus and Romulus (Rome… ulous) suckled by a she-wolf. Hannibal of Carthage marched elephants through Spain and across the Alps to destroy Rome, but failed: Carthage failed to resupply the mercenary, and Rome recovered, sailed across the Mediterranean, and razed Carthage literally sowing its fields in salt, plowing it into the earth and removing Carthage as a threat to future generations, much as Biblical authors discuss Christianity supplanting Judaism with: You are the salt of the earth (Mt 5:13, Jgs 9:13) (3); the new Jerusalem (Rev 3:12, 21:2).

Taking the lessons of Corinth and Carthage, Rome would confiscate or burn the library at Alexandria and Jerusalem (4), theologically inflicting the same on Israel or more precisely abbreviated, the Jews, the Northern Kingdom having departed in 722 BCE due to Judah's proclivity to human slavery (5). Rome would destroy Jerusalem, the city of peace founded by nomads on mountains high in the middle of the known world (Europe, Africa & Asia). The temple, previously destroyed by Babylon for seventy years, had been rebuilt in 525 BCE when Babylon had hoped to use repatriated Jews as a rearguard while invading the rich Egyptian Nile valley, the success of which was miserably misprophesied by both Ezekiel from Babylon and Jeremiah from Israel (6).

2 DAMASCUS 40 CE THE CITY OF BLOOD

Five Roman horsemen ride through the desert night along the Jordan valley through the Arabian highway from Jerusalem to Damascus far beyond the reach of Roman ships on the Mediterranean. Their leader, Paul, is blind. The five horsemen approach the gates of Damascus where two are granted entrance as emissaries of Caesar, Herod and the High Priest. In the morning Paul opens his scroll before the king discussing "innovation" and those most likely to cause revolution with a request to bring Aretas' daughter, Phaesalis, back to her ex-husband, King Herod. Ananias, Aretas' advisor, offers Paul the house of Judas on the street named Straight while the matter is considered (Ananias is family of the twenty-four courses of temple priests).

King Aretas, the Arabian King, is not a favorite of Caesar, yet Rome's administrator for the Decapolis, ten cities beyond Galilee. Aretas' capital, Damascus, is caught between two warring powers, Rome and Parthia (Iran, Iraq and Afghanistan), between Roman Antioch and Parthian Babylon*. Aretas' Decapolis runs the Jordan valley from Damascus to Gadara, through the Arabian desert east of the Sea of Galilee (the Sea of Tiberias) and east of the Dead Sea (the Sea called Asphalitis for its floating chunks of bitumen - medicinal asphalt or hardened oil(1)) – where John the Baptist denounced "this generation of vipers" (Lk 3:7). Incidentally the Herods were Edomite, closely related to Jews, and by my reading of their marriage practices, eligible to rule if married to a Maccabean like Herodias (Deu 17:15).

Phaesalis, princess of Arabia, King Aretas' daughter, Herod's ex-wife, stands to say, "His name is Saul (Paul). He has come here seeking my life, just as Herod's wife, Herodias, threatened by having John the Baptist beheaded in the warm springs of the fortress Machaerus on the Dead Sea where I fled to escape. Saul is the half-nephew of my ex-husband Herod, that **snake** who married his half-sister, Herodias, the richest woman in Israel, whose father stole his riches from king David's tomb. Herods are not true Jews! They are an incestuous **brood of snakes** whose gold-digging divorcees' pop up like **the heads of intertwined snakes from a pit**. Herod the Terrible fathered children by many Jewish wives, his sons intermarrying their half-brother's daughters. After Herodias' ex-husband Philip-Herod joined us in defeating Herod, Caesar's friend, Agrippa-Herod, **another snake**, replaced our friend Philip in Galilee. The Pharisees, those Roman accommodators, even shouted three times `You are our brother!'"

Two years later Paul, enlightened on Straight street by finding the backcountry a cauldron of rebellion, preaches. "I have seen the light of the world!" Ananias, advisor to King Areatas and temple zealot from Jerusalem, shouts Paul down. "Our Messiah is not crucified!" Judas, Paul's "host" whose hospitality must not be refused, betrays Paul, yelling. "King Aretas will be informed that revolution foments at our city gates!" A Roman soldier steps forward to protect Paul and Annanias cries out. Damascene city guards kill the Roman soldier and ask Paul if he is Saul, the brother of Herod. Paul responds. "My name is Paul. Rome would not be pleased with such hospitality." Paul hobbles bow-leggedly up into the city wall to plan his escape from the Jews of Areatas.

As Paul prepares to ride, it is night again and full moon. The surrounding hillsides are the desert of Arabia. Damascus stands in the hills with its high walls ready for battle, but only a night watchman standing guard at the gate. Two Roman soldiers sit on three horses waiting a short distance away as a candle appears in a window after which Paul is lowered to the ground by a red rope tied to a basket. Paul steps out of the basket, is picked up by the horsemen and rides away swiftly cursing: "Damn! Damn! Damn! Damn! Damn!"

/ Paul's Damascus enlightenment is of Sadducean xenophobia vs Roman and Parthian military science. Blood in Hebrew is "Damn". In Israel cups ("chos") are made by Rechabites, priests who call themselves "The Poor", architecting their lives so as to only have enough to live with nothing remaining to be taxed by Rome. Their sparse lives leave time for study and the craftsmen, carpenters, smiths or potters (like Joseph the father of Jesus), are revered as teachers, fostering or fathering knowledge, metaphorically referred to as their "babies" (as in the soon to be discussed murdered babies of Bethlehem). Wrath in ancient Hebrew, which has no vowels, is "chas". Damascus, the cup of wrath and blood, stands against foreigners. To keep this Parthian supply-line secret, all of Damascus seeks Paul's life, all except one lone prostitute named "Rahab" who lives in the wall of the city (Joshua 2:1,3, 6:1).

*Enemies of Rome/Herod include the "fugitives" of Philip Herod of Galilee, Aretas of Arabia (18.5.1 Antiquities Josephus), Abgarus of Edessa (3), Queen Helen of Adiabene and the Parthians of Persia in league with Rechabites (4), instigating rebellion in Jerusalem against Herod's High Priest (14.2.1 Antiquities, Josephus). Caesar's obsequious friend, Herod Agrippa, replaces Philip (10.6.18 Antiquities Josephus), and then Herod after complaining of Herod's stockpiling of armor for 70,000 (7.2.18 Antiquities Josephus) - probably made by Rechabites.

3 GADARA 42 CE HIGHWAY TO HEROD

After leaving Damascus the three horsemen travel the Jordan Valley desert backcountry to Jerusalem, taking the inland route around the Sea of Galilee, the route taken by Abraham from Ur of Chaldees (Iraq) through Gamala and Gadara. 'G' in Hebrew means bridge or camel, linking two places like heaven and earth, with Jewish names like lake Gesseneret, denoting the trade-route, the route which Rome attempts to control by building Caesarea Philippi (loves horses), the route through which Parthia (Iran, Iraq & Afghanistan) supplies Jewish rebels. Paul's journey will lead to safety at Caesarea on the Mediterranean, Herod's showcase for Rome with a Roman port, Olympic Arena, Icons and the Architecture Paul learned in Rome, but Paul will first complete his journey down the Jordan valley from Damascus through Gadara to Jerusalem before travelling back up the coast to Caesarea.

The area of Gadara includes Tarichaea, Magdala and Gesenera. Rome has spent much building Gadara's aqueduct to pasture horses on green fields and therefore shows no mercy when war starts in 66, killing Gadarenes after negotiating their surrender or selling them into slavery digging the canal of Corinth (Greece) (Ant 10.10). Sadly, by my reading, Biblical authors have Jesus in the 30s referencing this much later 60s massacre of Tarichaea through its graveyard, declaring, "Let the dead bury their dead (Mt 8:22, Lk 9:60)." The dead are left in tombs for a year by my reading in **purgatory** while flesh rots away where the worm never dies and children mourn, after which the **purified** and whitened bones are given a second burial, a second death (Lk 12:5, Rev 20), and moved to an ossuary, a stone box (1). Jesus implies this **year-long** worship of the dead sacrilegious, his authors metaphorically denouncing the practice by finding graveyard demoniacs (Mt 8:28) and a herd of two thousand swine (Mk 5:13).

Since leaving two years ago from the death of Jesus, Paul desires a stop in his family's ancient home, Jerusalem, seeking his half-uncle, Herod. After a night's sleep in Gadara Paul resumes his journey down the river Jordan from the Sea of Galilee (700 feet below sea level) to the Dead Sea near Jerusalem (1400 feet below sea level). By early afternoon Paul is starting to feel at home in Israel where the Arabian King Aretas of Damascus can no longer reach. Paul passes from Ephraim through Gad and into Reuben on the Dead Sea, the two and a half-tribes East of Jordan no longer extant even as Paul passes. In 701 BCE the Assyrians wiped out every tribe outside of the Southern Kingdom leaving only Judah with remnants of Simeon, Benjamin and Levi, hence Israelites now being called "Jews" (Judah). Afterwards in 587 BCE Judah was pressed into slavery in Babylon and the temple destroyed. Paul claims descent from Benjamin, possibly since his namesake, Saul, the first king of Israel, known as a large man like Paul, came from this tribe or possibly because Jews living outside of Israel, the diaspora, are derisively referred to as Benjamites, as is Paul for having persecuted the church (Gal 1:13).

Finally the three horsemen reach the Dead Sea. John the Baptist preached here on the Jordan by the Dead Sea, but was killed by Herod five years ago. The three horsemen cross the river and continue their journey up into the mountains of Jerusalem from the lowest place on earth.

Again an explanation is in order regarding the Crucifixion in 40: Pontius Pilate ruled 26/27-36/37. Per Josephus John the Baptist was beheaded by Herod in 37, after which Jesus began his ministry, picking up Philip and Nathaniel, John's disciples. To me Jesus was crucified three years later in 40; Paul was too active to have lain dormant after the crucifixion for ten years (30–40). And the death of Jacob (James) in 62, subsequent tax revolt in 66 (2) and fall of the temple in 70 would have been too far in the future to have been linked to a crucifixion date of 33 (3-5). In my opinion King Herod 36/37 – 41 crucified Jesus which was backdated to Pontius Pilate due to Herod Agrippa Galilee 36-44, Caesarea/Jerusalem 41-44, writing or editing the gospels in Rome in the 90's (6). Paul's earliest extra-biblically documentable activity will be his return from Antioch to Jerusalem for the famine 46-48 (Afterword).

On this last leg of the journey with Roman horsemen, Paul thinks about Jerusalem and the people there currently embroiled in discussion on how to live as brothers under a king who is not considered a brother (Deu 17:15). Romans consider the whole lot Jewdom from Herod down (7). Josephus will later regularly rail against slaves or innovators deposing kings. The Essenes, being the most numerous sect, lead this discussion, ostensibly per Josephus living in peace in linen garments, prizing a cold bath in the morning, owning nothing but a single pair of sandals and with diets either vegetarian or of food which grows of itself in the wilderness. These may be the people who later swear to eat nothing until killing Paul, meaning swearing off merely meat and wine (Acts 23:14) (8), but that will be for a later chapter as will be Paul's entrance into the beauty of Jerusalem with much debate upon Jerusalem's Messiah and prophesied rulership of the world (Ps 72:11).

4 JERUSALEM 42 CE THE CITY OF PEACE

After three days ride along the Jordan from Gadara to the Dead Sea, home to the late John the Baptist, Paul and his companions turn West to Jerusalem. The horsemen are tired and the road leads from the lowest point on earth to the city on a hill (Gospel of Thomas 32, Mt 5:14), the city of peace, in Hebrew, "Jerusalem", resting on its mountain. Paul approaches from the wilderness having left Jerusalem two years earlier after the crucifixion of Jesus while remembering the three groups of people with whom he will have to contend: Sadducees, mostly in charge of the temple except for the Herodian appointed High Priests; Pharisees, Roman accommodators, endlessly arguing fine points of the law (straining at gnats yet swallowing the camel of Roman rule Mt 23:24); and Essenes, like James, dedicated to peaceful resistance.

Jesus had been crucified two years earlier in 40, beginning his three year ministry around the age of thirty after which Paul had ridden to Damascus. The standard date given for the birth of Jesus is 0, but according to Luke, Jesus was born during the census of Quirinius of Syria which happened 6-7 CE. Jesus was born in 7, started his ministry around the age of thirty in 37 after the death of John the Baptist, took John's followers including Philip and Nathanael (Jn 1, 3:30), and was crucified three years later at the age of thirty-three in 40 under Herod, not under Pontius Pilate. Why was Herod not implicated? Herods provided Biblical documentation and reviewed the work (1, Afterword, Ch 27 The Gospel of Matthew).

As Paul and his companions ride through the desert from the Dead Sea, the lowest place on earth into the mountains of Jerusalem, Paul's thoughts turn to the Jerusalem he had left. Paul left after the crucifixion and a scuffle with Jacob (James), a celibate Essene vegetarian. Paul returns through the eastern gate, the gate through which Messiah is prophesied to enter. The eastern desert is also the lesser populated side although Essenes have set up camps along the way. Essenes live communally, prizing only a linen robe and sandals, carrying no money and vegetarian or even eating just wild plants (untaxable).

And then there are Sadducees (phonetically Zadok – Righteous), temple centered zealots, from whom Rome and Herod have much to fear. These are the Jews, who like Cephas (Peter) when told to carry a sword, would pull them from beneath robes explaining, "Here are two" (Lk 22:38). Currently Sadducees debate whether to raise the walls of the temple to hide the daily sacrifice from Herod's prying eyes while wondering how to defend the temple from the impending Roman invasion.

Herod, being a foreigner attempting to hold his kingship over Jerusalem (2), prefers Pharisaic families from synagogues in cities other than Jerusalem. Pharisees discuss the law endlessly while drawing power away from the temple. Pharisees do their best to live in peace with Rome and are known as "accommodators" to Roman plans for domination. Pharisees maintain a small representation of the temple or ark of the covenant in synagogues as do Catholic churches (3).

The current group in power, the High Priest and his supporters, have the support of King Herod and whatever remains of his Roman soldiers. Herod's fortress is on the mountain across the Kidron valley from the temple where Herod dines looking down on the daily sacrifice. The High Priest's vestments (clothes), a robe and linen crown, are kept with Herod and only dispensed as a blessing to whichever priest Herod chooses (4). Herod normally chooses a priest from one of the smaller families willing to pay a large bribe, thereby pitting Jewish political factions against each other and weakening all. Rome encourages this only wanting Herod to keep the peace and collect taxes.

After passing the Mount of Olives to arrive at the temple, Paul leaves his horse with his two soldiers and climbs the steps to where he meets Jacob (James). Although only of the low order of priests, Jacob's popularity with everyone and communication with Rome keeps Jerusalem safe and war at bay. Herod, hoping to avoid war has granted Jacob's Essenes tax waivers. Yet Jacob stands in the way of Paul's plan for peace.

5 JERUSALEM 42 CE JACOB (JAMES) TUMBLES

Finally in Jerusalem Paul (Herodian) climbs the stairs of the temple under the watchful eyes of Roman officers in Herod's fortress across the Kidron valley. Roman soldiers stand unobtrusively in a corner of the temple market. Bow-legged Paul wobbles through the marketplace of the Gentiles, through the women's courtyard, beyond the stone threatening death to foreigners (this "ancient" landmark only recently installed, which Paul inverts when calling Jesus a "stumblingblock" – for Jews rather than for Gentiles/Greeks I Cor1:23) and into the courtyard of Israelites where the priests sacrifice a bull and two doves upon the hill at the altar. The High Priest stands back by the temple conversing with an Essene dressed in white linen. After washing, though still in Roman garb, Paul gives the name of his Hebrew teacher, claiming to be a disciple of Gamaliel and asks someone what the High Priest would be discussing with the other man.

The Essene (pacifist) is Jacob (James), older now than when Paul had left for Damascus. Jacob is currently seventy-six and instructing Herod's new Sadducean (zealot) High Priest in his office. Jacob falls silent as Paul approaches in Roman garb, "Where is my Uncle Herod on this fine morning?" The Priest responds, "Herod is not in Jerusalem today." Paul then asks Jacob, "Do you normally discuss temple sacrifice without the captain of the guard?" The priest responds, "We were complimenting the soldiers for bringing no money into the temple, due to its violating the second commandment against graven images (Ex 20:4, Deu 5:8) and picture of the ruler Caesar who is not a brother (Deu 20:4) which would pollute the temple."

Two men approach and introduce themselves as Cephas (Peter) and John. Paul asks, "Have you still avoided swearing allegiance to Rome?" The High Priest speaks one last time before taking his leave, "Your Uncle Herod has excused the Essenes from the oath and taxes (15.10.4 Antiquities, Josephus), while my family has paid Herod heavily and appreciates the instruction of Jacob." Paul apologizes saying "It's been a long ride and I've come to honor Jacob for his years of study of languages to be able to minister to the multitudes during Pentecost and the loyalty his father showed in allowing the sacrifice of Jesus." Jacob remains silent, but Cephas pushes his way between Paul and Jacob while John gathers a small group of followers.

Suddenly the crowd in the courtyard erupts while Roman guards storm in led by the Romans who escorted Paul from Damascus. The followers of Jacob go to where Jacob is on the temple wall begging the crowd for peace, but Paul also goes to the top of the wall and Jacob falls leaving his cloak ripped in two from the hem by a Roman guard who throws it to the feet of Paul (Mt 14:36, Ex 20:26, Acts 7:58). After falling from the wall, Jacob does not get up. Roman guards escort Paul out of the temple and westward onto the road to Caesarea and Herod.

Paul is nearly beside himself as he rides with Roman guards down the road towards the safety of sunset, ocean and Caesarea. After two years of preaching in Damascus, he had hoped his reintroduction to Jacob and the Essenes would have gone well, but although Cephas seemed cordial after Jacob had whispered something, Jacob was now dead after Paul's Roman guards had started a riot.

Jacob does not die. His followers take him into the wilderness where he will recover, but he will never walk the same again, his knees having broken in the fall. With Paul's bowed legs from Roman horseback riding, the two will share similar limps, for different reasons, for the rest of their lives. Jacob, fearing the coming war with Rome, will eventually send word to Paul that Essenes seek only to live in peace.

On the road to Caesarea Paul's guards pass booths on the side of the road where craftsmen sell their wares. These Rechabite priests, like Jacob, purposefully live in poverty (untaxable) as skilled potters and carpenters spending time honing their skills for Judaism's Messianic revolt. All are wary of Roman garbed Paul and pray for the peace Jacob regularly discusses with his closest followers. Secrets abound. Herod's spies are everywhere, Herod himself occasionally dressing as a commoner to spy on the people (Josephus, Ant 15.10.4). No one discusses rebellion with anyone outside of the fold.

6 CAESAREA 42 CE THE GOOD SAMARITAN WOMAN

After three days' horseback journey from Jerusalem to Caesarea, Paul arrives at Jaffa on the Mediterranean with his Roman guard. A temple priest has joined the troupe too. The port of Jaffa in Samaria receives Jewish pilgrims from around the Mediterranean heading to the temple, while Caesarea in Samaria receives Roman dignitaries. Originally Samaria was only the tribe of Joseph west of the Jordan (called by the two sons of Joseph, Manassah and Ephraim), but now Samaria, despised by Jews, runs the entire length of Israel along the coast from Egypt to Phoenecia (Lebanon) including both Jaffa near Jerusalem and Caesarea up the coast, Herod's showcase, emulating Rome with Herod's palace, large port, and Olympic stadium.

Jaffa is therefore a resting place for travelers by the sea. A Samaritan woman waters the horses from a well. Noticing Paul's priestly garb she calls out, "my ancestor, Rebecca, watered the camels of strangers getting herself a near-kinsman husband from a foreign land (Gen 24). From your garb among these Romans you are a foreigner who should not be oppressed (Ex 22:21). Have you come seeking a wife for Isaac (in Hebrew, `laughter` - Gen 21:6)?" Paul, knowing that Jews despise Samaritans, yet claiming himself to be a Jew to the Jew and as outside the law to those outside the law, laughs (I Cor 9:20-23), agreeing that Samaritans are indeed the descendants of Jacob and close relations to the tribe of Judah responding, "Have you therefore gotten this water by striking a Rock as did our ancestor Moses (Ex 17:6)?" The Samaritan replies, "Moses did indeed lead both Jews and Samaritans out of Egypt. Jeremiah cursed those who escaped Babylon, yet he also fled to Egypt and returned (1)." She continues, "The temple councilor, the supervisor of the water supply, dug this well (2) serving travelers on both ends of the highway from Jaffa to Jerusalem."

Paul is aware that Jeremiah had cursed any not going into captivity in Babylon although escaping himself to Egypt doing that for which he had cursed others (1). Suddenly a soldier calls to Paul, "This Samaritan woman seeks a temple husband, Officer Herod." The woman is immediately silent when she notices herself agreeing with a Roman soldier. Her face goes white after hearing that Paul is Herodian, knowing she is now in danger from the Roman soldiers, the priest and Paul who are all mortal enemies of each other. Things have become strange and Paul says, "I'm Roman, Herodian, Edomite, Benjamite, Jew, Pharisee and Maccabean temple priest from Tarsus travelling from Jerusalem to Caesarea." All is silent while the horses drink until the good Samaritan woman asks the priest, "With whom do you travel?" The Essene priest says quietly, "blessed are the peacemakers, for they shall harvest righteousness (Mt 5:9/Ja 3:18)."

Paul and his soldiers turn north to the Roman port of Caesarea which Herod has turned into the family's Roman showcase with architecture Paul had learned in Rome. Paul looks forward to discussing his two years in Arabia (Damascus) with his kinsman, Herod. After journeying up the coast to Caesarea, Paul meets a group of young men running naked on the coastal road. These men are also Samaritans, but far from Jerusalem, training for the Olympics and to be Roman soldiers. Paul considers the good Samaritan woman near Jerusalem providing for travelers and oppressing not the stranger (Ex 22:21, Job 31:32) while hoping for a devoted Jewish husband (Zipporah, Rahab, Ruth) yet knowing the xenophobic danger she faced (Ezra 10:3, Ch 11 Queen Helen's Israel) and these Caesarean Samaritans, Roman subjects seeking citizenship through military service.

Herod greets Paul, his soldiers, and the priest before asking "How is Jerusalem?" – a flashpoint which might initiate rebellion against Rome. Paul explains that Jacob (James) may be dead and presents his plan for peace. The Essene priest tersely agrees, "Do well and you will be accepted (Gen 4:7)." Herod decides to send Paul to Syrian Antioch. Antioch's governor as a descendant of Mark Anthony (Marcus Antonius) is a strong supporter of the Herods. Herod sends Paul, his foster brother Manaen, and the Essene priest, Barnabas (Acts 9:27).

Paul watches the peaceful Mediterranean sunset from Herod's palace, over the great port of Caesarea where Roman ships unload soldiers. To the north a hill is covered with crosses holding Jews (5) accused by Samaritans of insurrection and to the east in the newly emptied synagogue, Romans have started bringing straw on which to sleep with their horses. Paul remembers the good Samaritan woman at the well near Jerusalem, proud of her ties to the temple. Paul wonders if she would do better continuing to claim a Jewish heritage like Herodians grafted into the lineage of Maccabean priests or if she would do better like the Caesarean Samaritans, claiming Roman fidelity. In the morning Herod's empty ships will be filled with taxes carrying Paul's group to Antioch too.

7 CAESAREA 42 CE BANISHED FROM ISRAEL

In the morning Herod Agrippa, the friend of Caesar, marches south hoping for peace with temple Sadducees rather than war with Rome. After a day Herod rests on the coast of Jaffa near a supply ship. Herod considers war with Rome knowing the Jerusalem temple stores will not outlast a Roman siege: Armies march on their stomachs in dire straits boiling and eating leather shields, belts and shoes from where we get our phrase "as tough as shoe leather". In the Essene Dead Sea Scrolls at the destruction of Jerusalem the besieged epithet is "**mud clinging to her feet**". Essene vegetarians despise riches and those who might afford leather sandals due to their creation in original sin. During the coming Roman siege, a rich woman will eat her shoes and lacking common wicker sandals, walk the streets barefoot, begging for food, her money despised.

The next morning Herod starts up the road to Jerusalem. Herod is considered Jewish by Rome, but while the Caesarean Samaritans, adore both Rome and Herod, here closer to Jerusalem Samaritans claim Jewish temple loyalties despising both Rome and Herod. The good Samaritan woman at the well has nothing to say to Herod although she is despised herself by xenophobic temple Sadducees, ineligible as wifely material like the wool of sheep or goats conceived and defiled in sex never to be mixed with plant-based linen (Lev 19:19, Deu 22:11), the linen worn by priests (Eze 44:17), or like a diverse crop never to be planted among homogenous seeds in a garden (Deu 22:9). While Roman loving Samaritans seek Herod's affections, like Pharisees who shout three times "You are our brother!" good Samaritans closer to the temple claim the heritage of Israel considering the family of Herods as foreign servants of Rome, ineligible for temple service, **dogs unable to separate the holy sacrifice from profane, strangled, bloody or unclean meat**.

While Herod-Agrippa marches to Jerusalem, Paul and his half-brother Costobarus board the ship with the Essene priest, Herod's letter and gifts for Herod's wife, second cousin to Herodias, Cypros, and her daughter, Drusilla, who are "guests" of Caesar in Rome. As Paul's ship departs for Antioch, the few remaining Caesarean Pharisees claiming loyalty to Rome are left remembering false Samaritan accusations, Roman crucifixions, and widows' properties confiscated by Roman soldiers. Only Roman sympathizing Samaritans remain in Caesarea the garrison that will become known as the bloodiest throughout Israel. Currently in Caesarea even Roman sympathizing synagogue-based Pharisees are presumed guilty of being temple-zealot-Sadducees.

Antioch, Syria is under the Roman control of Claudians (the family of Mark Anthony), good friends of the Herods. Paul and Costobarus will be safe in Antioch, and in addition to cutting marble sent for the plaza (1), Herod and Claudius Caesar have a further mission for Paul: To visit Queen Helen of Adiabene, six days by horse from Antioch. Queen Helen, it has been rumored, is sympathetic to the Sadducees (temple zealots). Her King Agbarus or King Aretas of Damascus joining Parthian forces with Sadducean rioters at the temple would mean war. While sailing to Antioch Paul explains to Costobarus a letter he is preparing, Heb 7:6-9, 12-14, 18-19, 8:10,13, 10:16, 13:24, the new covenant, Abraham's promise fulfilled, allowing all beyond the veil of the temple Heb 6:19, 9:3, 10:20. Paul then says to Barnabas (Joses), "My uncle Herod will bring a doctor with the Roman soldiers to Jerusalem. Do you suppose, if your brother Jacob (James) still lives, that he would allow a Roman doctor to review his broken legs?" Barnabas, trained in Essene silence, does not respond.

To maintain control of Jerusalem, Herod purposefully enrages the populace seeking trouble-makers on whom to unleash Roman soldiers. Herod's soldiers had earlier raised an eagle of gold desecrating the temple and killing 5000 until Herod's "mediation". Herod's spies seek small and violent factions which Herod secretly supplies with sicarii, small curved swords which are used to either circumcise or disembowel enemies. Herod's support of small, weak and violent factions keeps the temple embroiled in internecine fighting, weakening stronger sects with Roman interventions barely noticeable among the tumult.

    Two years earlier after much negotiation, the fighting had stopped: Jacob (James) as leader of the Essenes had allowed his younger brother, Jesus, to be crucified. Jesus even carried his own cross to show loyalty to Rome. After their other brother Cephas' (Peter's) rage and wailing in the temple threatened to undo negotiations, Jacob had sent Cephas to Caesarea and beyond, where Herod had now sent Paul. Herod, dreading Jacob's death and temple rioting, feels like the angel of death on his journey to Jerusalem, believing all is lost: The Temple's revolt and war with Rome seems inevitable.

8 BETHLEHEM 42 CE THE HOUSE OF BREAD

As Herod starts into the hills towards Jerusalem leading the Roman army from the sea into the mountains, he passes empty booths on his horse. Evidence of craftsmen, Rechabite priests who own nothing taxable lay on the side of the road, but the warning had been given. A soldier picks up a knife from among the booths exclaiming, "taxed!" By the afternoon nearing Jerusalem, Herod dispatches a guard on the road to Bethlehem, the rebellious city of the ancient Jewish warrior, King David.

Bethlehem means in Hebrew, "The House of Bread". However in allegory this stands for knowledge, or the house of education, just as bread sometimes means dough ($$$) – a spiritual knowledge of eternal life which per Rome "innovates" that all men are equal. Jacob's lineage (James' lineage) comes from Bethlehem, fearless Jewish Sadducean fighters claiming David as their root. Per the gospel of Matthew, Herod the terrible killed the babies of Bethlehem hating Jewish genealogical laws so much that he killed or married all of the Maccabeans diluting the priestly ruling lineage by raising kids, murdering their mothers and after raising grandkids, killing his Maccabean children: Joseph (Clopas, Alphaeus), a craftsman, carpenter and Rechabite (a priest vowed to poverty with no permanent home who studies a craft as a tradesmen Mt 10:10), fled to Egypt with his family.

Jewish law has no reference to a heavenly afterlife. The most that could be hoped for until Bethlehem was a record of a good life (a good name) and successful children to leave behind. The book of Daniel, backdated from Bethlehem, is the first to claim a resurrection. Ezekiel's bones represent a resurrection of Israel rather than a recalling of actual dead to life. A Psalm claiming Melchizedek as everlasting may have also been backdated by Maccabeans who took office from 167 BCE – 4 BCE claiming the High Priesthood through faith (Sadducean zealotry) and not having been of the lineage previously.

With the Bethlehem claim of everlasting life, kings come under judgement. Roman Samaritans near Caesarea might declare Herod Maccabean with a right to rulership, but not Bethlehem Sadducees. The meaning of Bethlehem is the knowledge that no one is better than another, taken from the Egyptian Pharaohs' hall of judgement where your soul is weighed against the weight of a feather and the pyramid opens only to the North Star, the Star of Bethlehem. Called "**witches**" by Herod these Egyptian astrologers also wrote of kings in Daniel: "You have been weighed (against a feather) and found wanting." Essenes would call no man lord since low or high death and judgement would come to all. Essenes bury their dead with their feet pointed not to the East like most Jews, but to the North Star. This gift of the Bread of Bethlehem (Bread of [Eternal] Life) is knowledge of eternity come down from Heaven, as the Egyptians claim their knowledge arrived, and upon which Paul architects his gospel.

Herod entered his fortress at Jerusalem with guards posted on the road to Bethlehem and orders to turn back all except the leaders should any arrive. His High Priest from the temple across the Kidron valley would soon visit with news that Jacob lived. Herod will relate that Paul had left Israel. Many are still unhappy with Paul's interference, despising both Herod's High Priest and Herod's visit to Jerusalem. Herod has rebuilt the temple without ever stepping inside and at his begging for reconciliation Sadducees had responded: "We will be reconciled to you in death!" However for the moment, due to all the Roman soldiers, nothing beyond murmuring is heard.

Herod sought the head rabble-rousers, usually of the Davidic lineage of Bethlehem, quelling disturbances by sending these to the Dead Sea with soldiers where hands and feet were bound. Due to the high salinity, people would float and drowning would take hours. From this we get our myth that **witches** float. Herod knew his Bible well taking Ecclesiastes 11:1 literally, casting his "Bread" upon the waters, those from "The House of Bread", with their innovation of equality for all, needing no Davidic or Roman king. Biblical authors will ironically encode this as "…Man shall not live by bread alone…"

(Mt 4:4). This is the knowledge of judgement and eternal life which came down from heaven (Jn 6:31-33). Bread fundamentally comes from G-d, and acknowledging that truth is the essence of Israel's Pentecost celebration (p565 Acts, A New Vision of the People of G-d. Gerald L. Stevens 2016).

9 ANTIOCH 43 CE PAUL'S ROMAN AMPHITHEATERS

Herod left Paul in Caesarea while rushing to get up to G-d's holy mountain of Jerusalem (2500 ft). Many find mountains spiritual with the ancient kings of Israel alternately supporting or destroying indigenous religious groves in high places. Samaria, also within the borders of Israel, is defined by mountains: Gerizim and Ebal where Abraham recited blessings and cursings on Israel. In Jerusalem on the temple mount, Mt Moriah, Abraham nearly sacrificed his son. Herod, a Maccabean Edomite, his family grafted into the root of Judaism, might therefore be said to be returning home to where his family is restoring the temple while simultaneously excluded as foreigners.

Paul, although Herodian, is banished from Israel by Herod for the trouble in Jerusalem. Herod sends Paul, his foster brother, Costobarus and Barnabas (Joses), to Antioch, the third largest Roman city (after Alexandria), an ancient city full of Greeks. In 44 BCE Cassius had picked up troops here for his battle against Mark Anthony (Marcus Antonius) in Philippi, however Mark Anthony reigned here afterwards becoming close friends of the Herods sending Roman troops from Antioch. Here in Antioch, Syria, in a city friendly to the Herods, yet well beyond the borders of Israel, Paul will practice the ministry he prepared in Damascus.

Paul arrives in 43 CE to a warm greeting from the governor Marsus who wants good relations with Herod and news of Jerusalem, Caesarea and Rome. "Herod sends you greetings", says Paul, "and the marble which weighs down this ship." Herod has many public works to his name in various Roman cities. After conversation Paul is able to set himself up as a marble craftsman improving the Roman road and building the amphitheater near the town square where he will review the comings and goings of ships, materials and emissaries. Roman ships carry craftsmen, tools, soldiers, grain from Egypt and taxes.

Rather than tent-maker (Acts 18:3) Paul prefers the title "builder" (Acts 4:11, Ro 15:20, I Cor 3:9). Paul doesn't make much from his craft asking for church donations and offerings, explaining that similarly farmers must not muzzle the ox that treads the corn (Deu 25:4). Paul's true work, his spiritual calling, is building his Plan for Peace, a Roman, Greek and Pharisaic cosmopolitan answer to the question of xenophobic temple Sadducees (*). Paul architects his religion to bring as many into his amphitheater as possible, arguing that he is Jew to the Jew and gentile to the gentile. Jerusalem temple Sadducees will learn of Paul's Plan for Peace. Pilgrims from Antioch will arrive on ships to tell his story returning with letters from Jerusalem. Ships also bring mysteries of Egyptian pyramids, the oracle from Delphi Greece and the temple of Diana in Ephesus.

In 45 CE times will change for Paul. Claudius Caesar of the family of Mark Anthony will hide his ancestry, claiming none from the family of Mark Anthony. The family of Cassius, despising foreigners and most especially Jews like Herod who supported Mark Anthony and married Egyptians (and a Greek named Cleopatra) will install Cassius Longinus as the governor of Antioch, who will then compel Paul to leave Antioch. Paul's revenge will take generations remaining in the gospel of Nicodemus: While every other gospel is peacefully and tax-payingly pro-Roman, in Nicodemus scorn is thrust upon a centurion who spears Jesus in the side (3). Blood and water run out of the wound. The Herodian author/editor of our gospels will name the centurion "Longinus", not after the Cassius killed by Mark Anthony, but after Cassius' descendant, the new Governor of Syria.

Paul will flee the Antioch of Gaius Cassius Longinus in 48, but first we must tell of Queen Helen of Adiabene with her two sons, their conversion, donations to the temple and martyrdom fighting for the Sadducees at Beit Horon, Paul's falling out with Cephas (the Rock, Peter) and Joses (the son of consolation, Barnabas), and of the death of Greek Stephen, some of which must wait for the story of how Herod authored the gospel of Matthew.

*The deacons of Antioch, "table servants", assisted in bringing Kosher Jews and gentile Greeks together at meals for communion. Far from mere table servants, deacons were and remain pastoral adjuncts, repositories of doctrine, apologists specializing in missions to Jew and Greek and extending the grace of church unity.

10 ADIABENE 43-48 CE QUEEN HELEN

Paul arrives in Antioch continuing his Herodian errands for Claudius Caesar and travelling inland to Adiabene as an emissary, an ambassador to the armies of King Agbarus who stands between the armies of Rome and Parthia. Paul takes Costobarus, his half-brother, and gifts for king Agbarus while preaching Paul's gospel: a non-circumcising transcendental Christ requiring no physical evidence of faith beyond baptism (no circumcision) (1). King Agbarus is not interested, but his wife, Queen Helen, listens. The son of Queen Helen, Izates, stands to say "I'll travel to the temple of Jerusalem with you to hear the words of the G-d of Israel." Paul, still banished from Israel by Herod, returns to and remains in Antioch sending Izates to Jerusalem with Joses (Barnabas).

In Jerusalem Izates speaks with the brother of Joses, the Essene (pacifist) Jacob (James) on theology until Sadducees (zealots) demand circumcision. Izates returns to Antioch with Joses, Cephas (Peter) and the Saducean priest, Eleazar. To Paul's great horror Izates says "I'm going home to Adiabene with Eleazar. You should stay here." Izates and Eleazar journey to the Adiabene of Queen Helen where Eleazar circumcises both of Queen Helen's sons, Izates and Monobazus (10.2.1 Antiquities Josephus). Queen Helen exclaims, "Prince Izates, the people will no longer accept your kingship!" On their escape to Jerusalem they pass through Antioch where Paul's disgust at their circumcision is apparent. And they stay in Jerusalem permanently with the support of King Agbarus, who hopes for war between Israel and Rome rather than between Rome and Parthia. The food sent to Jerusalem by King Abgarus through Antioch during the famine (46-48)(Acts 11:28), claimed by Acts as Paul's "donation", saves Essenes and Rechabites, known as "the Poor", from starvation. Queen Helen becomes a Jewish hero, or as much as will be allowed for a rich gentile with temple donations.

Governor Cassius of Antioch, explained earlier as a Roman xenophobe, banishes Paul in 48, liking neither the late Mark Anthony (Marcus Antonius) nor his friends, Herodians like Paul. Paul's first missionary journey therefore takes four from the Antioch church to Jerusalem with food for "the Poor" and donations for "the Brothers". Herod stops Paul at Caesarea due to Paul's Jerusalem riots, but supporting Paul's plan for peace, allows Paul's four evangelists to continue. The four have high hopes for their mission, the book of Hebrews having been more fully developed in Antioch. "Abraham promised to be a blessing to the world" they cry in Jerusalem, but Sadducees find the preaching blasphemous. Queen Helen, sitting quietly in a high chair in the marketplace, watches the murder of Paul's four evangelists. Four wives in Antioch, now bereft, become with much lamentation, "the widows of Antioch."

Biblical explanation is in order: The original "Brothers" are the four brothers of Jesus (Mt 13:55, Mk 6:3). Let's review how our gospels were written with eight or more of the apostles sharing the same four names: Cephas (Peter - Simeon) visited Antioch (Gal 2:11). Barnabas was named Joses (Acts 4:36). I'm suggesting that he, like Jude who left grandchildren in Antioch (2), is a brother of Jesus. "The Poor" is code for Essene or Rechabite who own no property having nothing for Rome to tax. Rechabites have a trade, like Joseph the carpenter, the husband of Mary. Essenes, like Jacob (James), mostly live in the wilderness. Famine or siege is especially tough on The Poor. However Sadducees and Pharisees enjoy riches, the zealot Sadducees with gold at the temple and Roman accommodating Pharisees running city-based synagogues. The Jerusalem famine runs from 46-48 where in one previously unintelligible story a rich woman's feet are caked with mud. In the metaphor of the times she is starving, having sold everything she owned down to boiling and eating her leather sandals, while the Rabbis who relate this story are unable to explain its meanings without violating Jewish courtesy.

Queen Helen will watch the murder of Jacob in 62, the succeeding Jewish revolt in 66 and its resulting Roman invasion. A key question: How did Jacob manage to preach in Jerusalem from the crucifixion in 40 until 62 with Paul fomenting discord from Antioch and Herod watching Jerusalem like a hawk from his fortress on the mountain just across the Kidron valley? The answer is: Jesus, Jacob's brother, crucified, proving the family's loyalty to Rome and promise to keep the peace, the Pax Romana. Queen Helen gets an apartment in Jerusalem where she will live for twenty-one years serving three sentences of seven years voluntary penance praying daily at the behest of Jewish priests for some unknown fault. Rabbi's will crow of Queen Helen's donations to the temple, for which her grand-sons will get the honor of serving Israel at the pass of Beit Horon where they will die fighting Romans fulfilling their father's hopes of instigating war. The three tombs of Queen Helen and her sons, Egyptian pyramids to be exact, stand in Jerusalem for some time afterwards describing the Bethlehem North Star promise of eternal life to those whose souls are lighter than the feather.

11 JERUSALEM 45 CE QUEEN HELEN'S ISRAEL

Queen Helen chose a xenophobic place to live out the remainder of her years. Jerusalem is in desert mountains at the center of three continents. Israel's story involves Abraham coming from beyond Babylon, nearly sacrificing his son Isaac on the Samaritan Mount Moriah (1), setting a stone, and buying the nearby field to bury his wife. When Israel returned from Egypt, Solomon killed an Israelite his father David had promised to spare (I Ki 2:5-6). Canaanite women who intermarried were abandoned by their husbands as foreigners (Ezra 10) along with an entire tribe, Benjamin, killed except for 600 men (Judges 20). A Jewish city which failed to participate in the fratricide was killed and their widows marched to Benjamin, xenophobically repopulating Judah's border… with Jews (Judges 21).

If Jewish prophesies attracted Queen Helen, her instructors might have been upset if she had asked why Jacob bowed to Esau upon his return (Gen 33:3) and if Esau ever became the servant of Jacob (Gen 27:37). Jewish secrets may include that the tribes of Israel escaping Egypt were few. Specifically historians mention Daniel as a tribe which may never have sojourned in Egypt (Myth 68 – 101 Myths of the Bible, Greenberg 2000). The tribe of Daniel split in two, one half living on the coast, the other half invading the mountains of the Golan Heights. As Joshua 19:17 puts it, "the coast of the Children of Dan went out too little for them: therefore the children of Dan went up to fight against Leshem, and took it." Although Jacob/Moses/Joshua supposedly handed out land according to ancient prophesies, all of a sudden one of the tribes extends these borders, the borders of Israel, to suit their needs.

Queen Helen may have been troubled by the Messianic prophesies of the non-departing scepter of David: In 722 BCE Assyria invaded, taking Northern Israel away into bondage. In 586 BCE Babylon invaded, taking Southern Israel (Judah) into bondage, destroying temple and throne. Further, Jeremiah first prophesized death to those refusing to go to Babylon, then that Babylon would kill everyone who remained in Israel, then that none escaping would return from Egypt, then more gently that those who failed to listen to his word and go to Babylon would die and finally, prophesying from Egypt himself, where two further Jewish temples would be built (1.1 Wars Josephus), that only a few would return from Egypt. Seventy years later Judah (Jews) returning from Babylon will find remnants of the Northern Kingdom, Samaritans, worshiping on Mount Gerizim, but refuse their offer of help to rebuild Jerusalem.

With her Mesopotamian origins Queen Helen might have heard that Jerusalem, Babylon's gateway to Egypt, was rebuilt when Babylon decided to invade Egypt. Both Jeremiah in Egypt and Ezekiel in Babylon prophesied victory for the invasion when Babylon gave the command to rebuild the Jewish temple and wall. Before the prophesy could be fulfilled, Media-Persia invaded Babylon (2).

Queen Helen's xenophobic Israel also destroyed Samaria. Samaritans, the remnant of the Northern Kingdom, claim as their root the Samaritan books of Moses differing only slightly from the Jewish books of Moses. Moses commanded Israel to recite blessings and curses on the mountains of Samaria (Gerizim and Ebal) and the road to Jerusalem starts on the Mediterranean, crossing the Samaritan pass of Beit Horon near Mt. Gerizim. After returning from Babylon in 522 and rebuilding the temple, Jews took notice of Samaritans claiming the preeminence of Samaritan (Northern Kingdom) scripture. Judah invaded in 128 BCE, destroying the Samaritan temple on Mt. Gerizim and killing its worshipers. Relations between Samaritans and Jews have been strained ever since with Josephus Antiquities 9.14.3 accusing Samaritans of only sometimes claiming Jewish heritage.

This was the Judaism in Jerusalem into which Queen Helen chose to seek the benefit of her immortal soul. Meanwhile Jews escaping the impending and previous Roman/Herodian invasions of Israel enjoyed the second temple in Alexandria. Per Josephus this was prophesied in Isaiah (13.3.1 Antiquities, Josephus, William Whiston, Is 19:19). Rome would eventually destroy the temples, killing the Jews of

Egypt and mangling records so badly with editing, overwriting and the burning of the library at Alexandria, that scholars wonder what happened to this day.

12 ANTIOCH 46 CE CEPHAS' (PETER'S) ARRIVAL

Antioch is a Roman city, the third largest Roman city after Rome and Alexandria (Egypt), whose inhabitants consider themselves Greek as do all Romans. Antioch was home to Mark Anthony (Marcus Antonius) in the previous century who sent the Roman army to support Herod the Terrible in his quest for the throne of Israel. Herod is only slightly Jewish, Edomite from Idumea, not the right kind of Jew to be allowed past the multiple exclusionary temple gates: foreigners, women's courtyard, Jews, low priests and finally the High Priest who was selected by Herod. A stone stands in the temple threatening death to foreigners in Latin, Greek and Hebrew. Some felt Herod was not a foreigner - Herod the Terrible killed or married all the Maccabeans (temple priest/kings), grafting himself into their root in the same way Paul grafts his Plan for Peace, like a wild olive tree, into the root of Torah (Ro 11:16-32). "Peace be with you", says Paul (Ro 1:7, I Cor 1:3, II Cor 1:2, Gal 1:3), greeting Herod's ship at Antioch.

Antioch rests on the Mediterranean in Syria on the route to Damascus, Edessa and Babylon (Armenia//Parthia). Jacob (James), as leader of the Jerusalem council, sends two of his brothers, Cephas (Simon Peter) and Barnabas (Joses) with Queen Helen's son Izates and the priest Eleazar. In twenty years Queen Helen's grandsons will die in Israel at the pass of Beit Horon fighting against Rome, but for now Eleazar and Izates continue on to Edessa where Queen Helen waits. Cephas cringes when Herod grumbles secret questions for Paul regarding Queen Helen whose husband, Agbarus, joined with King Aretas of Damascus facing and defeating Herod in battle after the death of John the Baptist. Herod leaves his guests at Antioch and sails up the coast to the summer home of Caesar at Corinth.

In Jerusalem due to his broken knees, Jacob waits for his brothers Cephas and Barnabas, and for the story of Paul's Plan for Peace. Paul desires a peace where Romans get Jewish taxes, are allowed into the temple (Ro 1:16), and the daily sacrifice is stopped (Ro 3:25, Heb 10:11). Herod, representing Rome, is grievously concerned about Sadducee hatred for himself. Herods have been remodeling the temple for decades. Herod begs priests regarding what he must do to be forgiven. Sadducees (temple zealots) reply that Herod should kill himself shouting: "We will be reconciled to you in death!", while Pharisees, Roman accommodators, shout: "You are our brother! You are our brother! You are our brother!"

Sadducees (Righteousness) are temple zealots (zeal of my house Ps 69:9, Jn 2:17), the word coming from the Hebrew root Zadock (holier than thou). S and Z are similar, followed by D and either C or K (Sadducee/Zadock). Sadducees make war in Jerusalem, while Pharisees accommodate Rome leading city-based Synagogues across the Mediterranean including Antioch, carefully studying Torah while wrapped in endless debate about whether camels, through the gate of the needle, should be allowed into the temple, due to whatever kind of hoof they have. Rome has significant input into Rabbinic/Pharisaic doctrine and after destroying the Sadducean temple, will build the Rabbinic school of Jamnia.

But back to our story: Jacob has sent Cephas (Peter) with Izates, Eleazar and Joses to Antioch to find out what Paul is doing. These arrive with Herod who continues in his ship onto Corinth, Caesar's summer home, leaving the ominous statement "take care of Queen Helen." The rest of Jacob's "emissaries" (uninvited Sadducees) will arrive later having walked from Jerusalem. When these, "some from Jacob", demand circumcision, Barnabas will leave for Cyprus and Cephas will swear off table fellowship with gentiles. The priest Eleazar converts Queen Helen, circumcising her son, while Paul laments, "all in Asia have abandoned me (2 Tim 1:15)." Paul's Plan for Peace had talked Queen Helen into donating a significant sum to the temple while seeking the temple's acceptance of foreigners: Romans (Greeks) and Herodians, but to Paul's great horror, Queen Helen converts to Judaism, continues donating heavily and moves to Jerusalem with her circumcised son (20.2.4 Antiquities, Josephus).

Bethlehem: The War of Jesus

13 JERUSALEM 48 CE THE FOUR EVANGELISTS

In every Biblical author's work, the travels of Paul present a singular challenge. While Luke's Acts report Paul's trips back and forth to Jerusalem with vociferous evangelization and riots, Paul's actual works report fewer and quieter visits including a fourteen year absence (Gal 2:1, 43-57(+-1)), necessarily including Paul's iconic famine (46-48) visit. To me Paul journeys to Jerusalem, yet stops at Caesarea sending his "presence", his proxy or representative, the church with the book of Hebrews and hefty donation - the four men reported in Acts shaving their heads at the word of James (Acts 21:23-24). Greek martyrs from Paul's church create the widows of Antioch where Paul and Jesus' laments originate: All in Asia have abandoned me (2 Tim 1:15). O Jerusalem…thou that killest the prophets (Mt 23:29-37). Paul's Antiochian church includes Barnabas, Simeon, Lucius, Manaen (Herod's foster brother), Saul (Paul), Stephen, Philip, Prochorus, Nicanor, Timon, Parmenas and Nicholas.

To me the three brothers of Jesus at Antioch were Cephas (Simeon, Peter), Jude (Judas) and Barnabas (Joses): Jude wrote the book of Jude noting his brother as Jacob (James). Jude's grandchildren are called before Caesar for claiming their rightful bishopric of Antioch. Barnabas means the son of consolation, a reference to his brother's crucifixion. These are the three brothers of Jesus who could walk. Jacob, making the fourth (Mt 13:55, Mk 6:3), broke his leg falling from the temple and was called "old camel knees" for his hours knelt in prayer.

After the annual High Holy Days with crowds dissipating and no revolt, Herod sails to the summer home of Caesar at Corinth. On the way Herod stops at Antioch where Paul paves the Roman road in marble. Caesar greets his foster brother, "Y'all stirred up trouble in Jerusalem. Jacob has sent his brothers with me. How is my road?"

Manean reports, "the road is going great. Paul cuts marble and rides his horse to its ends every day. Every night is spent teaching unity and building the plan for peace. In Hebrew Bethlehem means the house of bread. Deacons, table servants, school disciples on Abraham's promise to be a blessing to all, the bread of life, bringing Jews and Greeks together, breaking bread, and teaching that the Lord delights in mercy rather than in sacrifice."

Paul jokes that Cephas has come to judge the tribe of Benjamin. Benjamin is judged harshly in scripture although the favorite son of Jacob. Priests at the temple sarcastically refer to pilgrims who choose not to reside in Jerusalem as Benjamites, all the while enjoying their tribute, much as Herod enjoys the tolls he collects on Roman roads. Only the well-to-do can afford pilgrimaging more than once in their lives. After studying at Antioch, these "some from Jacob" recommend that Jews separate themselves from table fellowship with Greeks (Gal 2:12).

In 37 BCE Antioch's Mark Anthony (Marcus Antonius, who killed **Cassius**) provides Paul's ancestor Herod with Roman soldiers who destroy the first Sanhedrin. Per Rome, foreigners are perfidious barbarians. Any Roman crimes, sewing strife among all, are to be welcomed with joy. Rome sends Gaius **Cassius** Longinus, who despises Herodians like Paul, to keep all in subjection. After Paul's position in Antioch becomes untenable, Paul sends his church to Jerusalem during the famine (46-48) (Acts 11:27-30). Paul gathers his Antiochian Greeks sending four, shaving their heads with a vow and an offering (Acts 21:23-24), yet Paul can only accompany the evangelists to Caesarea, having been banished from Jerusalem by Herod in 42 after his trouble with Jacob at the temple.

After a week's travel with Paul left behind in Caesarea, Cephas (Peter), Jude, Barnabas (Joses) and Paul's four evangelists arrive in Jerusalem. The intrepid Stephen, with the Greek name meaning "crowned", claims that like Sampson his hair has begun to grow and with it his strength (Jdgs 16). The four don the white linen robes of the Essenes, enter the temple and begin to preach the book of Hebrews as had Paul six years earlier in 42 noting Esau as the first son like Ishmael, the rightful firstborn, but the promise carrying through the second, Jacob and Isaac, naming Paul as this second son. Paul had coached his evangelists well in Antioch.

Among the Sadducees are the sect of Sicarii who carry curved knives beneath their robes to kill or circumcise any who preach. Stephen was stoned, his white robe ripped from his naked body and returned to Paul. As for the remaining Greeks whose heads had been shaved, wearing the white robes of the Essenes, one runs away never to be heard from again. One is hung from a bridge. One is savaged by the Sicarii, his blood and guts spilling out onto a field the temple authority would buy with the thirty pieces of silver Paul's four evangelists had brought as a donation. Used for a while as a latrine for priests outside of the camp, this field of blood will become a pauper's graveyard for Rechabite burials, alms for the poor. The horror is written into the martyrs of our New Testament.

14 CAESAREA 48 CE BANISHED AGAIN

Joses (Barnabas) tells Paul that the four evangelists of the church of Antioch were murdered by the zealot sect of xenophobic Sadducees, the sicarii who carry curved knives with which to circumcise or kill any who preach for the Most High. Paul's two years with the book of Hebrews in Antioch has proven fruitless. Paul might have wished Roman accommodating Pharisees in charge of Jerusalem, or Jacob's (James') peaceful Essenes or even Rechabite craftsmen always studying to improve their skills. But perhaps the cosmopolitan Roman/Jewish historian Josephus puts the lie to these being separate sects, Josephus himself initiated into at least three of the four. In seventeen years Sadducees with Queen Helen of Adiabene will control Jerusalem after the death of Jacob catapulting Israel into war with Rome.

Paul sleeps in the Herodian safety of Caesarea. He remembers his Greek martyrs of Antioch. How did Paul create a cosmopolitan Antioch community of Greeks, Romans and Herodians? Paul was a Roman, a Greek speaking Herodian, an Edomite Idumean claiming Maccabean origins in Judaism from the temple. Paul spoke Greek in Antioch, although fluent in the Hebrew he learned as a Pharisee with an additional claim to being a Maccabean Sadducee from his great-grandmother's side. Paul's Roman teachers respected the Greeks praising the Greek philosophers. Paul's Roman teacher, Seneca, Caesar's secretary, is a known Stoic (Greek Philosophy) and Rome itself was named after two Greek twins, Rebus and Romulus (Rome… ulous). After Greece won freedom from the Media-Persian empire in 480 BCE, Greeks had gone on to invade and colonize Sicily before becoming subject to Rome.

Paul's plan for peace is an extension of Roman cosmopolitanism, acceptance of other cultures. Perhaps his Maccabean soul by his grandmother rages against his Roman/Herodian heritage from his grandfather who killed the Maccabeans he didn't marry. Perhaps Paul's Roman heart hated his Idumean/Edomite ancestry who Romans referred to as barbarians. Samaritans also handle mixed loyalties badly: At Lydda near Jerusalem Samaritans proudly declare their Jewish heritage like Sadducees while a day's journey up the coast towards Caesarea, Samaritans train to be Roman soldiers claiming Roman heritage. In Caesarea Samaritans even cheer crucified Pharisees while Roman soldiers sleep in their widows' Synagogue. Paul claimed being a Greek to the Greek and Roman to the Romans finding a catholic (universal), cosmopolitan (non-local) promise of peace in scripture: Paul's scripture declares our being a nation of priests (Ex 19:6), Abraham's descendants being a blessing to the world (Gen 22:18), all nations flowing unto David's throne for justice (Is 9:7), and our Lord having written the law in everyone's heart (Jer 31:33).

The murder of several of Paul's church from Antioch leaves widows in Antioch whose new Roman governor, Gaius Cassius Longinus, makes clear his disdain of anything foreign, Rome having expelled the Jews, and most especially any Herodians like Paul, Marcus Antonius (Mark Anthony) killing Cassius before befriending the Herods. The Roman governor of Caesarea notes Paul's Plan for Peace as having failed again and asks Paul to leave quickly. Paul's night in Caesarea with the Roman governor is tense, even with the governor desiring the support of Paul's uncle, Herod of Galilee. Although the governor supports Paul's plan for peace, the current riots in Jerusalem must be handled and so Herod will again send Paul beyond Israel and not wishing to face the remnants of his church at Antioch, Paul will go even further. He will be tossed before the four winds to his family home of Tarsus for a moment and then beyond where he has travelled in the past, not wishing to bring such passions upon his family's chosen home, ever beyond up the road through Turkey to Ephesus and Troas, sailing to Philippi. He will preach here briefly, stirring up passions, perhaps in retribution against Gaius Cassius Longinus, the new governor of Antioch (Marcus Antonius, strong friend of the Herods, having killed Caesar's assassin Cassius at the battle of Philippi). After teaching and practicing his gospel in Philippi and riding the Roman army's road to Thessalonica, he finds his true home in Corinth where he will re-author his Plan for Peace for Jerusalem and Rome.

15 PHILIPPI 48 CE ESCAPE FROM CAESAREA

As Paul sails from Caesarea, he considers the week's events. Three days before while anxiously waiting for news from Jerusalem, Herod had enjoyed watching Paul ride with the Roman army in Caesarea. Trained in the saddle since childhood, Paul hobbles bow-leggedly to the stables before outriding all but Herod's best. Paul was banished from Jerusalem by Herod after Paul's riotous encounter with Jacob (James) in 42, but with Herod's blessing Paul has sent his presence with four evangelists from Antioch. And so the two would wait.

In Jerusalem Jacob (James) was 82, his legs broken during his last meeting with Paul. Jacob is an elderly man of the priestly lineage leading the Essenes, although his dad, Joseph (Alphaeus, Clopas), is older. Herod knows that Jacob has been praying in the temple. Herod might stop this as Herod controls the vestments of the High Priest, but the family of Jacob, the Essenes and Pharisees, have been a peaceful counterbalance to the violent xenophobic Sadducees with their assassin Sicarii.

Herod and Paul wait for news from the temple. Paul and Jacob share many things in common, both born of high families, both Jewish, and both having trouble walking. Paul's troubles originate in bow-legged horse-riding as nobility and Jacob's from his tumble nearly a decade ago (Hegesippus circa 160 CE says that Jacob's knees were like those of a camel from his hours of praying in the temple).

News of Jerusalem returned with Joses (Barnabas) and Judas (Thomas, Didimus, the Twin) reporting that Cephas (Peter, Simeon the Zealot) had howled in grief remembering their brother's sacrifice until comforted by Jacob (these are the four brothers of Jacob). Paul had sent his presence to Jerusalem through four Greek evangelists from Antioch who had obediently recalled the crucifixion. Joses quietly wrings his hands showing Paul's evangelists dead. Judas weeps. Joses says the temple seemed ready to begin a revolt again with another of Paul's riots until Jacob comforted Cephas silencing the crowd. And that only a few had chased and killed Paul's evangelists with no further rioting.

Herod provides Paul a ship, because Paul is Herodian and a half-nephew of Herod, the Herods regularly fathering children by multiple women as did Isaac (Rebecca/Hagar), marrying more than one woman simultaneously as did Jacob (Rachel & Leah) and close kin like Egyptian Pharaohs as did Abraham (Sarah was his half-sister), intertwining lineages like a brood of vipers. Herod fathered many by Maccabeans through whom Paul is likewise Maccabean. The Gospel of Peter later confirms much, authored assumedly in Rome, referring to Herods as both Jewish and responsible for the crucifixion. Acts refers to the sisters Drusilla and Bernice as Jewish when visiting an imprisoned Paul in Caesarea, both daughters of Herod Agrippa and perhaps not viewed as Jewish by some. Sadducees note their renunciation of their Jewishness in divorcing their husbands to marry richer rulers, who may have needed their Jewishness for authority or legitimacy over Jewish subjects.

Joses departs at Cyprus. Jude moves permanently to Antioch to lead Paul's synagogue. Paul returns to Antioch to find much trouble at the hands of Gaius Cassius Longinus, the Cassian anti-Herodian governor and probably remembered as Longinus, the soldier who thrust his spear through Jesus on the cross, and the widows of the four evangelists Paul had sent to their deaths. Paul remembers better times when Claudius Caesar in Rome gave support to Paul in Antioch (Claudian Mark Anthony being good friends with Herods), but Claudius Caesar has been poisoned, hiding his heritage and evicting Jews from Rome, and Paul, "encouraged" by the soldiers of Gaius Cassius Longinus, rides his horse up the coastal Roman road, stopping in Tarsus with family for a bit and then escaping to the ends of the Roman empire through Ephesus and Troas to enter Macedonia (Europe) at Philippi.

16 PHILIPPI 48 CE THE PHILIPPI OF MARK ANTHONY

Paul, as a Herodian, has good reason to visit Philippi. Mark Anthony (Marcus Antonius), friend of Herod, retired soldiers here after the Battle of Philippi against Brutus and Cassius in 42 BCE. In Rome cosmopolitan Julio-Claudians of the family of Mark Anthony oppose xenophobic Cassians. With the good-will of descendants of Mark Anthony's retired soldiers, Paul hopes to perturb the governor of Antioch, Gaius Cassius Longinus.

Cleopatra Ptolemy, the last Pharaoh, married her half-brother before becoming the lover of Julius Caesar and Mark Anthony. The original Ptolemy was a general of Alexander the Great. Cleopatra's son by Julius Caesar, Caesarion, Julius Caesar's only known heir, is therefore a Greek/Macedonian Roman. Egypt is Rome's "breadbasket", supplying the Roman Empire with corn from the fertile Nile valley, which must be kept under control. After the assassination of Julius Caesar in 44 BCE, Cleopatra becomes the lover of Mark Anthony, giving him two children. She abandons Mark Anthony in battle twice: In 42 BCE Mark Anthony managed without her in Philippi, but in 31 BCE Mark Anthony loses at the battle of Actium off the coast of Greece retreating to Cleopatra's Egypt where like Romeo and Juliette, Mark Anthony and Cleopatra kill themselves.

General Julius Caesar came to power as a great writer for Rome. After his unauthorized victories in Gaul (France), Caesar was ordered to report to Rome. He plundered Gaul to supply his men and crossed the Rubicon with his armies, becoming the author of Rome's civil war, seizing control of the Roman Senate in 49 BCE, increasing the numbers of Senators from 400 to 900 of his closest friends, and setting term limits to ensure only his hand-picked men would remain. Like Alexander the Great, Julius Caesar set a policy of invading Parthia (Babylon/Iran/Afghanistan), sending troops to Antioch Syria for the task. Brutus and Cassius assassinated Caesar in 44 BCE, claiming love for Rome before fleeing to Macedonian (Greek) Philippi.

Julius Caesar's remaining generals, Mark Anthony, Octavian and Lepidus, fought each other for power in Rome before joining forces. This second triumvirate, like Julius Caesar plundering Gaul to supply his army, **killed and plundered the richest 300 citizens of Rome.** With these supplies Mark Anthony and Octavian marched on Brutus and Cassius in Philippi in 42 BCE leaving Lepidus in charge of Rome. Meanwhile Cassius had retrieved the legions of Syrian Antioch.

Mark Anthony begged Cleopatra to re-supply his troops during the battle of Philippi. She abandoned him due to "unfavorable seas". Octavian, Mark Anthony's right flank, retreated, leaving Mark Anthony to stand alone, but after the death of Cassius, Octavian rejoined the battle on the second day to defeat Brutus. It was the bloodiest of Roman battles with 200,000 troops participating and 40,000 dead. With the death of Brutus, Cassius, and the Republic, Octavian returned to Rome while Mark Anthony reigned from Antioch in Syria, gateway to the Parthians of Babylon/Iran/Afghanistan which Julius Caesar had been preparing to invade. Mark Anthony retired his troops in Philippi who are therefore loyal to the Julio-Claudians and graciously reconciled with Cleopatra on her ship at Tarsus (the Turkish Tarsus of Paul's family), although many say he should have made her debark to have met on land at his glorious headquarters.

Herod was only minorly involved in the battle of Actium 31 BCE. Mark Anthony had assisted Herod's rise to power, killing the Sanhedrin, for which Sadducees would hate Herod forever. After Lepidus disloyally married the sister of the late Cassius, Octavian removed Lepidus from office becoming emperor. Mark Anthony planned on invading Rome with his troops and those of Herod and Cleopatra, but Cleopatra asked, "Send Herod after the Arabians who have given us no end of troubles." Herod was only able to send grain and money to support Mark Anthony's war. Octavian chose Agrippa as his admiral and Cleopatra's ships stood with Mark Anthony until the height of battle when she fled in her flagship, again scuttling Mark Anthony's battle plans.

After defeating Mark Anthony, Octavian would take the name "Augustus Caesar" and the month after Julius Caesar (July - August). Cleopatra had kept the rest of the world out of Rome's civil wars. Herod sailed from Israel to Rome exclaiming, "My loyalties lie with Rome!" diplomatically naming a son after Caesar's general Agrippa. Augustus' Roman navy sailed to Israel to be generously resupplied by Herod before attacking Cleopatra and Mark Anthony in Egypt. The Cassians remain in Rome continuing their hatred of Claudians including Mark Anthony and his friends, foreigners like Cleopatra and barbarians like Herod, yet the Claudians of Rome and soldiers of Philippi remain loyal to the late Mark Anthony. Paul looks forward to inspecting buildings peacefully in Philippi.

17 CORINTH 50 CE CASTAWAY

Paul leaves Philippi needing access to scribes to write **Paul's bible** and goes to Caesar's summer home of Corinth half-way between Athens and Sparta, the Greek cities of peaceful democratic philosophy and war. Corinth sits between the Adriatic and Aegean seas on an isthmus of land connecting the Peloponnese to Thrace and Macedonia (Thesslonica). Rome had razed Corinth a hundred years earlier (ch 1) and maintains an army busily cutting a canal where Paul will quarry stones for amphitheaters across four miles of stone mountain (the work will be completed in 1889).

Paul arrives home in Corinth during the reign of Claudius Caesar (40 – 54). Claudius is a relative of Mark Anthony (Marcus Antonius) and strong supporter of *Paul's Plan for Peace* where Jews and Greeks worship together in the temple. Paul architected most of **Paul's religion** before Antioch where he edited the book of Hebrews. From Antioch, Paul's four evangelists including Stephen took Hebrews to Jerusalem leaving their soon to be widows. Afterwards Paul retested *Paul's Plan for Peace* in Tarsus, Ephesus, Philippi, Thessalonica and now in Corinth where Paul will build his church, there being a natural division between architecting and building. Corinth is Paul's true home, perhaps not a natural setting for a Maccabean, Idumean Herodian, but the only safe place to write **Paul's gospel** for the Herodians scattered from Rome to Caesarea. In Rome a very pregnant Herodias' niece Mariamne is held hostage and in Caesarea Herod's Roman building projects continue unabated. Herod is even remodeling the Jerusalem temple, training Rechabites as masons for marble since Herodians, who keep the priestly vestments, are not allowed into the temple (15.11.5 Antiquities, Josephus).

Paul is acquainted with at least Hebrew, Aramaic and Greek, developing Paul's religion around the Greek version of love called philia, brotherly love as in Philippi (love of horses). Paul develops this love with his communities. First however the Roman governor Gallio (50-52) has to beat Sosthenes, the leader of the local synagogue, into submission. With the synagogue leader in compliance with Paul's plan, Paul applies his Pharisaic knowledge gaining the acceptance of most, many of whom regularly travel from Greece to Jerusalem for the annual High Holy days, so much so that the mouthpiece of Jacob (James), Cephas (Peter) will be called the founder of a church in Rome also sending his presence into Greece without ever having left the Levant.

We look at Paul through the lens of 2000 years, but the question must be asked, how much difference was there, at the time, between Catholicism and Judaism? The answer is that there is more of a difference between Sadducees (temple zealots) and Pharisees (synagogue-centered Roman accommodators) than between Christians and Jews. Some linguistically equate Christians with Sicarii, the penultimate Sadducee in their assassinations (erudite RHE?), however Christianity only separates from Judaism in 137 when Bar Cochba (Son of the Star) becomes the messianic hope of Israel once again and Christians, opposing the proposition, claim Jesus. Meanwhile every assembly tied into the temple with annual pilgrimages has some believers in Joseph's Bread of Life (Knowledge of Eternal Egyptian Judgement), a belief in a reward in the afterlife, the Egyptian Hall of Judgement or Zoroastrianism's angels and demons that make all men equal before their creator including kings. As priests say: From whom much has been given, much will be required (Lk 12:48).

18 CORINTH 50-58 CE THE POLITICS OF ROME

No place seems safe for Paul. Egyptian Alexandrians mock Herodians like Paul (*Against Flaccus*, Philo). Syrian Antioch has four widows (including Stephen's) whose husbands Paul had sent to their fate evangelizing in Jerusalem with donations for the famine. Herod is despised in Jerusalem while paying to remodel the temple. For his gospel Paul has been kicked out of Philippi, Thessalonica and Athens. Yet Paul travels to Corinth, the summer home of Caesar, where Paul will discuss his gospel with Seneca, the Stoic philosopher who believes that in greatness, men find immortality (On Tranquility of Mind).

Paul arrives in Corinth in 50 having followed Roman roads through Cappadocia and Macedonia, inspecting buildings while worried about his aunt Mariamne and her young son Aggripinus being schooled in Rome (held hostage). When he arrives in Corinth, Paul preaches and is hauled by Rabbi Sosthenes before the Roman governor, Gallio. Paul declares, "I am a Herod, a Roman building inspector here to review the canal quarry and all public buildings for cod and to meet Seneca, Gallio's brother, to review my gospel bringing Jews and Romans together with the Stoicism he taught me in Rome."

Gallio encourages Sosthenes to be hospitable to Paul (Sosthenes is beaten). During the eight years Paul remains in Corinth, Sosthenes will become a good friend (I Cor 1:1) along with fellow builders Pricilla and Aquilla who have been expelled from Rome as Jews (Acts 18:2). Paul's Roman teacher, Seneca the Stoic, Caesar's secretary, meets Paul in Caesar's summer home and says: "Long ago I trained you in Stoicism in Rome. Teach me now of your Hebrew doctrine of unity with Romans. Caesar wants peace and taxes." As Paul talks, Seneca begins to author a letter for Paul to the Romans.

Seneca provides scribes for Paul, including Epaphroditus, Seneca's successor, to copy and edit Paul's works. For eight years Paul writes in Corinth, preaching in the synagogue and practicing in Ephesus. Claudius Caesar supports Seneca's efforts. The goal, as always, is to find a method of peace for temple zealots, the Sadducees, the Sicarii, who carry curved knives under their robes in the temple courtyards. Seneca and Paul will rail against temple zealots as will Epaphroditus and Josephus decades later.

Unfortunately in 54 Claudius is succeeded by Nero and Seneca must leave Corinth, quietly returning to Rome where Nero persecutes Christians and Jews. Therefore Paul gathers his belongings, demanding Jewish synagogue donations, beginning his journey once again to Jerusalem with never a place to lay his head (Lk 9:58). Jewish pilgrims returning from their annual journey tell of Jacob's (James) leadership in Jerusalem. From Rome with the aid of Seneca and Epaphroditus, Herodias' niece Mariamne has escaped Nero's rages, coming to Corinth with her son Herodion (Agrippinus) to accompany Paul to the relative safety of Jerusalem. Herodion has never seen their hereditary Maccabean temple (the Jerusalem temple).

Before beginning the journey with synagogue donations from cities ringing the Aegean, Paul, Mariamne and her son Herodion ride the four miles across the isthmus of Corinth on horseback to perform a ceremony in secret. Paul's nephew Herodion, raised in Rome, is uncircumcised, which in Jerusalem would be a death sentence. Romans consider circumcision to be castration and a backwards Jewish custom. Roman law views circumcision as mutilation - child abuse. Rome and Jewdom are willing to come to violence over the flesh (Ro 7:5). Afterwards, boarding a ship with his very sick nephew, Paul finds a returning pilgrim carrying a letter in Hebrew. It is currently 58, fourteen years after Paul has visited Jerusalem and seven years after the leader of the Corinthian synagogue was beaten to ensure Paul's preeminence. Jacob (James) in Jerusalem has mostly recovered from Paul's last visit in 44, his knees gnarled from his fall from the temple, his beard grizzled at 92, but his eyes seeing across the world to Corinth. Paul snatches the letter sent to the Jews of Corinth and sails to meet its maker.

19 CORINTH 58 CE THE LETTER OF JACOB (JAMES)

To the Pharisees of the Synagogue of Corinth from the Council at Jerusalem:

Dear Peacemakers,

Greetings from Jerusalem (the Jerusalem council), from our beloved High Priest (selected by Herod), from Pharisees (Roman accommodators) who wish you the freedom found in Torah, from Essenes (pacifists) who wish you humanity, from Sadducees (zealots) who wish you the liberty to live in Jerusalem, from Bethlehem (the city of David) wishing you eternal life, from Rechabites (Craftsmen) remodeling our temple,

We write you by the kind permission of Rome, through the grace of the family of Herod, descended from priestly Maccabees, who kindly remember the sacrifice of our beloved Jesus, our dear son sacrificed for peace, as was Isaac by Abraham [or nearly so Gen 22:10]. Just as Joseph sought peace for our people in Egypt, leading us into safety, so too does Clopas, the father of Jesus, Simon, Jude and Jacob (James/Israel). For his son's sacrifice giving peace with Rome, our father [of Israel] is called first among us, in Greek, Alphaeus by name*. Our High Priest sends greetings praying that Jesus' death might preserve all Israel (Jn 11:50).

Over the last seven years, pilgrims to Jerusalem have related many of the happenings in Corinth. We have heard of a Roman mason or building inspector filled with the spirit**. Please come have dinner with us. As you are aware we invite the shepherds of every Synagogue in the known world to visit every seven years, bringing offerings of first-fruits and leaving fields fallow to review our common orthodox doctrine while recording the births, deaths, joys and sorrows of our people and sending our letters of recommendation for your service.

To the Peacemakers of Corinth from the House of abundant Bread (Bethlehem) by the hand of [Israel] Jacob (James): Egyptian pyramids point out the North Star eternally guiding souls, like Joseph guiding Israel into Egypt saving Israel, like my father leading us into serving our most benevolent and world ruling Romans. Please remember as you watch our Star [from Jacob] (Num 24:17)*** that Joseph served Israel as we serve you.

Silence be with us,

rs Jacob/Israel (James),
the son of Joseph (Clopas) whose sacrifice we will always remember.****

*Jesus sacrificed himself (Ch XX The Power of Rome through History, Understanding the Bible, Ray Shortell 2013). Jesus' brothers were Jacob (James), Simon, Joses and Judas (Mt 13:55). Jacob is Israel (Gen 32:28).

**Paul in Corinth here is referenced as "filled with the spirit" or "hot air", the words breath and spirit being the same in Hebrew. Or the word "windbag" used for Paul referencing old used wineskins, like a wrinkled old man's privates (stones) filled with emptiness (childlessness), "Wine" sounding the same as "Greek" in Hebrew suggesting that perhaps Paul is not adhering to good doctrine and even now bringing outsiders, Greeks, into Judaism wholesale (ibid Ch XXII The Cup Of Blood, Ch XV Letters).

***Essenes like Jacob were buried with their feet pointing to the North Star under the dome of heaven much as Egypt's pyramids have a star chamber pointing the soul's way to the North Star. Queen Helen literally had three pyramids made in Jerusalem for her and her two sons to have a proper burial. Num 24:17 says a star will come from Jacob. Jacob and his father (Joseph) known as "the Egyptian", struggle for peace amongst intense passions.

****rs means "Respectfully Submitted" on behalf of the Jerusalem Council (ibid About the Author).

20 TARSUS 58 CE I COR 13 ASTROLOGY

After sailing for some days Paul's ship comes to rest on the shores of Tarsus which Paul claims as his hometown. The group has arrived at a most auspicious time, just as when Cleopatra joined Mark Anthony (Marcus Antonius) here after the battle of Philippi. Tarsus has spent months preparing to re-enact the myths of Hercules. In the evening at his family's mansion, Paul visits with Herodias' niece Mariamne and her son, Herodian. Herodion asks, "will the play happen tomorrow?" Later Paul sleeps in an upper room. In the morning Paul meets his family for breakfast before stepping out onto the porch to take in the reenactment.

Hercules is performed in the town square by a large man dressed in a cape surrounded by all. The narrator calls to the crowd in the West-South-West. All of the audience in this section have been born in April – what our current calendar would call March 19 – April 20th, the month of Aries. At the end of the first trial, the crowd screams, "Love is Hope!" The next section, from May, screams at the end of the second trial, "Love is Trust!" Paul's family's home was fortunately located in the South-South-West of the town square keeping the sun at their backs for better viewing and June Gemini babies cry with Paul, "Love is Forgiveness!" How the actors manage to get all of the animals through the crowd is another story. The July Cancers yell, "Love is a Feeling!"

The narrator continues that each sign will carry all the qualities of the signs behind it. The crowd's roars get longer and longer as hours by the sundial held by Hercules pass in minutes teaching children to tell time. When the August Leos come up, Aries people cry, "Love is Hope!" Taurus people cry, "Love is Trust!" Gemini people cry, "Love is Forgiveness!" Cancers cry, "Love is a Feeling!" Until Leos finally cry, "Love is Freedom!" Through each test the narrator turns counter-clockwise like reading a horoscope as the man playing Hercules tells about the challenges he faces in each of the signs he crosses, supported by farmers with a lion, a deer, horses, a wild boar, chickens and a dog walking onstage to each point on the compass in turn for the twelve signs like the twelve hours of the day.

Paul explains to Herodion that the twelve tribes of Israel and the twelve stones upon the breastplate of the High Priest are also about the twelve months of the year. Virgos scream, "Love is Humility!" Libras scream, "Love is Beauty!" and Scorpios cry, "Love is Harmony!" It was getting up around noon, both literally and metaphorically as Hercules went through each of his trials and so after the Sagittarians cry, "Love is Honesty!" The crowd breaks for intermission and lunch with three signs left to go. Stage-hands run back and forth carrying fences and moving all of the animals needed for the play.

After lunch the people born in January cry, "Love is Loyalty!" And the narrator concludes that Hercules' ten tasks have been accomplished and that Hercules is free to go, but the crowd cries "No!", sending Hercules onto his next tasks after noting his having cheated at two tasks by getting assistance. Hercules is given two more tasks: taking the world on his shoulders while Aquarians yell, "Love is Unselfish!" And visiting the underworld, the valley of the shadow of death while Pisceans yell, "Love is Faith!"

Paul watches with his nephew, Herodion, remembering how it felt to get the letter from Jacob (James) for the Corinthian Synagogue which was possibly intended to shred Paul's credibility. Paul begins to compose his letter to the Corinthians. Meanwhile Hercules is placed on a bier, a ten-foot tall stack of firewood, his funeral pyre, which is lit. Only the actors and stage-hands know how the star of the play manages to crawl out of the bonfire.

Paul's letter to the Corinthians will include chapter thirteen (I Cor 13), the love chapter, from this play. Children in Tarsus are given this play as the best the town can do for their education. I Cor 13 starts with Taurus, "Love is Patient" and combines Capricorn and Aquarius into one statement: "Love rejoices not in evil, but rejoices in the truth." I Cor 13 (my paraphrase): Love is patient. Love is kind. Love is not envious. Love is not puffed up. Love is not ill-mannered. Love seeks not its own. Love is not easily angered. Love remembers not past grievances. Love rejoices not in evil, but rejoices in the truth. In the end these three remain: Faith, Hope and Love and the greatest of these is Love. If I were to give everything and have my body burned, but have not love, it profiteth nothing.

21 TARSUS 58 CE THE UNKNOWN G-D

Paul, Herodias' niece Mariamne and Herodion say goodbye to family in Tarsus and go to the sea at dusk where the captain, a Roman marine, says, "We sail at daybreak." The Captain doesn't like Paul and doesn't like waiting, having been charged by Seneca, Caesar's secretary, with escorting Paul to Caesarea. "Our delays including at Miletus, waiting for Trophimus to bring the donation of Ephesus has brought winter weather," says the captain. Six synagogue treasurers voyage with Paul, but sick Trophimus was left behind with his donation at Miletus.

Nero's rampages have begun in Rome and Paul and the Herods seek the relative safety of Caesarea with well-crafted documents, after seven years explaining in Corinth that Judaism is meant for all, because G-d promised that Abraham would be a blessing to all. Paul prays his mission will preserve the temple and Herodian family. Like the Roman accommodating Pharisees, **Paul's Plan for Peace** desires good relations with Rome, praising meekness and temperance in disciples (Gal 5:23). Jesus teaches in the Gospel of Thomas 42: Become passers-by.

Paul is thankful that Seneca, Caesar's secretary, had returned to Rome to assist Mariamne and her son, Herodion, in their escape. Seneca and his protégé, Epaphroditus, will eventually convince Nero to give **Paul's Plan for Peace** another review. Epaphroditus will publish Josephus' *War of the Jews*, the final days of Jerusalem.

During Paul's last evening on the shores of Turkey a young man on the beach prays to a statuette of Diana of Ephesus. Paul recalls the Herculean effort of Tarsus passing on the best education it can muster for children, a play about Astrology possibly originating in ancient Egypt or in the earlier Hittite (Turkish) or Sumerian (Babylonian) civilizations. A young man kneels on a platform on a rocky outcropping staring into the sea. When Paul asks, "Which g-d hears your prayer?", the man points to the rocky shore where Paul notices figurines.

The man says, "The weather is turning. I pray to all the powers that be for our safe journey to Caesarea." Paul looks at his ship's bow with its figurehead, the heavenly twins, the Dioscori Castor and Pollux, the constellation of Gemini, laughing at the world. Paul finds the sculpture another sign of people searching for meaning. The young man says, "I sought spiritual knowledge from the Oracle of Delphi (Greece) who has sent me to Egypt to seek a teacher to learn the mysteries of the pyramids."

Paul considers the young man's search as like a fisherman casting his net, first into one spiritual tradition and then into another. Paul wonders at G-d who is present everywhere (Ro 8:35, 38-39) asking why people must seek G-d in Delphi, in Egypt, in the story of Hercules, in this altar on the ocean or even at Jerusalem. This is **The War of Jesus**, whether religion will be defined by the temple caught in a proxy war between Rome and Parthia or by a greater context. The Gospel of Thomas 48 says when two (Jew and Greek) make peace in the house (the temple) then they might say to the mountain (Mt. Moriah, the temple mount, a fortified city on a hill 32), "Move from here!" and it will move. Paul prays that his transcendent and cosmopolitan vision of Judaism, **Paul's Plan for Peace**, will allow peace between Jerusalem and Rome preserving all.

In the morning Paul, Mariamne and Paul's nephew, Herodion, are again on the ship bound for Caesarea. The captain has observed the sky and is working hard to beat the weather, but due to rough seas, plans an unscheduled stop in Antioch to reseal the ship's hull. Paul dreads Antioch, his famine mission to Jerusalem having left Greek widows there ten years earlier in the care of whomever he could muster: The deacons - table servants, those dedicated to the proposition that regardless of keeping kosher, Jews and Greeks should eat together.

22 ANTIOCH 58 CE WIDOWS' REVENGE

Blown before a furious wind that settled later that afternoon, Paul's ship soon makes port needing maintenance. Paul chooses to not get out of the boat and reviews his notes on what he will soon be preaching in Caesarea and Jerusalem, Paul's book of ***Hebrews***: The religion of Abraham is a blessing for all and temple has been opened. The second covenant of faith given by the prophets is better than the first, which is close to disappearing. G-d's chosen one has arisen from the grave and the rest of the world now comes to Jerusalem, not for its antiquated sacrifices, but for faithful spiritual leadership.

Paul reads his scrolls knowing the hefty donation he carries will grant him an audience in Jerusalem. The Greek philosopher, Seneca, Caesar's secretary, has listened to Paul's speech, improving Paul's command of Stoicism with its patient view of life. Pragmatically, Seneca has ordered the ship's captain to get Paul safely to Caesarea and collect the taxes from Herod, although ironically Paul carries a hefty donation in the opposite direction to the temple. Paul watches the soldiers on board, knowing their lives are at stake protecting his safety. But the church of Antioch has noted Paul's arrival and waits on shore to talk.

Paul steps onto the dock to meet the church and smells boiled pitch being pounded into the hull. The church leader is Jude, one of the four brothers of Jesus (Jacob/James, Cephas/Simeon/Peter, Barnabas/Joses and Jude/Judas/Thomas). Jude is dressed only in a white linen robe, an undergarment and sandals and says, "Jacob (James) has called for you to be heard, however first there are the widows." Jude requires Paul to honor the widows of Antioch, whose husbands were martyred preaching Paul's gospel in Jerusalem ten years ago. Jude asks whether Paul would like to meet the widows and Paul replies, "time is short and the journey most pressing." Jude does not handle the money. Paul gives his donation to two Roman soldiers, sending them with two deacons to the church. Paul invites Jude aboard knowing that Jacob, the leader of Jerusalem, is the brother of Jude.

In 115 Jude's grandchildren will ask of Rome their rightful bishopric in Antioch, but for now their father, a deacon, Jude's son, serves Jude, carrying Jude's lone small bag aboard filled with dried pulse – grain needing water to be edible. Once underway Jude pulls out a scroll and sits on the deck for days, never going below, reading and praying out loud from dawn until dusk and lighting a candle at midnight to do the same for an hour. This grates on Paul's nerves, but Paul knows that Jude is not a man with whom to trifle. Paul retreats to the other end of the ship with soldiers and looks forward with great trepidation to meeting Jacob, the brother of Jude.

Paul and Jacob share the doctrine of eternal life which is foundational to Christianity. In Jewish metaphor knowledge (da'at) is referred to as "bread" (lechem), the currency of theology, much as in English the euphemism "bread" can be used for "money". Jews claiming knowledge of eternal afterlife remember the Egyptian Hall of Judgement, referring to this knowledge as a special privilege granting fearlessness in the face of death, "the Bread of Life", as Jesus said, 'I am come that they might have life, and that they might have it more abundantly. Fear not … him who has power to destroy the body' (roughly Jn 10:10 & Mt 10:28). The leaders of "The Way" are descendants of David from the town of Bethlehem, David's hometown, finding their metaphors happily intertwining with scripture making straight their paths, leveling mountains and filling valleys. "The Poor", Essene pacifists like Jude, carry no money due to its graven image, its sculpture of a king who is not a brother, rejecting the world and anything Rome might tax. As Jesus said, "be in this world, but not of this world (monetarily)(roughly Jn 16:33, Ro 12:2, Mt 10:16)."

23 JERUSALEM 58 CE THE BOOK OF HEBREWS

Everywhere else Paul supports cosmopolitanism as the apostle to the gentiles. However at this meeting with James, Paul knows he must speak directly to the Hebrews, justifying a Messiah prophesied by and superseding the covenant. Rather than rebuffing Cephas (Peter) for refusing to eat with Greeks, Paul will argue against the Hellenists (Greeks/gentiles) while teaching a Christ greater than Angels, Abraham, Melchezidek and the temple.

Paul remembers ten years ago, banished from Jerusalem by Herod, waiting in Caesarea while sending his presence onto Jerusalem with four Greek evangelists from Antioch. Jacob (James) and the Sadducees had not accepted Paul's gentiles. The evangelists were murdered, as it is said: Jerusalem kills her prophets. Paul preached fourteen years afterwards in Greece until Paul's "spirited" preaching had reached Jerusalem, where in Hebrew "spirit", "wind" and "breath" are the same word implying "windbag" (hot air). Preparing for Jerusalem, Paul has brought temple donations from Greek cities and a sealed scroll from Seneca, Caesar's secretary.

Walking onto the dock in Caesarea, Paul again notes Roman crosses filled with Jews. Samaritans have not yet taken over the empty synagogue. Drusilla greets her sister Mariamne who has returned from Rome with uncle Paul, "Our brother Herod Agrippa is with soldiers collecting taxes in Galilee for my husband, Felix." Drusilla continues, "And who is this young man? Could this be Herodion?" She confides, "Your grandmother, Cypros, will fuss at Agrippa for not being here to greet everyone. Come inside, Herodion, let me put up my swollen ankles while aunt Bernice tells you a story. I've suddenly morning sickness again."

Inside, Bernice, the eldest sister suggests the importance of harmony telling the story of Herod: In the year 37 in Caesarea, Herod gave a piece of property to a centurion to keep him close, hiding the price of this property from Herodias for which they both died, like Ananias and Sapphira (Acts 5). Herodias was an ambitious woman, berating Herod for his indiscretion and brow-beating him into travelling to Rome to beg a promotion from Caesar. She was furious that Agrippa Herod, our father, who she despised, had been given her ex-husband Philip's Galilee. In Rome, our father Agrippa reported Herod's 70,000 suits of armor for which Herod was retired to Spain, chastised for failing to lead for his wife. Dad was given all of Judea and Caesar even asked Herodias to marry Agrippa for her riches and Maccabean lineage. Per Deu 17:15 only a brother might reign in Israel. However Herodias refused, loving her husband or despising us, and was `retired` with Herod.

The next morning Agrippa has returned and Paul explains, "In my cosmopolitan Judaism, *(Paul's Plan for Peace)*, the temple accepts people of many beliefs including us Herods and Romans. We will have the Pax Romana!" Governor Felix reads the scroll from Seneca, and Paul rides away with Herodion, following the road to Jerusalem through the pass at Beit Horon. Paul's cosmopolitan plan will ensure the safety of Jews around the Mediterranean who annually visit the temple. After four days on beautiful Roman roads, Paul is surprised to meet Jacob with his broken knees nearly healed fourteen years after Paul's first attempt at preaching to Jerusalem.

Jacob greets Paul warmly with few words, "Welcome traveler, we have heard rumors that you and your disciples struggle with the law, however the peace which surpasses all understanding speaks more here. Let me help with your re-introduction to Jerusalem by your taking a temporary vow of silence with four others for whom you will pay according to the traditions of our fathers. Afterwards these four, whom you will know intimately, will be sent to care for the widows you've left at Antioch." Paul considers saying something about Cephas's (Peter's) escape to Antioch and the execution of his Roman guard, but Jacob's silence is an unrefusable offer.

After four days of silence in Jerusalem, Paul opens his parchments and begins preaching the book of Hebrews just as his four evangelists had ten years earlier. Jacob listens politely until Sadducees again intervene, "You have polluted this temple by bringing in the gentile dog Trophimus the Ephesian! Only your blood will atone! Only afterwards may our temple once again atone for the blood spilled butchering our daily meat!" Paul rejects having invited Trophimus as having left him sick in Miletus. Paul claims the eternal spirit of Bethlehem as his propitiation.

Herodion, Paul's nephew, storms in with a Roman guard. Like a fox without a den (Lk 9:58), Paul has nowhere to lay his head. Nero has banished the Jews from Rome. Alexandria's pogrom continues. Corinth and Greece are unsafe and Antioch has Paul's four grieving widows. The family home of Caesarea becomes a prison to Paul while he waits and writes.

24 CAESAREA 58 CE PAUL, THE WRITER

In Caesarea Paul watches empty Roman crosses staked to the hill and is essentially imprisoned in his room, staring hopelessly at the sea through narrow windows from the walls of the Herodian palace. Paul remembers his Herodian family's attempts at acceptance, controlling of the High Priest's vestments, selecting the High Priest from the twenty-four courses (High Priestly families), and even paying to refurbish the temple. Paul himself, after his education in Rome in masonry, had taught priests how to cut stone, yet was not allowed to review his students' work in the temple. Finally, Paul's books of Hebrews and Galatians have failed to lay a theological foundation for the introduction of gentiles, Greeks and Herods into the temple. ***Paul's Plan for Peace*** has failed.

With deep despair, Paul writes from his "prison" the books of Galatians for gentiles, sending I Corinthians from Caesarea as well. Paul feels betrayed by Jerusalem, by Antioch and Ephesus. II Timothy 1:25 sums up Paul's experience thus far: **All they which are in Asia have turned away from me.** However his words betray a hope that somehow, elsewhere, Paul's gospel might be heard, and return to bear fruit.

Paul spends a few years in Caesarea discussing theology with family and Roman governors. The three sisters of Agrippa II are Mariamne, Bernice and Drusilla. Rather than meeting with the church, the widows of Anitoch or the Sadducean temple zealots, Paul meets with Bernice and Drusilla before Agrippa II visits. Both sisters have traded up in husbands for money and status. Therefore, although these Herodian women are seen by Rome as Jewesses (Acts 24:24), they are despised by temple Sadducees who are enamored with their Three Nets of Belial: Fornication, Riches and Pollution of the Temple.

The Herods are marvels of athleticism and charisma. Josephus noted Herod the Terrible's donations to and participation in the Olympic games (Wars I 21:12) leaving his posterity a great name. Agrippa Herod was named after Caesar's general who defeated Mark Anthony (Marcus Antonius) and Cleopatra in battle. The Herods are masters of politics with Drusilla married to the Roman governor Felix of Judea from Caesarea.

In 59 Caesar sends a new Roman governor Festus to replace Drusilla's husband Felix. Felix returns to Rome with his wife and new baby. After Sadducees demand Paul's presence at the temple, offering to pay handsomely, Festus asks himself why previous assessors had missed this revenue, before asking Paul, "Paul, wouldn't you feel more at home in Jerusalem where your family's Maccabees have lived for ages?" Paul knows the temple Sadducees there will make his journey and stay unsafe.

Festus' decision is made when Seneca, Caesar's secretary, sends to Caesarea demanding Paul. It is time for Paul to go. Festus, pandering to the Sadducees in Jerusalem promising a "trial", asks Paul to make a quick trip to Jerusalem. Paul appeals to Caesar and Herod Agrippa II, the son of "Caesar's friend", travels from Galilee to Caesarea with taxes for Rome and to discuss the fate of Paul. Festus is convinced, and Paul begins the long journey to Rome with the taxes brought by Agrippa. Seneca plans to convince Caesar that ***Paul's Plan for Peace*** will bring temple Jews, Sadduceans, under Roman control, including the extreme Sicarii zealots, allowing for Rome's interests, the Pax Romana and taxes.

25 ROME 60 CE JOSEPH THE EGYPTIAN

Upon arriving in Rome Paul meets with Christians, a small subset of the Jews of the new small Roman synagogue (rebuilt after Nero's Jewish expulsions) who have pilgrimaged to Jerusalem learning of the Bread of Life (knowledge of eternal life come down from heaven). The euphemism "Bread" can sometimes means money. In this sense, the currency of theology is knowledge (bread). Its teacher in Israel is Joseph (the father of Jesus), also known as Alphaeus (Mt 10:3), also known as the father of Israel, also known as the Egyptian, but his name is Clopas who per the gospels spoke with Jesus after the crucifixion on the road to Emmaus (Lk 24:18). Sometimes Biblical dissimulators call him the uncle of Jesus since John 19:25 refers to Clopas as the husband of Mary, the sister of Mary, the mother of Jesus.

secretary, eventually meets Paul, asking to understand warriors of Bethlehem to enforce **Paul's Plan for Peace**. Paul begins his story for Seneca, explaining the warriors, the descendants of David from Bethlehem who frustrate Rome's plans for warriors fear not death and yet fight with peace, rising in the morning to welcome the linen of priests and rarely breaking their code of silence. Seneca knows only Caesar's ear and so settles in to listen to the tale of Joseph the Egyptian.

ian, whose real name was Clopas, took his young family from Bethlehem of the escape Herod the Terrible before 4BCE, leading his family into Egypt as did the (Mt 2:13-15; Gen 50:24). Rechabite priests, like Joseph, are tradesmen, masons, scribes and it was with these skills in Egypt that Clopas was able to make a living. returned from Egypt with the Egyptian theology of the "Bread of Life". The four Jacob (James), Jude (Judas), Cephas (Simon, Peter), Jesus and Barnabas (Joses). father of Israel because his son, Jacob (James) was given the name Israel in the first 28). At the crucifixion, Joseph prayed with Jacob's Essenes for peace and Jacob ing father being father to all Israel, just as the High Priest consoled Joseph for giving servation of all Israel (Jn 11:50). Therefore Jacob preaches peacefully in Israel and the patron saint of fathers.

thlehem refers to the Egyptian Hall of Judgement where your soul is weighed against ather. If your soul is lighter than the feather, it goes to heaven. As previously noted this nids pointing to the North Star, the prophesy of a star coming from Jacob (Num 24:17), rial of the Essenes with their feet pointing north towards the center of the great ceiling where our North Star never moves, eternally present even remaining during our day dowed by our sun.

Daniel is backdated from Bethlehem, this school of knowledge of the Bread of Life. rophesies written in the past tense (some refer to this as the prophetic tense, written as if y happened), Daniel missing his immediate rulers while knowing minutiae about the me of Bethlehem, Daniel being the first book of the Bible referencing an eternal e soul and now this proof: Daniel 5:25 is notable for having non-Hebrew writing: Mene, Jpharsin (You have been weighed and found wanting), making no Hebrew sense, the e's soul mentioned nowhere else in Torah or Prophets. This metaphor comes from the of the Dead where your soul is weighed against a feather and if lighter passes into heaven orth Star. The fingers writing upon the wall in Daniel would have used an unmentioned feather.

holds the title, "Alphaeus", the first, for having brought back this knowledge of the Bread of Life. In my opinion he is called in Josephus, "the Egyptian". Dr. Eisenman notes The Egyptian made his home base the Mount of Olives as do the followers of Jesus above the Garden of Gethsemane. According to Josephus this Egyptian led 4000 followers, assuredly undercounted, into the wilderness, the desert, to escape Rome much as our Bible says thousands were added to the church at Pentecost.

After listening to Paul's story, Seneca asked Paul for copies of Romans and Hebrews, copying and editing Paul's previous books for the Bible. Paul writes II Corinthians and Philippians after hearing tales of woe from these synagogues and sends them with Philemon, a run-away slave from Corinth, a scribe Seneca returns to Corinth with Paul's books Philemon, the second letter to the Corinthians and a letter for Thessalonica further up the coast of Greece.

26 ROME 62 CE JACOB'S (JAMES') KISS OF DEATH

The Mafia works in mysterious ways. Paul had expressed an intention to visit Spain where the brothers Seneca and Gallio are retiring (Caesar's Secretary and Paul's governor of Corinth), but Rome's plans for Judea have taken shape and Paul is conscripted one last time to entreat Jacob (James) to remove Jewish exclusivity (xenophobia) and pay Roman taxes like good citizens. And so Paul returns to Jerusalem with an embassage. Now the word embassage comes from the Latin for servant and along with the ambassadors, Rome sends a laundryman, a cleaner… from the family of Cassius.

After travelling to Jerusalem Paul holds his final debate against the silence of Jacob. Jacob's name is not James. James is a "mistranslation" of Jacob. Jacob might remain silent regarding the mistranslation, but assuredly does not call himself James. Lacking a direct quote, calling someone other than what they call themselves is ignorant. Jacob's father is Joseph who is sometimes called "the Egyptian" (maybe Alphaeus or Clopas).

Jacob has aged and is now ninety-six. Paul, decades earlier, had unsuccessfully preached the book of Hebrews, that the new priesthood promised in the order of the immortal Melchizedek supersedes the daily bestial sacrifice. Upon failing, Paul taught Greek cities faith, to which Jacob had replied that faith without works is dead (Ja 2:17). Paul now preaches Galatians, Corinthians and Romans: That G-d has promised Abraham children like the sand of the desert and the stars of the sky, blessing all nations (Gen 26:4), that the covenant belongs not to Israel, the first-born, but to the second like Seth (Abel, Cain), Isaac (Ishmael) and Jacob (Esau). Paul says, "Moses watched the first-born of the Egyptians die (Ex 4:10). Hear his voice and harden not your heart (Ps 95:7-8). The new covenant is a stumbling-block, a rejected cornerstone as prophesied (Ps 118:2), like a short-sheeted bed where the covers don't fit until you understand (Is 28:20), its teachers not making haste (Is 28:16), while speaking with stammering lips in a foreign tongue (Greek) (Is 28:11), laying precept upon precept as prophesied (Is 28:10), of a servant wounded in the hands (Zech 13:6), sold for thirty pieces of silver like Paul's four Greek evangelists (Chapter 13, Zech 11:13), like the good shepherd (Zech 7) who arrives on an ass, with the foal of an ass (Zech 9:9), wearing clothes washed in the blood of grapes (Gen 49:11), the rest of Israel not understanding (Zech 10:2), the pools of the river (knowledge) drying up (Zech 10:11, Seneca's mentor burning the library at Alexandria Chaper 29), never justified by the law (Ps 143:2), all nations calling Jesus blessed (Ps 72), the Davidic fountain of living waters for sin and uncleanness (Jer 17:13, Zech 13:1-8, Jn 4:10), not like a forsaken Israel with a Roman invasion, a vineyard destroyed (Is 5), branches marred (Nahum 2), planted in a desert with withering branches (Eze 19), but becoming a nation of priests (Ex 19:6), with no oppression of strangers (Ex 22:21), giving access to the temple (the body of Jesus Mk 14:58; the church I Cor 12:12) to which all nations flow (Is 2:2). The Law is now written in our hearts says Paul (Jer 31:33), "grafted" into the root of Torah (Rom 11:17). If now is not the time to become a nation of Priests to the world (Ex 19:6), says Paul, then when?

Such is Paul's passion and knowledge of scripture that Paul's Roman servants are astounded, but even more so with the silence with which Jacob confronts Paul. Jacob believes in actions and peace more so than words (Ja 3). Paul preaches cosmopolitanism and acceptance of Romans asking for Jacob's blessing as Essau had asked of Jacob's father Isaac, but Jacob remains silent, until as silent as a lamb, Jacob is thrown again from the pinnacle of the temple, praying for his murderers while beaten to death with a fuller's club (laundryman's club, Ch 31). The cleaner had followed Paul from Rome under orders from Nero to ensure the acceptance of Paul's cosmopolitan mission or the elimination of Jacob. Cephas (Peter) weeps bitterly, wailing again in the temple for the death of another brother, first Jesus and now Jacob, and is ordered to take up his complaints with Caesar in Rome.

Footnote: Eusebius is our premier church historian writing around 300 and preserving the works of

Hegessipus who wrote of the death of James around 160 <below>. Per Dr. Robert Eisenman the story of the death of James is retold in the stoning of Stephen (Ch 14, James, the Brother of Jesus 1998). Stephen likewise observes the heavens opened and begs G-d for the forgiveness of his murderers for "they know not what they do".

Hegesippus in his *Memoirs* - "The aforesaid Scribes and Pharisees, accordingly, placed Jacob upon a **wing of the Temple**, and cried out to him '**O thou Just One, whom we ought all to credit, since the people are led astray after Jesus that was crucified, declare** to us **what is the door to Jesus that was crucified**.' But he answered with a loud voice, 'Why do you ask me regarding Jesus the Son of Man? **He is now sitting in the heavens on the right hand of Great Power, and is about to come on the clouds of Heaven.**'…

And they began to stone him as he did not die immediately when cast down; but turning round, he knelt down, saying, 'I beseech Thee, **O Lord G-d and Father, forgive them, for they know not what they do.**' Thus they were stoning him, when one of the **priests of the sons of Rechab**, a son of the Rechabites spoken of and by Jeremiah the prophet, cried out, saying, 'Stop! What are you doing? The Just is praying for you.'

Thus one of them, **a fuller, beat out the brains of the Just with the club he used to beat out clothes.** Thus he suffered **martyrdom**, and they **buried him on the spot where his tombstone still remains, close to the Temple.** He became a faithful witness; both to the Jews and to the Greeks that Jesus is the Christ. **Immediately after this, Vespasian invaded and took Judea.**" (Hegesippus as quoted in Eusebius, *Ecclesiastical History,* Book II, xxiii)

http://www.biblesearchers.com/hebrewchurch/primitive/primitive15.shtml

27 CAESAREA 62 CE HEROD'S GOSPEL OF MATTHEW

After Jacob's (James') cruel death Paul begins his final journey to Rome, finding more soldiers in Caesarea than expected. The soldiers arrive under orders from Rome finding Paul's Plan for Peace failed. They arrest Paul making an example by tying him to the crosses Herod uses for Caesarean Pharisees accused by Samaritans. While Paul is lashed with whips and in agony, the Cleaner talks: His name is Gaius Cassius Longinus, Herod's ruler from Antioch and named after the Cassius killed by Mark Anthony, the family in Rome hating Mark Anthony and all Herodians like Paul. "You take too long to die." Impatient, Longinus mercifully sticks a lance in the two Pharisees crucified on either side of Paul, to hurry death listening to the sucking wounds as they gasp their last. With a silent cry like a lamb being slaughtered the two on either side of Paul die.

Longinus and the temple embassage heading for Rome have a discussion. Longinus asks Cephas (Peter), Josephus and eight other temple priests how they feel about Paul's impending death explaining that Rome is doing everything it can to accomplish peace knowing that Sadducees have not appreciated Paul's double-talk: claiming to be a Jew to the Jew and otherwise elsewhere. "Paul speaks with a forked tongue", says the Cleaner, referencing John the Baptist's denunciation of the Herodians as a brood of snakes and Paul's Herodian lineage. "Herod will take the news of Paul's death back to Jerusalem", says Longinus, but then has soldiers take Paul down from the cross and bind his wounds. "Remember this", says Longinus to Paul, "and be silent" as Paul is loaded on the ship.

Longinus says to Herod, "Caesar asked me to take care of Jacob (James) if Paul failed, giving me power over all including you, up to your life and the life of Paul, for whom Caesar's contentious wife, Poppea, begged. As the embassage with Paul returns to Rome for a trial, take these soldiers to Jerusalem seeking peace and await word from Rome. My family, the Cassians of Rome, are currently displeased with Caesar's and your handling of this affair, for Rome's plan to invade Parthia may be thwarted by Jerusalem. Can you tell me any more about the prophesies of Messiah?"

Herod, Paul's half-uncle, writes all the Messianic prophesies of his priestly Maccabean lineage, which Herod himself fulfills: Messiah would descend from Bethlehem (Micah 5:2) as a star and scepter of Jacob (Num 24:17). The child would signal the birth of a new order. He would be called out of Egypt which Herod had visited after Caesar's accession. Messiah would be of the seed of David and of priests (Psalm 110). From Psalm 22 and Isaiah 53 Herod explains the gospel of the Messiah to whom all nations will bring treasure, who will rule the world from the throne of David in Jerusalem and upon whom all Israel waited. Herod who enters Jerusalem on branches (37 Gaius, Philo), adorned with the wisdom passed down through his Maccabean lineage with its progenitor, King David, outlines the prophesies of Torah as related to Jesus explaining that when Messiah is come, Jerusalem would not accept the good shepherd as king, for he would not be a pretty man and his story would be like a short-sheeted bed which fails to cover everything (Is 28:20). Herod explains that Messiah, Israel's cornerstone, will be as rejected as himself (Is 28:16, 22).

Herod again leaves for Jerusalem hoping to stop the riots after Paul's multiple visits, this time with news that Paul would no longer be working to introduce Greeks like Trophimus the Ephesian into the temple (Acts 21:29, 20:4, II Tim 4:20). The Jewish embassage to Rome, ten Sadducees including Josephus (the Roman historian) and Cephas (Peter), hope for Caesar's favor. Rome takes an intense interest in the prophesies of Messiah, having worked until Paul's most recent failure to accommodate zealots, the xenophobic Sadducees, if in any way peace and taxes might be accomplished. Rome's cosmopolitan charity (tolerance, munificence) seeks the welfare of all subjects, although the Cassians of Rome dispute which Romans should be considered more than barbarians and Josephus will later declare of Jerusalem, "You are the only people who think it a disgrace to be servants to those to whom all the world hath submitted. You are not freedom fighters, but recalcitrant slaves." Temple zealots work against peace, incessantly finding righteousness lacking everywhere outside of the temple, especially among the Herodian brood of snakes. Sadducees describe Rome as Egypt (the land of sin) or Babylon where Judah was exiled from the temple and busy themselves finding reasons to reject even their own as not pure enough.

Paul's visit to Jerusalem is therefore Rome's final attempt to reconcile Jacob and Paul, temple zealots and Romans. With Paul's failure, Rome's intended purpose has failed: The dream of a unified church, *Paul's Plan for Peace*, where zealots pay taxes and Romans visit the Holy of Holies. Rome will blame Herod, furious at his having rebuilt the temple, having prepared Israel for war, yet never having demanded his own or Roman admittance.

"You have failed," says Longinus to Paul, "you and yours (Herod), have robbed Rome of her glory in rebuilding a xenophobic temple which refuses entrance to Caesar, a fortified isolated enclave which cannot be ignored (Thomas 32). Your Sadducees (zealots) have stolen the taxes of Rome, hiding gold in the temple, while your Essenes (pacifists) have stolen the glory of Rome in failing to render tribute; scumbags holding no taxable property, much as your priests often accuse the synagogue in Rome of stealing from the temple in failing to render tithes and offerings (Mal 3:8). Rome will repay your temple's insolence and your Herodian naiveté at having prepared Jerusalem for war using the riches from the tomb of King David, which belongs to the public and should now reside in Rome. Your half-uncle Herod never even demanded the entrance of Roman officials!"

Sicarii, the penultimate Sadducees (zealots) in their xenophobic assassinations, refer to Herod as their robber in chief, the tax-collector, the compromised Edomite king, the sister-marrying Roman accommodator (the three nets of belial being fornication, riches and pollution of the temple). Therefore Rome names the Hebrew prophesies written by Agrippa Herod, "Matthias" (the gospel Matthew), after the robbers of Judea, Jewish mountain guerillas striking fear into the heart of pilgrims on their way to the temple. The gospel of Matthew, this gospel of the Messiah, is the first gospel, although as yet incomplete. Rome will edit out the most xenophobic and Zionist of prophesies to create the gospel of Mark. A later Alexandrian editor will rework the gospel of Matthew as the most anti-Semitic of the gospels, declaring the crucifixion a Jewish fratricide, consenting to the genocide and avenging the royal lineage of Cleopatra for Herod's assistance to Rome.

28 ROME 63 CE THE TEMPLE WALL AFFAIR

When the Jerusalem embassy of priests arrives in Rome to complain to Caesar, they meet Seneca, Caesar's secretary. Seneca tells Paul, "You have spoken enough. As the Essenes suggest, you seem to have a spirit full of hot air. Remain in solitary in your room until Caesar sends for you. If you're lucky, Caesar may retire you to Spain with Herod and Herodias. Let us hear from your opponents now." Seneca requests a written report. In ancient Hebrew script Josephus writes the story of Jacob's (James') last days. Years later Seneca will overwrite the death of Jacob to hide the commotion with only a slight deviation. In Seneca's story, Paul's hot air comes from the backside of a Roman soldier standing on Herod's porch overlooking the temple:

The fortress of Herod faces North on a hill overlooking the Kidron valley and temple. Jewish families vie for the High Priesthood for which Herod keeps the temple vestments. Herod would select a priest from one of the lower ranking families to cause rancor, unless a higher ranking family paid him handsomely. Herod's High Priest would become the bane of other high-ranking families who would bide their time waiting for opportunity, for the death of the High Priest or an odd opportunity for replacing the High Priest, such as when Rome left a lack of leadership. For instance as in 54 when Nero succeeded Claudius or in 58 when Nero killed Messalina, his first wife, bringing her head on a platter as requested by his mistress and future wife, the beautiful and crazy Poppea.

Josephus continues his litany against Herod, while Seneca daydreams his story of the fart: Herod reclined in his fortress with guests eating and drinking while watching the happenings in the temple below thereby sacrilegiously desecrating the temple. The Three Nets of Belial were always on the minds of Sadducees (zealots): Fornication, Riches and Pollution of the Temple. The Herods regularly married their half-nieces, divorced and re-married, and were rumored to have slept with their wives and sisters during their menstrual periods. Herods also sent taxes to Rome, taxes graven with the image of Caesar violating the second commandment, while failing to provide for the poor during the famine (Acts 11:28), perhaps because The Poor had previously vowed poverty to avoid taxes (Mt 19:21, 22:21). Still, regardless of Herod's choice, not even a Jewish Maccabee like Herod himself was righteous enough to be High Priest. No one was actually righteous enough to be High Priest, not Davidic enough, nor Sadducean enough (zeal of my house), nor even the right kind of Davidic Sadducee, xenophobia knowing no bounds.

And so priests erect a higher wall to avoid the prying eyes of Herod. In Seneca's mind, a Roman soldier, munching on a pork chop with a glass of wine, drops his drawers breaking a glorious wind from the wall of Herod's fortress aimed in the general direction of the temple. From Herod's BBQ, Herodian ladies laugh to see such a sport. Meanwhile the real story is that Jacob had been murdered. The ensuing riots raise a big stink, Romans being overly sensitive to riots or anything preventing taxes. After Herod demands the wall be torn down, a Sadducean embassage will make its way to Rome, including Cephas (Peter) and the young priest Josephus.

Rome's editorial rewrites do away with Jacob a decade earlier (Acts 12:2), killed and replaced with another Jacob, Jacob the lesser (Mk 15:40). The riot at the death of Jacob after the speech of Paul will be overwritten with the stoning of Stephen by Paul (Acts 22:20). And Josephus will write of his experiences in Rome with Poppea, including the Temple Wall Affair, while neglecting the death of Jacob, overseen by the secretaries of the Caesars, caretakers of Rome's sole library, Sulla, Seneca and Epaphroditus, neglecting the embassage's denunciation of the death of Jacob and the atrocities of Herod. Indeed Herod Agrippa II, the original author of the gospel of Matthew, will edit Josephus for Rome.

Upon finding Nero's wife, Poppea, enamored with the temple, Josephus explains his religion, "the laver represents the sea, the temple the land and behind the curtain where no man can enter, the ineffable heavens." And Seneca's plans for Jerusalem have changed. Josephus will replace Paul as Rome's chief negotiator, attempting to work from within the temple authority, for Josephus has learned that Jerusalem might never withstand the Roman army with its unsurpassed military science.

Josephus and Seneca rewrite the book of Esther for Poppea to gain the ear of Caesar. Esther (Ishtar/Easter the g-ddess of fertility, Hebrew having no vowels) becomes the Heroine, like Poppea, married to the king for her great beauty, yet hiding the secret of her Jewishness. Esther teaches how the Jews survive lawfully by following the edicts of the king. Mordechai, Esther's uncle, too old to fight, yet with the wisdom of Seneca, is named after Marduk, the Sumerian g-d of war, representing a vulnerable Parthia. Jews arm themselves in the wee hours of the very day, killing their well-armed executioners. Seneca sends the book of Esther to the Roman synagogue which becomes our modern celebration of diaspora, an ironic Jewish victory explaining why Romans must kill Jews before Jews gain the upper hand in politics. With Poppea's blessing Josephus returns to Jerusalem. Poppea will soon find herself having family troubles for her secret Jewish conversion and love of the temple.

29 ROME 64 CE ROME BURNS

The Cleaner, the man responsible for tying up loose ends, Gaius Cassius Longinus, arrives back in Rome to give Seneca, Caesar's secretary, the messianic prophesies sent by Herod. For 150 years, Sulla, Seneca and Epaphroditus are Caesar's official curators, destroying private libraries while fighting to maintain the official records of the world in Rome. Caesar's library includes scrolls collected by Sulla before he burned the library of Alexandria. Sulla's successor, Seneca, despises private collections (On Tranquility of Mind). Epaphroditus, Seneca's successor, will support the writings of both Paul (Phil 2:25, 4:1) and Josephus (2 Preface Antiquities).

Gaius Cassius Longinus is filled with rage at Paul's failure. "That barbarian Paul and his Plan for Peace have been rejected by Jerusalem! The temple continues to hoard gold to pay for war! Our auditors will never be permitted to collect our taxes! Rome only wants peace, but Paul has started a riot! To avoid taxes Herod's Essenes own nothing worth taxing, while calling themselves `The Poor`. For some `service`, Herod has forgiven their taxes to Rome!"

The Cleaner is like a roaring dragon knowing his time is short. In an age without printing presses, keeping secrets is not an insurmountable obstacle (*). The Cleaner has taken care of the Jerusalem leaders: Jacob (James) is dead, Cephas (Peter) in Rome waiting to complain about Herod, and Paul imprisoned, waiting for an audience with Caesar too. Judas is in Antioch and Joses (Barnabas), when last heard, was somewhere in Cyprus.

However Poppea, Caesar's mistress become wife, fails to recognize the trouble Longinus will create. She is so excited to meet the remaining leaders of the church of Jerusalem, that she sneaks Cephas and Paul into the synagogue of Rome. The synagogue leader asks her, "How is Josephus? We are so grateful that Caesar has allowed us back into Rome thanks to you." To Paul he growls, "Please be aware when preaching that this synagogue has heard of your half-uncle, Herod's having stolen his riches from the tomb of David."

Paul preaches first, "Learn from Jesus humility, unity and obedience to Caesar." A low rumble starts from the usually reverent crowd. Before the riot can begin, the leader thanks Paul for his presence and asks for silence for the synagogue to hear the preaching of Cephas.

From the same pulpit Cephas proclaims, "My brother Jacob (James) died to Caesar's poor choice of rulers for Judea, namely, Paul's Herods. My dad, Joseph the Egyptian, teaches the dignity of the eternal soul, the pyramids pointing to the Star of Eternity, the North Star. Our prophesies of this Star from Jacob (Num 24:17) have passed through my family's ancient lineage in David of Bethlehem Ephrathah (Micah 5:2) where my father brought the mysteries of judgement based on how each person chooses to live their life, echoing longer than the eternity of Stoic immortality which only lasts as long as its retelling."

Gaius Cassius Longinus' informants tell the issue immediately and Nero Caesar knows his life is held in the balance. Beside himself rage, he prepares his guard and has Cephas crucified. This very night Nero fiddles on his roof for Poppea, while in the small Jewish quarter of Rome, overseen by The Cleaner, Nero's soldiers prevent firemen from doing their jobs. The Cleaner returns Paul to his prison saying, "In the morning we will discuss your future and your sponsor Seneca's too." The morning sun falls upon bodies charred beyond recognition. Rome was not built in a day, but in one night the fire of Rome has eliminated the Jews who have heard both Cephas and Paul. Caesar's edict pronounces death to those of The Way in Rome.

That evening Gaius Cassius Longinus visits Nero to discuss the previous night's events and notices

Poppea's remorse. Feigning sympathy The Cleaner says, "my g-dson died in the fire." Poppea explains her grief with the synagogue destroyed as swayed by the doctrine of eternal life, the bread or knowledge of life as taught by the House of Bread, Bethlehem, she has converted to Judaism (**). The Cleaner looks at Nero with one eyebrow raised and the die is cast.

Before Gaius Cassius Longinus departs, Nero responds, "You will not be allowed at her funeral." Nero comforts his wife knowing this night will be their last. He says to his wife, "bring Seneca to read to us once more your tale of Esther and remember to be brave." Caesar hopes to make his wife's last night on earth happy. When Seneca arrives, Nero whispers, "after tonight we'll have one last task for you."

Seneca and his scribes have written Ephesians in Paul's name. Paul's review has added only one change. The letter's acceptance in Ephesus proves the Bible will continue. With Esther and Ephesians as tests, Seneca and scribes will begin another daunting task: Toning down the warrior Messiah of Israel into a peaceful, tax-loving prophet who fails to quench the smoking reed and is led by Rome to his death on the cross as quietly as a lamb. The Stoicism of Seneca and his student, Epaphroditus, will weave its way into the gospels.

*One example of how Rome controlled documentation may be found in the writings of the bishop Eusebius of Caesarea who around 300 CE rants on how horrible Josephus was to list the destruction of Jerusalem as due to the death of Jacob (James) rather than Jesus. However our current Josephus has no mention of this, recording the death of Jacob followed by seemingly inane stories probably overwriting the truth.

**Bread – Fundamentally comes from G-d, and acknowledging that truth is the essence of Israel's Pentecost celebration. p565 Acts, A New Vision of the People of G-d. Gerald L. Stevens 2016

30 ROME 65 CE DEATHS OF PAUL, SENECA & POPPEA

"…you have caused the word `Roman` to belong not to a city, but to the name of a sort of common race, and this not one out of all the races, but a balance to the remaining ones…"
Aelius Ariestides (155CE) quoting Thucydides paraphrasing Homer
pg87 Acts, A New Vision of the People of G-d, Gerald L. Stevens 2016

Paul's prison is dank and yet the presence of the former governor of Antioch casts an even darker gloom over the guards: The Cleaner, Gaius Cassius Longinus, hisses at Paul, "This will be the last time we speak. You failed to cause peace and taxes in that backwater fortress of Jerusalem – whose barbarians are worse than the Germans and English! At least the Egyptians are disorganized and able to be controlled! Roman authors will take over your work now. I had no power of death over you in Jeruslaem or last night, but by dawn tomorrow your executioner will be at hand. Your disciples will fight for Rome against the Jews. Even now Herod writes for Rome. For I will increase while you will decrease (Jn 3:30)."

After watching Paul's execution in the morning, The Cleaner listens in the Senate to Nero Caesar's declarations, opening the public coffers to provide for those whose homes had been destroyed in the fire and planning a new public plaza on the area which had been cleared. The Cleaner remembers Nero's secret instructions to kill Cephas (Peter), set the fires, and prevent firemen from quenching the flames. The uninformed Senate praises Caesar's wisdom in providing for the poor of Rome.

In the Spring Gaius Cassius Longinus returns to Nero's home. Seneca, Caesar's tutor and then advisor, speaks. "Poppea, the mistress and then wife of Caesar, had asked for and received Messalina's head on a platter, Caesar's first wife, receiving it as though it were her engagement present and dancing with Nero. As her due reward, shortly after the fire Nero kicked her and their unborn child to death."

Seneca continues. "Nero has slowly gone crazy." Lead poisoning from tomatoes served on pewter dishes poisoned the Caesars. Tomato acid dissolves lead pewter, cumulatively lowering intelligence. Longinus, the Cassian, had carefully monitored Caesar observing that as his intelligence lowered he returned to his base desires and yearnings, speaking the thoughts of his heart – murder, theft and covetousness, no longer deceitful as lead lowered his mind's capacity like a truth serum.

Seneca has stoically accepted his fate, demanded of Nero by the cleaner. "After the death of Poppea, Nero wandered the Palatine (palace grounds) for weeks until he found a soldier who looked like his late wife. Imagine the terror that man faced when the Praetorian Guard, Caesar's guard, explained the soldier would be castrated. Nero had the soldier's head shaved and called him by the name of Poppea."

"Poppea was trouble. Josephus brought a book which he and I rewrote calling it Ishtar (Esther). We unfortunately patronized Poppea. She therefore wheedled Nero into donating to the Jewish temple, like Paul's donations, while we were attempting to work with the Herods for peace and taxes. Even Sosthenes, the leader of the synagogue of Corinth sent a donation through Paul, although my brother, Gallio, had previously beaten him for delaying Paul. Poppea went crazy and Nero was unable to control her. The Sadducees eventually rejected our offerings and sent Josephus as the Northern General in charge of the defense of Israel."

Seneca finishes. "My time is short, having been given a few months to work with our writers on a few projects. My student Epaphroditus, who has worked extensively with Paul, has been trained and I assume you, Gaius Cassius Longinus, have come to witness my death."

Seneca returns home to his wife and Nero sends a guard to oversee Seneca's death before banishing the Cleaner, Gaius Cassius Longinus. However after the death of Nero, Vespasian will return to Rome with the legions of Antioch and Gaius Cassius Longinus will return to Rome with honor, loved by the legions of Syria over whom he governed during the early riots of its district of Israel.

Philemon, a run-away slave returning to his owner at Paul's instigation, takes Paul's last writings to Corinth although Roman authors will continue to create letters in Paul's name advising peace and taxes. War takes time and Rome, having killed the Roman supporters of the Jews, has begun its final solution for xenophobic Sadducees living in their fortified city on a hill which cannot be ignored (Thomas 32, ~Mt 5:14). Later, the book of Esther will be canonized by the accommodating Pharisees, supporting and supported by, Rome. Epaphroditus, Seneca's student, will publish Seneca's legacy as II Timothy stoically guiding the future of the church.

31 GALILEE 66 CE JOSEPHUS SURRENDURS TO VESPASIAN

Josephus is still a young man of thirty-five, born a Sadducee, but having joined the Pharisees and Essenes before travelling to Rome in 62 with the embassage to complain about the death of Jacob (James). In Rome Josephus made friends with Caesar's wife, Poppea, whose friendship would serve him well even after her death, through the end of his life authoring the Jewish histories from Rome, adopted by the family of the Roman General Vespasian to whom Josephus will surrender: "Vespasian is the prophesied Messiah! He will come out of Judea! He was not born, but forged in Judea, and will rule the world!"

When Jacob (James) was murdered at the temple in 62 as an old man of 96, his knees broken from an earlier encounter with Paul in 42, a slow fuse was lit and war with Rome inevitable*. Josephus was sent to Rome with the Sadducean embassage while Jerusalem cried, "Herod is an oaf! Fie on the house of Herod! Rome must find better!"

The War begins in 66. Sadducees take over, stop paying taxes and accepting polluted Roman donations for sacrifice on the holy mountain. The Battle at Beit Horon lead by the martyred grandsons of Queen Helen defeat Rome gives Judea hope, but Rome will inevitibly invade and destroy everything. Josephus has returned from Rome with presents from Poppea, Caesar's wife. Priests murmur, "Josephus is a great negotiator, although perhaps suspiciously pro-Roman." The Sadducean temple authority gets Josephus out of the way sending him north as a general to defend Galilee – "You're a big man and have seen the power of Rome. Go down to Galilee. Fortify and protect our flock. Be sure to send the best soldiers and supplies to Jerusalem, for if Jerusalem falls, all is lost."

Josephus carefully catalogs the strengths and weaknesses of the cities and towns of Galilee, never mentioning Nazareth, the suspicion being that Nazareth never existed, the prophesy originally for a messianic Nazarite - no sex, no wine, no hair cutting**, while the current Nazareth may have been started by Carmelite monks long afterwards. At Tarichae the city fights until surrendering. General Vespasian promises, "If you will but open your gates and throw down your weapons, all will be well." Generals argue with Vespasian that the people will escape to other cities where they will fight again, and General Vespasian turns his back on Tarichae, avoiding the argument and travelling to Jerusalem. Refugees are promised unarmed escape but slaughtered on a forced march through a valley.

By 67 facing imminent defeat, General Josephus holes up in a cave with forty soldiers. Afraid for their immortal souls, Josephus denies the Romans victory, exhorting his men to kill each other like Moses ordering Jews to kill every man his brother (Ex 32:27), like the Jews at Massada fearing slavery and/or Roman victory, saving their souls unpolluted. Josephus later authors their murders by lot with himself remaining one of the last few. Suddenly, a vision appears to Josephus who is told that Vespasian will be the Messiah. Josephus is given a mission abrogating his pact. Denying his fate, knowing that Rome preserves the kings and generals of conquered peoples for the triumphal parade and thumbs up slavery / thumbs down execution in Rome, Josephus kills the remaining soldiers who are intent on his murder and calls out for the Roman commander, "Vespasian!" Josephus and one other survive. Josephus, begging to not be sent to Rome for the triumph, prophesies Vespasian, Caesar and as Vespasian's translator will beg Jerusalem to surrender.

*Eusebius, who writes in 300, our primary church historian through whom all documentation was filtered, feverishly attempts to attribute the War as tied to the death of Jesus in 40 rather than that of Jacob in 62.

**Paul's "polling" Acts 21:24, shaving his head and the heads of four others for a cost with a vow of silence for a period of time and the Hindu "offering of joy" where after something joyful one shaves one's head at the beginning of a vow, suggests the Jewish laws of not cutting one's hair may not be understood at this time (Lev 21:5).

32 JERUSALEM 70 CE TITUS BURNS JERUSALEM

You are the only people who think it a disgrace to be servants to those whom all the world hath submitted.
2.16.4 The Wars of the Jews, Josephus (William Whiston 1998)

Rome focuses everything on destroying Sadducean Judaism – xenophobic temple focused zealots – any Jew loyal to the temple over the Pax Romana. The temple, an isolated enclave, cannot be ignored. In addition to failing to worship Nero Caesar as G-d and Savior, the Jews seek their own Savior (Joshua, Yeshua and Jesus are the same word in Hebrew meaning Savior). To solve the problem of the Jews who have rejected Rome and fortified their mountains, Rome sends Vespasian, the best general, with a legion from France and Germany, to join the legions of Antioch (Syria), the third largest Roman city, invading the district of Syria known as Judea. Vespasian's son, Titus, leads a legion from Alexandria (Egypt), the second largest Roman city joining the legion of Caesarea Maritima (Israel). The legion of Caesarea is known as the bloodiest of legions, of whom Romans would declare, "We ought to rejoice in that evil done by Romans in foreign countries."

Rather than attacking Jerusalem immediately, Vespasian stalls after capturing Galilee. After much discussion Josephus is freed having surrendered in hopes of telling his story in Rome and declaring Vespasian the Savior, the Messiah from Israel. Titus proposes, "let us not merely unlock the chains of Josephus." A smith smashes the chains of Josephus who is presented by Vespasian with golden chains.

Using Josephus as his chief negotiator, Vespasian begs Jerusalem to capitulate under his mercy. And yet Vespasian waits far away in the plains of Galilee, his armies eating the food gathered and stored by the Jews killed or sent to Corinth, his cavalry feeding on grass watered by the Roman aqueducts of a desolate Gadara. Vespasian receives joyous news as Jewish refugees surrender to his armies: the Jews in Jerusalem have destroyed their local support, storing grain in the temple while ravaging Jewish villages to prepare Jerusalem to defend against the imperator (emperor Nero Caesar). Josephus reports that the Jewish leaders of Jerusalem, following the Roman model, each struggle to become King while pitting their armies against each other. There is even a Jewish faction of Roman loyalists which fights to install their King to surrender the city. Vespasian might have noted, 'A house divided cannot stand.'

Finally Vespasian can wait no more. The armies of Rome arrive in Jerusalem and build a wall around the temple and city. Josephus begs the city to capitulate noting Jerusalem as subject to Rome for generations writing: "Those who rebel against their masters are not lovers of freedom, but recalcitrant slaves." A Jewish `slave` standing on the wall of the temple hurls a rock, knocking out Josephus and giving pause to his rant. Josephus will later write of a `prophet` who marches around the city yelling, "Woe, woe, woe to Jerusalem!", much as had the prophet Jeremiah before the invasion of Babylon. Lastly this prophet prophesies, "And woe to me also!" before stuck by a stone from a Roman catapult, much like Josephus struck by a stone from the wall.

Starvation besets Jerusalem while Sadducees guard the gates seeking to prevent defections. A rich woman having sold everything walks barefoot, her feet caked with mud after boiling and eating the leather of her sandals. Although it is the Essenes who despise riches, she is even scorned by Pharisees for believing her riches might save her, while the Jesus of John will wash the feet of his disciples. One Rabbi makes it out of Jerusalem in a coffin carried by his students. Sadducees pray for the Messiah to come down upon the Mount of Olives, open the Eastern Gate and destroy the armies of Rome by the heavenly host always present, as on the mountain of Elisha where the servant's eyes were opened to chariots of fire driven by angels and led by invisible horses (II Kings 6:17).

Messianic hopes run high while Rome undermines and burns the first of three defensive walls defending the city. A Roman hero and his cohort mount the second wall, goaded by Vespasian's promise of reward, only to discover the supposed weakness to be a trap. Surrounded by fire some plummet from the wall while others return through the fire, their burnt hair smelling worse than their charred legs as they gasp their last. Generals berate their troops' ambition, begging future prudence and making an example of some leaders. Vespasian knows that if his troops capture the city, they will loot the treasures of Jerusalem, rather than Jewish leaders giving the rightful tribute to Vespasian's triumphal parade of victory in Rome.

Suddenly, Nero dies. News reaches Vespasian that three generals have declared themselves Caesar, while Rome is thrown into civil war. Josephus advises Vespasian, "You are the Messiah, the chosen one of Israel. Go and become emperor." But Vespasian is already gone, leaving his son, Titus, in charge of a small force for the siege of Jerusalem. Vespasian travels first to Antioch where he is approved as imperator and sent to Alexandria to gather another legion for the travel to Rome. Roman walls and the Praetorian guard prevent armies from fighting in the streets of Rome, but many outside the city welcome Vespasian as his legions march over the bodies of fallen and falling soldiers - the current Caesar still upset with his assassinated predecessor's armies. Vespasian's legions march into Rome with their banners where Vespasian finishes the year of four Caesars as Emperor.

In Jerusalem the second defensive wall has fallen. Starvation has beset the populace. Starving Jews storm about the city seeking any who would hide their stores of food behind locked doors, explaining the food must go to those most able to fight, stealing grain from the weak and elderly and eating the bread of women and children. Josephus' writings begin centuries of persecution, facetiously telling that poor mothers cook and serve their babies (6.3.4 Wars Josephus), the charge of sacrificing babies used against Jews in the 1490 pogroms of Spain. The book of Esther, in my opinion also written by Josephus, likewise justifies the killing of Jews - before they can return the favor. Although a favorite of diaspora, Esther explains that in the few hours before dawn, supposedly peaceful Jews will gather arms for a slaughter of their enemies.

Herod had spent the gold from David's tomb remodeling the temple which is beautiful. The cedars of Lebanon, carefully imported for the project, support the roof of the temple which is covered in gold reflecting the sunlight. Priests trained to handle the intricate stonework have rebuilt everything. Although Jerusalem lacks food, Josephus writes that one sect, holding to the Messianic prophesy, burns another sect's stores of food, hoping to create an unwinnable war, thereby forcing the return of the Messiah. Per the prophesy the Messiah will only return when all is lost, turning the tide of war and reserving the glory for himself, as when a mere three hundred of Gideon had won the war for Israel (Judges 7). Perhaps a Roman spy does toss the ember which sets the stores of grain on fire, but more likely it is the firestorms set by Rome on the defensive walls. The fire burns furiously in the dust-filled air over the grain and then will not be put out. Priests throw what little rationed water can be gathered on the fire, knowing that mold will start immediately within wet grain. They also try to smother the fire with dirt. The fire burns slowly, but is unstoppable. Starvation sets in as Titus, the son of Vespasian, has reinforced the wall around the city.

The wall falls. The temple burns. Gold from the ceiling melts into the walls while priests hand their precious books over to Josephus, their angst palpable, remembering this Roman turncoat as a Sadducean priest, hoping at the very least to preserve the sacred books of Judaism. Roman soldiers pry apart every stone, to gather the precious metal, crashing the stock market. Not one stone is left upon another. The temple, the banking center of Israel, is destroyed. A few days later, like Jesus rising from the grave, Simon shockingly rises from hidden underground chambers into the rubble, clothed in purple robes, and is taken to the triumph of Titus.

Josephus takes all the books he can preserve back to Rome where he records the genocide. City by city Rome has destroyed Israel killing 1.1 million, the entire population. Rome enslaves 100,000 building the canal at Corinth, sending 20,000 to build the coliseum in Rome and killing another million Jews in Alexandria, Egypt where Jewish priests have built another temple. Josephus records the number of Jews killed around the Mediterranean with their property taken by the state or for politicians. Nothing so much angers Rome as non-tax paying subjects.

The followers of Jacob (James) flee into the wilderness by the thousands following Joseph, the Egyptian, the father of Jacob, eventually becoming the second exodus of Israel. A thousand climb up to the mountain fortress of Masada on the Dead Sea, which Rome besieges, engineering a monumental ramp, until like Josephus at Jotapata, the Jews deprive Rome of victory, murdering each other by lot until only two women and five children are left to tell the tale. Thousands flee to Kurdistan becoming known as bathtists (daily bathers). The followers of Jacob and Joseph are barely recognizable according to the biblical authors who describe them, but if my understanding is correct, our biblical authors were fourteen hundred miles away in Rome. There is no remnant left in Israel. Sadducees flee, are killed or sold into slavery. Titus takes the temple treasure back to Rome giving Jewish gold to the overseers of Jewish slaves fated to build the coliseum in Rome.

33 ROME 125 CE THE WAR IS FINISHED

Roman power… was the principal reason no one ever returned… No one could have, because no one survived.

pg xxii James, the Brother of Jesus, Robert Eisenman 1997

In Roman mythology Mars is the g-d of war, but Pluto is war in its higher orbit. Mars takes the field as did Vespasian, but Pluto overturns the battlefield as do the authors of the gospels. Rome has a history of preserving authors of conquered peoples like Polybius of Corinth (Greece 200 BCE) and Josephus. The strong-hold of Jerusalem was not its fortified temple, but rather its people. Paul's works grafted in Greeks, just as Herod grafted his family onto a Maccabean root. Paul aimed at finding peace for his grafted Herodian half-Jewish/Maccabean family. The Plutonian authors of the Gospels and posthumous pseudo-Pauline letters use Paul's unifying works as Cassian foundation justifying genocide while outraging Jews with discussions of peace. For example Stephen, a Greek Christian before Paul preaches as a gentile, preaches uncircumcised in the temple, where he wouldn't have been allowed, to the High Priest on Jewish history. As another example Jesus weeps while calling down hell-fire on Chorazin, Bethsaida and Capernum.

The Plutonian gospel is written on top of the peace seeking works of Paul riding Paul's unifying peace-seeking works as foundation. Our earliest copy of a gospel dates to 125, the gospel of John. When the soldier in chapter one of this book is asked in what language he is speaking, when the preamble to this book focused on metaphor as a method of communication, the point is that metaphor, such as is found in the Bible, can ride on top of the ostensible story. For instance from Chapter one, The Language of Rome, what kind of a question is "in what language are you asking?". Can you come up with three possible interrelated meanings? Metaphor should be considered its own language, in the case of the Gospels setting a context for genocide (The End of Israel, Sin Sacrifice, Heaven & Hell, Ray Shortell 2017).

With the first miracle in John, Jesus turns water into wine and the steward notes it is better than the first wine ("wine" in Hebrew a homophone for the word "Greek"). The woman at the well explains the water comes from Jacob (metaphorically explaining the six waterpots as Jewish no longer). Nathanael implies the whole lot "unpleasing" (Jn 1:24)(1). And with such the authors of the Gospels take away everything Jewish, metaphorically turning Judaism into a shadow of things to come as when Moses veiled his face (II Cor 3:13, Col 2:17, Heb 8:5, Heb 10:1). Jesus decries worshiping at the temple, honoring the Sabbath, scribes, lawyers and doctors of the Law like Jacob (James), allows unclean food and eats with sinners. Jesus says we will not worship at the temple, but in spirit and truth. Peter apparently forgets the food message later needing either a tablecloth vision or reproof from Paul in Antioch to remember. Heretical Gospels, apparently opposing or revealing too much of the authors, were burned (Acts 19:19), authors killed, books lost to the sands of time until some were recently found (Dead Sea Scrolls, Robert Eisenman… this is a topic rather than a text, although it's kind of a text too).

In an age without printing presses Seneca had copied Paul's works in Corinth, early copies probably residing in the Vatican to this day. The Sadducee Josephus will soon follow in Paul's footsteps authoring the history of Israel for Epaphroditus. Josephus and Herod Agrippa II will also assist in creating the Gospels.

Epaphroditus probably wrote the gospels taking fifty years after the destruction of the temple and calling upon the works of Josephus, Roman history, Isaiah 53 and Psalm 22. Jesus as described by Epaphroditus would walk peacefully through Israel discussing peace with whores (incestuous and gold-digging Herodian divorcees… much as does Paul), tax-collectors (Roman soldiers or kings), with invalids bathing in temple pools (invalids were not allowed nor even people with flat noses Lev 21:18). Paul's writings sought to bring Greeks into the temple, but the authors of the Gospels stepped beyond Paul's peacemaking attempts suggesting followers must carry a sword (Mt 10:34, Lk 22:36) and those who refuse to submit must be killed (Lk 19:27, Prelude End of Israel (Salt of the Earth), Sin, Sacrifice, Heaven & Hell, The Meaning of Christianity, Ray Shortell 2017).

Clean-up continued with Eusebius in the 300s decrying the heretical heresy of earlier church authors. In 125 Rome (Domitian) hunted down the remaining Davidic line, the grandchildren of Jude of Antioch who were crucified by Trajan a decade later. Augustine's (~400 CE) ten commandments neglect the second splitting the tenth into two making the commandments hard to remember for Roman Catholics, most especially the second (no idolatrous busts of Caesar on money)(Mt 22:21), intending Catholics to live a good life.

EPILOGUE 2017 AMERICA

This novel is the best I can come up with around the story of the Bible never having visited Gadara. I've spent years wondering whether I've missed a cross-reference: Did James refer to the sacrifice of Jesus? Does Paul claim a resurrection? What are Paul's credentials and family? Who was Stephen's evangelist? Who were "the Brothers" at Three Taverns in Rome? I'm also a bit fuzzy on what is "family" per the Bible. To some, second or third cousins are part of daily life. To others a brother has been disowned.

I'd like to see the back-side of the temple mount where Rome breached the walls, look at Herod's fortress from across the Kidron valley and visit Rachel's and Sarah's tombs and Queen Helen and her sons' pyramids. I'd like to visit Caesarea, ride horses from Gadara to the sea of Galilee, look at the fisherman's boat found from that time in the sea of Galilee, ask that one professor if she really believes that no one in Israel could read and if so who preserved Hebrew, drive down the Jordan, cross the pass at Beit Horon visiting Lydda (and Lod) and Jaffa, visit a statue of Diana in Turkey and Greece and a Hittite city in Turkey, look at some Sumerian cuneiform, boat through the canal of Corinth, visit Three Taverns in Rome and have a tour guide tell about the arch of Titus.

For further details:

James, the Brother of Jesus – Robert Eisenman 1997
Crucifixion and Turin Shroud Mysteries Solved – Pierre Krijbolder 1999
The New Testament Code – Robert Eisenman 2006
Understanding the Bible – Stephen L. Harris 2011
The Ancient Historians – Michael Grant 1970
The Christ Conspiracy – S. Arachya 1999

My first book, Understanding the Bible, Ray Shortell 2013 noted Astrology as underlying I Cor 13. This finding was previously published by me elsewhere. Understanding the Bible recounted the works of others through my Roman Catholic eyes finding the Bible removing everything testifying to Jewish authority.

My second book, Sin, Sacrifice, Heaven and Hell, Ray Shortell 2017 continued reviewing Roman attacks on Jewish authority by deciphering the Salt of the Earth metaphor as Rome committing genocide (Lk 19:27) along with finding the Bible developing topics rather than divinely communicating a developed topic. Money as an idol is a focus. Perhaps others have taken the violation of the second commandment as assumed (fornication, riches, pollution of the temple), or perhaps a Catholic viewpoint was required: When Luke says G-d or mammon, when Augustine's Roman Catholic ten commandments fail to include the second with the tenth split in two, when Essenes carry no money submitting to neither Caesar as not a brother nor Roman coins as idolatrous with graven images, I'm guessing Herod would have accepted livestock, clothes or anything to have appeased Rome.

EPILOGUE: EDITING THE TALMUD

History is written by the victors. <Anon>

Rome was greatly concerned with Jewish Messianism sending warriors and scholars to oversee a review of religious writings. There would have been a few things Rome wanted removed from Pharisaic Messianism, those things tending towards a populace ready to revolt. The warrior messiah was toned down in the Talmud. Pharisaic Jews allowed this knowing Rome would have destroyed anything else. Vespassian Caesar built Yochanan ben Zakkai a Pharisaic center for study at Yavneh which became the hub for rabbinic Judaism under Gamaliel II, grandson of Paul's rabbinic teacher. Herod Agrippa II authored/edited the gospels in Rome.

ca. 90-150	Writings (third and last division of Jewish Scriptures) discussed and accepted as sacred scripture.
69	Vespasian gives Yochanan ben Zakkai permission to establish a Jewish center for study at Yavneh that will become the hub for rabbinic Judaism.

http://www.jewishvirtuallibrary.org/rabbinic-jewish-period-of-talmud-development-70-500-ce

The rabbinic Jews (former Pharisees) reorganized after the defeat, around 90 CE, under Gamaliel II at Yavneh (Jamnia), a city on the coast of Palestine, to organize a final canon of their writings and reformulate a religion based entirely on the synagogue. They chose to define the canon by including only works written originally in Hebrew, thus excluding a number of books in the Greek translation of the Hebrew Bible (Septuagint) that had been used by Jews in the Diaspora (=outside Palestine) since the 2d century BCE. The Septuagint was also the Bible of the Christians.

http://www.religion.ucsb.edu/faculty/thomas/classes/rgst116b/JewishHistory2.html

Note: "(former Pharisees)" is part of the quote and not my interpolation.

Paul's Dream: Paul dreams of the murderer Constantine who welcomed absolution on his deathbed and setting the cannon, deciding which remaining texts to keep and which to destroy. In 373 the council of Laodicea declared: Christians shall not Judaize by resting on the Sabbath, but shall work on that day resting on Sunday instead ([anti-christ] shall think to change times Dan 7:25). Paul's nightmare continued from generation to generation until the Dead Sea Scrolls, Thank You, Dr. Eisenman, opened a new world against the hegemony.

APPENDIX: THE QUESTIONS

Does the Bible condemn homosexuality? Does the Bible condemn abortion? Does the Bible condone women preachers? Why do some get excited over I Tim 4 in regards to priests?

The Bible is written in multiple layers. One author may have an opinion and others may have another. Regarding homosexuality let's start with Josephus who I take to have an overarching view of Sadducean, Pharisaic and Essene Judaism at the time, along with writing nothing to upset the Roman position. In Antiquities 4.8.40 Josephus notes that gelding is unlawful in Israel (castration) which is of course gainsaid in Mt 19:12 for which Origen apparently castrated himself. In Antiquities 3.12.1 Josephus notes death as punishment for men lying together proposing that this comes from the scripture of Moses, although some of the texts to which Josephus had as reference have apparently not passed down to us. Rom 1:18-26 to me speaks against unnatural lust diplomatically so as not to promote violence, essentially a discussion for homosexuals to have amongst themselves and not to be wielded by non-homosexuals. In I Cor 11:14 Paul similarly speaks against long hair on men. And there's the Epistle of Barnabas 14:8 Neither shalt thou corrupt thyself with mankind (The Lost Books of the Bible and the Forgotten Books of Eden, 1927). My understanding of the Roman Catholic position as per chapter 3 of Sin, Sacrifice, Heaven & Hell is that the church has no issue with non-practicing homosexuals.

Abortion: I'll go with Lk 1:44 …"the babe leapt in my womb"… However Ex 21:22 says: If men strive and hurt a woman with child, so that her fruit depart from her, and yet no mischief follow: he shall surely be punished, according as the woman's husband shall lay upon him, and shall pay as the judges determine. By which I wonder whether a husband's opinion should change the severity of the offense. Paul, of course, claimed himself as essentially an attempted abortion: And last of all he was seen of me also, as one born out of due time (I Cor 15:8). And there's the Epistle of Barnabas 14:11 Thou shalt not destroy thy conceptions before they are brought forth; nor kill them after they are born (The Lost Books of the Bible and the Forgotten Books of Eden , 1927).

Now for women preaching, Deborah was a judge of Israel, Judith was an Israeli ambassador (heh, heh) and Zipporah spoke to G-d on behalf of her husband, Moses, but priests were men. The dispute, I guess, comes from Paul's I Cor 14:35: "If there is anything they desire to know, let them ask their husbands at home for it is shameful for a woman to speak at church." However Paul had praise for Phoebe, a deaconess (Rom 16:1) and also another powerful church woman at Philippi, Lydia (Acts 16:40). Other authors note Roman society as unaccepting of female leaders, but as for myself I go back to Kaballah, as Paul would say in I Cor 7:6 myself "speaking by permission rather than the Spirit.": Women are on the pillar of Understanding, Judgement and Thought with men on the pillar of Wisdom, Mercy and Feeling. To me women sometimes ask the congregation more than they should about what to preach and send out more judgement than required from the pulpit. On the other hand men, being karmically younger, sometimes preach on subjects which don't interest the congregation. I'm comfortable suggesting advisors to both.

I Tim 4 - …in the latter time some shall depart from the faith… forbidding to marry, and commanding to abstain from meats… Or Mt 23:9 And call no man your father upon the earth; for one is your Father which is in heaven. Lent, in Ireland historically meant no meat except for St. Patrick's day.

APPENDIX: THE QUESTIONS

What say you in regards to snakes and tongues?

In the Appalachians a church touts its faith by handling deadly snakes explaining as per Mark 16:18 that the faithful shall handle snakes and drink poison with no ill effects. They probably note Paul's getting snake-bit before shaking the snake off into the fire (Acts 28:3-5). Perhaps they exclaim that Moses raised the snake in the desert in order to heal those who had been bitten, pointing to Isaiah that the knowledge of the heavenly kingdom fills the earth while explaining that out of the mouths of babes, followers becoming like children (Mt 21:16) came the insight that snakes, infused with the knowledge of the kingdom would not bite a believer and that children of the kingdom (Mt 18:3) might put their hands on such a den in the mountains (Is 11:8-9).

Many strange beliefs have come from people reading and interpreting the Bible. The church's position is that it is the church's purview alone, to interpret the Bible. Indeed the church believes that within its purview another book may be written, condoned by heaven and added to the cannon if the church should so desire, the church being the sole author of the Bible. The church understands that during the course of one lifetime a person might come to understand much of the mystery of the Bible, but that by themselves one person is not enough to read and interpret the Bible which must be done in community under the guidance of a Priest across generations.

Snakes are dangerous. People have died at this heretical church. Now it is one thing for the pastor of such a church to have died, as Paul would say: Neither let us tempt Christ, as some of them also tempted, and were destroyed of serpents (I Cor 10:9). But when a member dies, the Bible would hold such a pastor responsible: Not many should become teachers knowing that we shall be judged more harshly (Ja 3:1). Paul explains leadership by example (I Cor 8, Rom 14) explaining that to those weak in the faith, eating meat is a sin and therefore Paul himself would eat meat nevermore. Paul gives this lesson twice in order that churches might not be swindled by such hucksters (Mt 5:19).

Isaiah is sandwiched between two mythical passages: The Cockatrice was a mythical being with the body of a snake and the head of a cock. My mother was raised on a chicken farm and regularly relates how when collecting eggs, the peckers come out of nowhere and pinch your skin like a snake. On the other side of the passage, lions aren't eating meat, but eat straw. Between these the author lays the passage of children being safe while playing on top of the dens of snakes on the mountain of Jerusalem – the promise arguably only for this one place while the children neither pick up, grab nor even observe a snakes. If the followers of Jesus are to be like children (Lk 18:15-17) then it were better to have a millstone tied about one's neck to be drowned in the depth of the sea than to offend one such as these (Mt 18:6).

Jesus responds that one should not tempt fate (my word, but a Greek g-d) when the devil, having taken Jesus to the pinnacle of the temple, asks that he be worshipped, that Jesus use his power for himself, and that Jesus jump off to be borne up by angels (Mt 4:1-11). Now if Jesus had jumped, it might be assumed he would have bruised his heel as some relate the serpent of Eden was cursed to do (Gen 3:15) and as apparently happened to Jesus upon the cross. But the healing snake identified with Christ upon the cross, which Moses lifted in the desert, was made of brass and unlikely to harm anyone.

Which brings us to the hermeneutic (the interpretation) of Mark: We shall lift up snakes. It does not say this is something which should be done. According hermeneutics, with which the church does not agree, scripture must interpret itself. There are no supporting passages. Matthew and Luke, written after Mark, each include negative commandments regarding this issue: Matthew asks if a child were to ask their father for bread would they be given a stone, or if a fish would they be given a snake? Do not parishioners ask this of a pastor or at least of Jesus on the sea of Galilee (Jn 6:1-27)? In Matthew the snake is then interpreted as evil or at least a bad gift (Mt 6:11). Luke, on the other hand, interprets the passage piece by piece: *Behold I give you power to walk on snakes and scorpions, and over all power of the enemy. Notwithstanding don't rejoice in this, that the spirits are subject unto you, but rather rejoice that your names are written in heaven.* Luke interprets the creatures as metaphoric explaining that one should keep quiet about overcoming evil while seeking good things instead.

Tongues are a reference to the Mebakker (overseer), James, the Bishop of Jerusalem who learned the multiple languages used in the fortified enclave of Jerusalem at the center of the known world in the usual way (p196 & 206 James, the Brother of Jesus, Robert Eisenman 1997). Paul had the gift of tongues, which was one of my main points of chapter one, but a point which mainly comes out only in sources. I could say something about Paul's requesting an interpreter before allowing tongues in public in church (I Cor 14), but my focus is on the difference between works (study) and faith (tongues). Please review Education Denounced by the Bible, Sin, Sacrifice, Heaven and Hell, Ray Shortell 2017 or Sources for Chapter one.

AFTERWORD
Was Jesus Crucified in 40?
If Jesus died before John the Baptist, then what are we to make of these scriptural accounts at all?
--p107, James, the Brother of Jesus, Robert Eisenman 1997

Was Jesus crucified in 40? Herod the Terrible died 4 BCE so Jesus would have had to have been born before then to be whisked off to Egypt (Mt 2). However the census of Quirinius of Syria happened in 6-7 for a difference of about ten years. If Jesus was born in 7 and about thirty when he began his ministry preaching for three Passovers, you get year 40 (Dating the Bible, Understanding the Bible Shortell 2014). Joseph Raymond in Herodian Messiah 2010, notes 40 as one of the few years when a Friday was also considered the Sabbath due to Passover (Jesus spending three days in the earth, raised on a Sunday yet interred on a Sabbath's eve).

Pontius Pilate reigned in Judea 26/27 – 36/37, but I contend Jesus was crucified afterwards under Herod 37-41 who beheaded John the Baptist in 37. John the Baptist preached against the incestuous marriage of Herod and Herodias because she divorced their half-brother, Philip Herod - Yes, I know some scholars argue against the terminology "Philip Herod". I'm guessing these are mainly Roman Catholic and call their debate "obfuscation". (Philo in Flaccus ~48 calls him Philip the Tetrarch and uncle to Herod Agrippa (26). Josephus calls him Philip in Wars 18.5.1 plus (Mt 14:3, Mk 6:17, Lk 3:1,19). Although per Dr. Henry Abramson Jospehus was known to borrow from Philo and per Robert Eisenman the Gospels may have borrowed from Josephus.) War between Herod/Herodias and Philip Herod/Areatas cost Herod his Roman army after which Tiberius Caesar 4 – 37 sent the army after Areatas, but Tiberius Caesar died before the army's task could be accomplished. After the death of John the Baptist in 37 Jesus picked up the disciples of John the Baptist (Jn 1) and preached three Passovers (Jn 2, 6, 11) bringing us to 40.

For a more detailed timeline, Agrippa Herod did not do well in his younger days, but later moved to Rome for college. The Herods paid exorbitantly to have children schooled in Rome (1.31.1 Wars Josephus) as I believe was done for Paul. Herod Agrippa was named after the famous Roman general who destroyed the fleet of Cleopatra and Mark Anthony. Herod Agrippa became good friends with Caius, the son of Tiberius Caesar and was imprisoned for wishing Caius to be Caesar quickly, which was taken to imply the death of Tiberius. After Tiberius died in 37, Herod Agrippa was released and installed as governor over the Galilee of Philip Herod and then over Judea too, becoming known as the friend of Caesar (Jn 19:12) and later retiring to Rome to work with Josephus.

Herodias divorced Philip Herod of Galilee for Herod whose first wife Phaesalis escaped Herod to Macherus, where John the Baptist was beheaded, and then to her father, King Aretas of Damascus with whom Paul later had problems. John the Baptist decried their divorce calling the Herods "a brood of snakes" since you couldn't tell when the next would raise their heads from the pit and they were all half-brothers/sisters and intermarried with their half-nieces (their half-sister's kids). Herod imprisoned and beheaded John the Baptist at Macherus after which the father of Phaesalis, King Aretas, joined with Philip Herod in destroying Herod's army (18.5 Antiquities Josephus). Paul then travels to the Damascus of King Aretas where he stays for three years before escaping, while Herodias drags Herod to Rome to ask for Galilee (2.9 Wars, Josephus) (Herodias despised Herod Agrippa after his younger days). Herod Agrippa notes Herod's 70,000 suits of armor (7.2.18 Antiquities) to Caesar and Herod/Herodias are retired to Spain, while Herod Agrippa is given Judea in 41.

My contention is based upon the life of Paul who I am unable to understand having sat still for too long. To me it was the beheading of John under Herod followed by the crucifixion proving the loyalty of the family of Jesus, followed by Paul's journey to and rejection by Damascus and rejection by Jerusalem before starting Paul's church in Antioch. The Antioch famine visit (46-48) and Paul's rejection by Antioch under the new Cassian governor (47-) force my timeline, as does the death of James in 62, tax revolt in 66 and fall of the temple in 70 (related by Eusebius to the crucifixion p83 Eusebius, The Church History, Paul Maier 2007). I can't find a crucifixion in 33 tied to the death of James in 62 which started the war in 66, but a crucifixion in 40 makes this timeline plausible to me.

And some bad timelines to consider: Irenaeus proposes Jesus to have been 50 at his crucifixion (something about being a master teacher and having been scolded for not yet being 50 and yet having seen Abraham Jn 8:57-58 (p160 Against Heresies Irenaeus 2015)). Luke 3:1, writing on Jesus' birth, notes Lysanias of Abilene reigning who ruled in 40 BCE (Dating the Bible, Understanding the Bible, Ray Shortell 2014).

\

AFTERWORD
Was Paul Herodian? Was Paul a Roman Building Inspector? Did Herod write Matthew?

Two authors strongly suspect that Paul was Herodian: Dr. Robert Eisenman of the Dead Sea Scrolls research p502 James, the Brother of Jesus 1997 and Joseph Raymond, author of the book Herodian Messiah Ch 7. Beyond Paul being a Roman Jew (Acts 22:27) of whom there were few (1), let us first note a few indicators of Paul's Herodian heritage before reviewing his claim of being a Benjamite and then follow with my additions to the discussion: The governor of Antioch, Gaius Cassius Longinus, probably being an enemy of the Herods and an indirect argument based on Paul's avoidance of Alexandria.

Paul was a Pharisee taught by Gamaliel (Acts 22:3). How many Jews were taught by Gamaliel? Gamaliel was head of the Sanhedrin in Jerusalem (2). This is a strong indicator to me that Paul was of no average family. Indeed Paul is sent to Damascus with orders to arrest and imprison certain people in Jerusalem (Acts 22:4-5). Who gave him this authority? Was it Manaen, the foster brother of Herod who was in Paul's church in Antioch (Acts 13:1)? Was it Paul's nephew who collected the guard at the temple to protect Paul (Acts 23:16)?

In Corinth Sosthenes, the Synagogue leader, is beaten by Gallio, the brother of Seneca, Caesar's secretary (Acts 18:17)(3). Sosthenes later travels with Paul (I Cor I) with the offerings Paul took from Corinth to Jerusalem (Acts 24:17) – Paul traveled with several on this journey with their offerings from many cities including Ephesus. Paul waited at Miletus for the offering from Ephesus (Acts 20:16-17) apparently due to an issue with Demetrius the silversmith (Acts 19:24), although the Ephesian offering seems to have been sent by another ship with Trophimus, who although Paul claims to have left in Miletus (2 Tim 4:20), seems to have caused Paul problems in Jerusalem (Acts 21:29). How does Paul get the offering of all of the other cities? With what authority did he travel?

In Romans 16:11 Paul makes direct his Herodian kinship: Salute Herodion my kinsman. The book of Romans was written for Rome. Herodion was the son of a Herodian woman, probably being "educated" (held hostage) in Rome – There were several Herodians studying in Rome (4). I'm thinking Herodion was a hostage, as was Paul under Felix in Caesarea (Acts 24:26), and as were two of the ten Sadducean ambassadors detained by Poppea (5). Paul was probably tutored in Rome by Seneca (6). If Paul spent time in Rome under a teacher, Seneca would have been the best and would have wanted to oversee Caesar's charges in Israel (Herodians). Seneca was a Stoic who tutored rulers. Some have noted similarities between Paul's writings and those of the Stoics (7). Epaphroditus, who Paul calls a brother and fellow-worker, was Seneca's protégé (8).

How would a Herodian have Benjamite blood? First remember all the Benjamites except 600 men were killed. These married Jewesses, repopulating Judah's borders with, by definition, Jews (Jdgs 19-21). Also temple Sadducees referred to diaspora, derogatorily, as "Benjamites" (9). During the first century there were no discernable Benjamites among the Jews (10). Joseph Raymond suggests Paul's Benjamite lineage was through his mother (11). However both of these arguments are weak, Paul having been originally called Saul, either Paul calling himself a Benjamite (of diaspora) trying to make some point to the temple about the equality of all, himself being a Hebrew of Hebrews (whatever that means) or that perhaps there was some Benjamite lineage through either side of his family.

Paul leaves Antioch after Claudius Caesar decides to hide his family genealogy (ties to Mark Anthony and his friends the Herods) eventually hiding even himself. The Cassians install Gaius Cassius Longinus as the governor of Antioch. The Cassians despised foreigners like Cleopatra, her beguiled lover Mark Anthony and the Herods. Which to me is the reason why the gospel of Nicodemus, at least influenced by the Herodian Paul and probably edited by Herod Agrippa excoriates Longinus as the Centurion who spears Jesus upon the cross in the side exclaiming as no Cassian would: This man was innocent (Lk 23:47) and truly the son of G-d (Mk 15:39)!

Another indirect support for Paul's Herodianism, involves why Paul, after being banished from Israel, would travel to Antioch, the third largest city of the Roman empire, rather than Alexandria, the second largest city of the Roman empire. Alexandria was home to the Jewish Philo who gives us our Biblically Greek interpretation of Hebrew scriptures, a philosophical and allegorizing interpretation, much like Paul's interpretation. Due to the Roman destruction of documentation (Thesis), it is tough to decipher what was happening in Alexandria where Jews had built a second temple based on a biblical prophecy (Is 19:19). Philo lived from roughly 20 BCE to 50. One of his nephews was Berenice's first husband (Herod Agrippa's sister). Another nephew, Tiberias Julius Alexander, led the Egyptian army as part of Vespasian's Roman destruction of the Jerusalem temple in 70.

Perhaps Paul avoided Alexandria due to the riot caused by Herod Agrippa there in 38 (12). Herod Agrippa had just been appointed governor of Galilee after Herod Philip's apparent demise - Philip having joined with Aretas in the war against Herod and Herodias after the death of John the Baptist. Agrippa's riot may have been caused by Alexandrian Jews despising an Idumean like Herod Agrippa becoming king of Israel. Or it may have been caused by Egyptians despising an Israeli Jew like Herod Agrippa supporting a Jewish temple which excluded women. Afterwards the Jews sent ambassadors to Caesar and the governor Flaccus was removed from office, but regardless of the causes, a Herodian in Alexandria would probably not have fared well and regardless of the similarities to the work of Philo, Paul avoided Alexandria giving an indirect argument for his Herodianness.

Was Paul a Roman building inspector? Paul worked at all the sites where Herods were paying to install public works such as the marble street in Antioch (Wars 1.21.11) and I'd guess Ephesus (it had a marble street too). With all the pictures in Gerald L. Steven's book of Roman Amphitheaters while describing Paul as a "builder of stage properties", I find Paul accompanying Herodian money (mostly stolen from David's tomb (13)). Also the way Paul travels, these three missionary journeys, are to me a trip through cities inspecting buildings and amphitheaters and then returning a few months later to inspect the work which was done. Per Adam Hamilton's book, The Call pg 159, Paul rents a lecture hall in Ephesus where he probably taught other civil servants – they go out to various cities and to me, inspect stone works too. According to Tacitus Annals 4.62-63 in Fidena, Italy, one such amphitheater collapsed. Its foundation was unstable and wooden super-structure was weak killing 50,000. With this in mind, my timeline for Paul staying in Corinth with Aquila and Pricilla eight years digging the canal, rather than travelling, training others in Ephesus and returning to inspect recommended repairs would more closely follow the three missionary journeys.

Was the gospel of Matthew authored by Herod? Please read chapter 27 of Bethlehem the War of Jesus and Paul's Plan for Peace. Essentially Dr. Eisenman proposes that the chief tax collector

(Matthew) would have been Herod and notes Eusebius raving that Matthew first wrote the prophesies which the Messiah must fulfill. I figured we would eventually find a Herod in Rome editing the gospels as mentioned in my introduction to Sources and as found in Dr Gerald Stevens Acts, A New Vision of the People of G-d p486/496 2016 (14).

***********Notes and Sources***************

I'm guessing Jewish Herodians would have been expelled from Rome in the multiple (as near as I can tell) Jewish expulsions. And so I have Herodion, his mother Mariamne, and Paul escape Corinth with the assistance of Seneca and the donations Paul carried to the temple in Jerusalem: p360 & 386 Acts, A New Vision of the People of G-d, Gerald L Stevens 2016, with the Fire of Rome & "Christian" persecutions.

"this imagery relates to both the `Herodian` family itself and the Establishment they sponsored, not to mention to a certain extent, `the Liar`. If the latter is Paul, he probably also carries `Herodian` blood even if Paul is not identical with the `Saulos` in Josephus – which we think he is." P758 the New Testament Code, Robert Eisenman 2006

"The case for Paul as Herodian-Hasmonean" – Chapter 7 Paul of Tarsus, Herodian Messiah, Joseph Raymond 2010

---Jesus may also be Herodian: His brother, Jacob (James) had the Maccabean/Priestly Ps 110:4 applied to his actions – a priest forever in the order of Melchizedek p313 James, the Brother of Jesus 1998 – The only Maccabeans were the descendants of Herod the Terrible - Herod the terrible married or killed all of the Maccabeans, raising children who married their nieces after which Herod's Maccabean children were killed. Finally in Herodian Messiah, 2010 page ii, Joseph Raymond 2010 argues that Herod would write "the King of the Jews" upon no one but a Herodian.

1) "Few Jews from outside of the house of Herod were Roman Citizens." Pg126 Herodian Messiah, Joseph Raymond 2010
2) Gamaliel head of Sanhedrin - p128 Herodian Messiah, Joseph Raymond 2010
3) Gallio is brother to Seneca, Caesar's secretary - p527 James, the Brother of Jesus Robert Eisenman 1997)
4) Herodians being educated in Rome - 1.32.2 Wars, Josephus – William Whiston 1998
5) Poppea's hostages - Josephus Antiquities 20.1.11 (William Whiston AM 1998)
6) Paul … was tutored in Rome by Seneca – p235 Herodian Messiah, Joseph Raymond 2010
7) Paul's writings were Stoic - p547 Acts, A New Vision of the People of G-d, Gerald L. Stevens 2016
8) Epaphroditus was Nero's secretary, appears intimate with Paul and encouraged Josephus – p35 James, the Brother of Jesus, Robert Eisenman 1997 / Seneca was Caesar's tutor – p800 ibid
9) I don't remember where I read this.
10) No Benjamites - P765 The New Testament Code, Robert Eisenman 2006
11) Paul's Benjamite lineage might have been through his mother - p150, Herodian Messiah, Joseph Raymond 2010

12) In 41 Agrippa received the kingship of Judea in Rome from Caesar. He stopped in Alexandria on the way home where there was a riot. Philo, the alabarch, presents a Greek interpretation of Jewish scriptures but berates Agrippa and Flaccus fails to prosecute Jews who riot and the subsequent pogrom. Minutes after 35 - Who Was Philo Judaeus of Alexandria? Dr. Henry Abramson Oct 10, 2013 htttps://www.youtube.com/watch?v=U6zvpUK7Gi8
13) Herod steals from David's tomb - 7.15.3 Antiquities Josephus
14) Herod Agrippa edits literary works in Rome – p486 Acts, a new vision of the people of G-d, Gerald L Stevens 2010

AFTERWORD: Paul's Infirmity

Paul says he prayed upon his infirmity three times:

Ye know how through **infirmity** of the flesh I preached the gospel unto you at the first. And my temptation which was in my flesh ye despised not nor rejected; but received me as an angel of G-d, even as Christ Jesus (Gal 4:13-14).

And lest I should be exalted above measure through the abundance of the revelations, there was given unto me a thorn in the flesh, the messenger of Satan to buffet me, lest I should be exalted above measure. For this thing I besought the Lord thrice, that it might depart from me. And he said unto me, my grace is sufficient for thee: for my strength is made perfect in **weakness**. Most gladly therefore will I rather glory in my infirmities, that the power of Christ may rest upon me. Therefore I take pleasure in infirmities, in reproaches, in necessities, in persecutions, in distresses for Christ's sake: for when I am weak, then I am strong (2 Cor 12:7-10).

Some feel Paul had eye problems:

And Paul earnestly beholding the council (70 men plus probably secretaries, guards and stragglers), said, Men and brethren, I have lived in all good conscience before G-d until this day. And the High Priest Ananias commanded **them that stood by h**im to smite him on the mouth. Then said Paul unto him, G-d shall smite thee, thou whited wall: for sittest thou to judgest me after the law, and commandest me to be smitten contrary to the law? And they that stood by said, Revilest thou G-d's High Priest? Then said Paul, I whist not, brethren, that he was High Priest: for it is written, Thou shalt not speak evil of the ruler of thy people (Acts 23:1-5).

And Paul was struck blind on the road to Damascus in Acts 9.

My feeling is that Paul's "infirmity" was not his eyes:

Because the scales fell from the eyes of Paul in Acts 9:18 and Paul "received his sight".

Because Paul regularly had "visions", "saw" people and worked as a builder (or even tentmaker Acts 9:18). To me Paul traveled Cyprus reviewing Roman Amphitheaters, possibly paid for by Herodian money like the marble road at Antioch and the work happening in Corinth. To me, "sight" was not Paul's "infirmity".

Possibly Paul had eye problems, but to me Paul travelled too much for this. My assumption is that Paul, as a Herodian, rode horses regularly. Philip Herod, who I believe was a relative, named a city Caesarea Philippi – Phillippi means "loves horses", through which Paul would have ridden on his journey to Damascus, much as Paul would have traveled the road through Turkey from Antioch to Ephesus, not to mention Paul's travel through Philippi itself. To me this rules out eye problems as Paul's writings would have otherwise noted further accommodation, more so than the Romans he dictated as well as further restrictions. How could Paul work if he couldn't see well enough to write?

To me Paul's infirmity came from riding horses:

In my opinion Paul was bow-legged. As a member of the Herodian family, my expectation is that Paul rode regularly. Paul prayed for release from this infirmity, an inability to walk easily, unable to mention this "infirmity", this dis-ease with his foundation when standing, unable to discuss it directly in his writings without directly linking himself to Herodians and riches. Paul therefore found comfort in a Roman saddle, riding Roman roads at a time when saddles did not include stirrups. Paul's legs, to me, were strong, able to grip a horse easily, able to lunge quickly. Paul was able to cut stone or sew tents, but was unable to walk very far without pain. Paul therefore sat among the throng when the High Priest spoke, unable to see, able to stand and fight but not for long, unable to run from soldiers and prison guards, commanding respect in all other aspects of his being while not even having an "infirmity" which would prevent his being present at temple gatherings (men who could not fight in war and eunuchs were excluded – Acts 8:27, the treasurer of Ethiopia, would not have been allowed – Ch 7 Ethiopian History, Understanding the Bible Ray Shortell 2013).

AFTERWORD: THE GOSPEL OF THOMAS

In my opinion, the Gospel of Thomas was not primarily Gnostic, a separate tradition from Antioch, as proposed by some. Other authors have noted a strong "Thomasine" tradition from Antioch. As my story has noted, there is indeed a strong Thomasine tradition in Antioch. Specifically three of the four brothers of Jesus, all who could walk, spent time in Antioch. Paul puts Cephas (Peter) there when some arrive from Jacob (James) (Gal 2:11). Jude's grandchildren are rounded up by Trajan. In my opinion Barnabas was Joses (Acts 4:36). And per Robt Eisenman in Jesus, the brother of James, the apostles were the brothers (Judas Thomas). However, the Gospel of Thomas was found in Coptic (Egyptian), in Egypt (Alexandria), and in my opinion was the work of Alexandrian authors attempting what would become the wisdom of Jesus in the Gospels. To me these are unedited rough drafts later shipped to Rome. My job as a typesetter observing editors making rough notes bland comes through here:

It was first directed at the temple: A city built upon a high mountain (and) fortified cannot fall, nor can it be hidden (32).

It explains that Romans want taxes: They showed Jesus a gold coin and said to him: "Caesar's people demand taxes from us." He said to them: "Give to Caesar the things that are Caesar's. Give to G-d the things which are G-d's and give to me that which is mine" (100).

It discusses a plan for Jews and Gentiles together and for men and women in the temple together: …When you make two into one and when you make the inside like the outside and the above like the below – that is to make the male and the female into a single one… (22) When you make the two into one, you will become the sons of man. And when you say: "Mountain move away," it will move away (that Jerusalem will no longer be necessary) (106). If two make peace with one another in the same house (Jews and Gentiles in the temple) they will say to the mountain: `Move away,` and it will move away (48).

Alexandrians were apparently pretty upset that women were not allowed in the temple: Peter says that women are not worthy of life. Jesus says that he will draw them in and make them male spirits. And further that every woman who makes herself a mane spirit will enter the kingdom of heaven (114).

It discusses the first purpose of the Bible directly (unity; Jews and Gentiles together): A person said unto him: "Tell my brothers to give to me what is mine." Jesus replied: … I am not a divider… (72).

It heaps disgrace upon the temple: Twenty-four prophets have spoken in Israel (24 courses of high priestly families led by their patriarchs – Josephus Antiquities 7.14.7). You have pushed away the living (one) and begun to speak of the dead (52). …there are many around the well, but the well is empty (74) (Woman at the well, living water/wine from Jesus, well from Jacob – Jews and Gentiles). The ten virgins (Mt 25:1-13 – NIV) similarly represent the new and old covenants with the first five commandments, focused on our relationship with G-d "foolish". Verse 16 explains this Jewish obsession with numbers: with the house divided standing two against three (witness against manifestation) (Mt 12:25 household divided) By my interpretation Rome wanted Jews fighting Jews… as happened while Vespassian waited in the temple itself (Josephus Wars).

It discusses whether circumcision is beneficial concluding: …if it were beneficial, their father would beget them circumcised from their mother… (53)

It begs the temple to recognize the greater reality that G-d may be present in the xenophobic temple but surely displays craftsmanship and unity across the world: Jesus says: Why do you wash the outside of the cup? Do you not understand that the one who created the inside is also the one who created the outside? (89)

It puts down city-based Pharisees (dogs being despised by the Jews for not discriminating unclean, unkosher, profane meat from the holy): Woe to them, the Pharisees, for they are like a dog sleeping in a cattle trough, for it neither eats nor allows the cattle to eat (102). A vine was planted outside the vineyard (temple; Jerusalem) and since it was not supported it will be pulled up by the root and perish (40).

It tells of the second purpose of the Bible (War): …I have come to cast dissension upon the earth: fire, sword and war. For there will be five in one house: there will be three against two… (16) I will destroy this house and no one will be able to build it again (71). …The person who is near me is near the fire… (82)

It tells of its method (deceit): …Whatever your right hand does, your left hand should not know of its doing (62). Do not give to dogs what is Holy lest they throw it on the dunghill. Do not throw pearls before swine lest they turn them into mud (93).

And it explains the mystery of living water (Jn 4:10): Whoever will drink from my mouth (words) will become like me… and what is hidden will be revealed to him (108). …I am not your teacher. For you have drunk, you have become intoxicated at the bubbling spring I have measured out… (13)

And it wraps up with a promise: …The one who seeks… when he finds, he will be dismayed… he will be astonished. And he will be king (rule) over the all (2). There is nothing hidden that will not be revealed (5).

Source of quotes: The Fifth Gospel, The Gospel of Thomas Comes of Age, Stephen J Patterson, James M Robinson, Hans-Gebhard Bethge 1998

Source of women being considered equals in Alexandria (owning property, running businesses): Assassin's Creed Origins.

Pharisees per the Gospel of Thomas with my interpretation (city based). Tom rather than Gospel of Thomas indicates my interpretation of how the authors should have translated, based upon my knowledge of the metaphors being discussed rather than any knowledge I might have of Coptic:

Jesus says: "A grapevine was planted outside (the vineyard) of the Father. And since it is not supported, it will be pulled up by its root (and) will perish." (40)

Jesus says: "A vine growing outside of the vineyard will be weeded." (Tom 40).

Jesus says: "Whoever knows all, if he is lacking one thing, he is (already) lacking everything." (67)

Whoever claims to know, but lacks the smallest thing, knows nothing (Tom 67; Tu no sabe nada!).

He said: "Lord, there are many around the well, but there is nothing in the <well>."(74)

The well (of Jacob) is empty though many labor at the winch (Tom 74).

Jesus says: "Woe to them, the Pharisees, for they are like a dog sleeping in a cattle trough. For it neither eats nor [lets] the cattle eat." (102)

Jesus says: "Woe to them, the Pharisees who, like a dog sleeping in the cattle trough, neither eats nor allows the cattle theirs (Tom 102).

THESIS

Understanding the Bible 2011 shows that the purpose of the Bible is to remove all authority from the Jewish Temple Sadducees (zealots) who didn't want to pay the tax (i.e. Essenes [pacifists] like Jacob [James] had nothing taxable) against whom the biblical Jesus railed telling his followers to pay the tax while not touching money himself. Sin, Sacrifice, Heaven and Hell, the Meaning of Christianity 2017 shows that the purpose of Biblical Christianity was to remove/justify removing Sadducees and their traditions from the face of the earth. Bethlehem: The War of Jesus explains how Paul (Pharisee - Roman accommodators) authored the first purpose and Rome authored the second. Bethlehem: The War of Jesus further explains that Judaism, far from being based on a rich prophetic tradition, was primarily based on both Ezekiel and Jeremiah who prophesied that Babylon would defeat Egypt garnering crops from the rich Nile delta while Jerusalem stood as a rear-guard of loyal Jewish Babylonians (Ch 11 – Queen Helen's Israel). The Old Testament was first set in writing during the 70 year Babylonian exile according to Gary Greenberg (pg xxix 101 Myths of the Bible). The Babylonian defeat of Egypt did not happen, but the walls of Jerusalem were re-erected, remaining standing until Rome.

Further charges of Bethlehem: The War of Jesus: Upon the Babylonian return, Jews found Samaritans with their own biblical tradition which was destroyed by Jews 125 BCE. Daniel was backdated as related by other authors. My contribution around Daniel with its first biblical reference to eternal life is surmising that a quill was probably used to write upon the wall from the Egyptian Hall of the Dead, due to the words "being weighed" as happens there yet mentioned no place else in scripture. My contribution around the book of Esther and the holiday Purim is suggesting that these were written by Rome (or highlighted/modified) or by someone like Josephus wanting to impress Poppea, Nero's wife, with her ability to impact history. Perhaps Poppea was part Jewish, but this is doubtful as a Jewish woman would not have been impressed by being referenced as Isthar. According to other authors Purim is a modern feast not recognized by traditional Judaism at the time. And that even Psalms were backdated with the one regarding everlasting Melchizedek having been added to support Maccabean priesthood which Dr. Eisenman has charged was not descended from Levi (Postscript: Failed Messianic Propheises, Understanding the Bible, Ray Shortell 2011).

Finally the thesis of Bethlehem: The War of Jesus is that the Roman destruction of evidence was purposeful as noted in Sin, Sacrifice, Heaven & Hell: Salt of the Earth. See also in SSHH Education Denounced by the Bible: Rome burned the library of Alexandria (it was rebuilt and Muslims burned it again an aeon later). Seneca, Caesar's secretary, was at the burning and picked up whatever he thought hopeful in regards to scholarship, assumedly stored in the Vatican archives just as Josephus preserved the books of the Jerusalem temple. Rome killed a million Egyptian Jews and destroyed the second Jewish temple in Alexandria. Rome killed 1.1 million Jews in Israel burning the temple there and killing another thousand zealots at Massada. Josephus records Romans killing Jews and confiscating their property around the Mediterranean much as Mark Anthony (Marcus Antonius) and Octavian (Augustus Caesar) had done to Rome while pursuing Brutus and Cassius in Philippi. And as Julius Caesar had done in France before Marching on Rome (crossing the Rubicon).

Questions still remain: What covered-up or hidden prophesies led to Messianic hope and rebellion? My strong suspicion is that there are prophesies for which we either lost the key, as in warrior David's Bethlehem meaning the Bread of Life, knowledge of the afterlife come down from heaven, from the Egyptian Hall of Judgement weighing one's soul against a feather before allowing passage to the North Star pointed out by pyramids of Egypt with even Paul showing his knowledge of Astrology in I Cor 13, Daniel being the first to mention an afterlife, the feet of Essene burials pointing to the North Star, with the Jerusalem pyramids of Queen Helen whose husband I argue probably instigated the war between Rome and Parthia in Israel with these messianic references much as Cleopatra wished War between Israel and Arabia to weaken her enemies. Could Rabbi Yochanan ben Zakkai, leader of the Roman school of Pharisees, have left any writings he knew Rome wouldn't get or decipher?

By the way, I adore Robert Eisenman of California State University and would like an honorary Masters from him. My current degree is a bachelor's of Computer Science, College of Engineering, University of Illinois.

INDEX OF METAPHORS

Prelude – Mark Anthony, Paul the Herodian, Cleopatra, Fore-skin, Scrotum, Longinus
0 – Scribe, Longinus, Gnostic, Knowledge
1-Historians, Stoicism, Rome means destruction, Jeremiah
2-Tomb of David, Brood of vipers, King/brother, Rechabites, Oath of Meat, Bow-legged, Taxes, Poor, Philip
3-Purgatory, Crucifixion, tax revolt, King is not a brother, Herod is Jewish, Oath to kill Paul before eating… meat
4-Crucifixion 40CE, Temple Wall Affair, Sadducees/Pharisees
5-Exclusionary gates, Bow-legged, Money, Languages, James' Camel Knees
6-Samaritan, Maccabees, Taxes, James broken legs
7-Costobarus, Leather sandals, Dogs, Crucifixion means loyalty
8-Bethlehem Bread of Life, Joseph the Egyptian, Daniel, Witches float, Taxes
9-Mountains, Letters, Mark Anthony, Tent, Architect, Muzzling the ox, Nicodemus' Longinus
10-Alms, The Poor, Widows of Antioch, Rechabites, Pharisees, Sadducees, Barnabas
11-Xenophobia, Sadducees, Isaiah, Jeremiah, Babylon, Samaritans, Second Temple at Alexandria
12-Exclusionary gates, Grafting, Sadducees, Roman editing, Alms
13-Bread, Brothers, Benjamin, Barnbas son of consolation, Herod fornication, Sicarii, Widows
14-Widows, Paul Roman, Herodian, Maccabean, Stoic, Seneca
15-Bow-legged, Horses, Sending Presence, Brothers, Camel's Knees, Bernice, Drusilla, Herod, Paul, Brood of vipers
16-Cleopatra, Augustus
17-Paul's gospel, Sadducees, Pharisees, Catholics, Bread of Life, Egyptian Hall of the Dead, Mom/Dad
18-Mark Anthony, Longinus, Seneca, Epaphroditus, Herodias, Herodion, Sicarii, Letter, Peace Plan
19-Letter, Wind bag, Essenes, Rechabites, Joseph, North Star, Pyramid, Grave, Herods, Maccabeans, Wine/Greek
20-I Cor 13, High Priest's Twelve Stones, Hercules, Corinthians, Deacons, Herodion
21-Herodias, Herodion, Seneca, Nero, Vatican Archive, Diana, Hittite/Sumerian/Babylonian-Gemini, Delphi, Pyramid
22-The Way, The Poor, Essenes, Jude, Jacob, Widows, Bread of Life
23-Sending presence, Killing all of her prophets, Seneca, Herod & Herodias retired to Spain, Herodion, Cosmpolitan, Poppea, Nero, Cephas, Alms, Bernice, Drusilla
24-Bernice, Drusilla, Jewesses, All in Asia have turned away, Cosmopolitanism, Mark Anthony, Cleopatra, Seneca, The Peace Plan, Taxes, Philip
25-Bread of Life, Joseph/Jacob, Crucifixion, Egyptian Hall of the Dead, Daniel backdated, Seneca, Philemon
26-Mafia, Cleaner, Seneca confiscates Alexandrian Library, Paul's Peace Plan, Death of James
27-Cleaner, Paul Crucified, Herod's Gospel of Matthew, Cosmopolitanism
28-Temple Wall Affair, Seneca, Three Nets of Belial, Book of Esther
29-Seneca burns Alexandria Library, Temple gold, The Poor, The Cleaner, Death of James, Paul, Poppea, Cephas, Joseph the Egyptian, Pyramids, Star of Bethlehem, Star from Jacob, Nero fiddles, Rome burns, Seneca, Esther, Ephesians, Warrior Messiah, Gospel of Thomas, Gospel of Barnabas, Nero lead poisoning, Epaphroditus, The Cleaner
30-Nero, Submit to Rome, Poppea, Josephus, Seneca & Epaphroditus, Esther, Gallio & Sosthenes, Bread of Life, Cassians, Pewter & Tomato, Philemon, Sadducees & Pharisees, The Stoicism of II Timothy
31-Josephus surrenders, Death of Jacob (James), Nazareth, Cleaner
32-Vespasian, Sadducees, Josephus, Rabbi in coffin, Grainery burns, Temple gold market crash, Titus, Genocide, The Egyptian, Flight to Antioch (Syria)
33-Mars, Pluto, Historians, Genocide, Stephen, Gospel of John, Vatican archives, Eusebius
Epilogues: Salt of the Earth, Talmud, Pharisees, Rabbinic Judaism, Vespasian, Rabbi Yochanan ben Zakkai, Augustine
Afterword – Was Jesus Crucified in 40 - Philip
Thesis: Maccabees as Zealots by Eisenmann
Epilogue America – Augustine
Sources – Mafia (Handlers)
Bibliography
About the Author – Augustine

SOURCES

Hopefully you've enjoyed reading my book, Bethlehem: The War of Jesus. This is the best I can do regarding what was happening and going through the minds of Paul, James and the Roman (Greek) authors of the Bible. Unfortunately metaphors are tough to untangle and the authors of Christianity, Paul and his Roman handlers, purposefully hid their authority and purpose. SOURCES may help understand what I was communicating, if you would have a question regarding a particular chapter.

First there is the question of Paul's not visiting Jerusalem for fourteen years (per Galatians) while Acts has Paul traipsing about the Levant like a tourist. Acts has Paul in Corinth until going to Jerusalem before 58. This means Paul's previous visit would have been before 44, but the famine visit (Acts 11) was 46-48. I put Jesus' crucifixion in 40 with Paul's Damascus return in 42 followed by moving to Antioch (Appendix: Timeline, Sin, Sacrifice, Heaven & Hell, Ray Shortell 2017) (Chapter 5 – Dating the Bible – Understanding the Bible, Ray Shortell 2014).

How did Paul manage to be present in Jerusalem for the Famine Visit and Jerusalem Council and yet be able to say he was absent from Jerusalem for fourteen years? Interestingly, based off of Fr. Good??? From All Saints in Dunwoody who gave an ecumenical talk at the Jewish Community Center in Dunwoody around 2005 with a Rabbi, Fr Good??? said there was no Jerusalem council. As per "About the Author" in Understanding the Bible, the Catholic Serendipity Bible does title the section as "the Jerusalem Council", but Paul argues with "Hellenists" (Grecians Acts 9:29) totally unlike himself as always arguing against the temple (against those who commend themselves 2 Cor 10:12). My belief as Per Fr Good…? is that the Jerusalem Council didn't happen and that Paul was banished from Jerusalem by Herod.

Regarding the Famine Visit, my men's team has an answer as per our standard: Be present at every meeting. When unable to attend we "send our presence" in the form of asking someone to let our team know how we're doing and sending something to add to the meeting such as a joke. My belief is that Herod banished Paul from Jerusalem, but that Paul managed to send his presence from Antioch for the famous famine visit, possibly even accompanying his church to Caesarea while waiting for news from Jerusalem. And perhaps Paul similarly considered himself present at the Jerusalem Council, generally knowing what James' ideas and pronouncements were. The author of Luke/Acts was not Paul and probably didn't join Paul until later in Paul's career.

Another key point in this book is the word "Herod" which I use freely. Josephus, from whom most of our timeline comes, noted that historians often praise winners (Rome) and vilify losers (Jerusalem, Cleopatra). As there were many Herods running around like a brood of snakes and Josephus wasn't even alive for early happenings, my use of the terminology "Herod" should be taken as generic along with my liberal interpretation of Acts in regards to whether and when Paul visited a particular city. Dr. Robert Eisenman proposes Paul as Herodian in James, the Brother of Jesus 1997, Appendix: The Herodians and also in Paul as Herodian: The Dead Sea Scrolls and the First Christians 2004 and notes Paul as a "foreigner" in the Ascents of Jacob on pg762 of The New Testament Code 2006 with Herod Agrippa II similarly called a foreigner on pg 759 noting foreigners bringing gifts which Paul did (Acts 24:17) which pollute the temple on pg 757. Joseph Raymond in Herodian Messiah, Case for Jesus as Grandson of Herod 2010 has a different suggestion for Paul's Herodian lineage, and further supporting arguments in his Chapter 7 – Paul of Tarsus.

Regarding the names I've chosen, as I note in chapter 26, calling someone by other than what they would wish calling themselves is ignorant Jacob (James), Barnabas (Joses), Jude (Thomas, Didymus, Judas), Cephas (Peter, Simeon the Zealot), Jesus … to the best of my abilities.

Also, as praise to our creator, I started this book trusting I would find my last couple of references, needing someone from the family of Herod as a Roman editor (p496 Acts, a New Vision of the People of G-d, Gerald L. Stevens 2016) and something about Rome controlling the authorship of the Pharisees (Epilogue, Editing the Talmud).

Enjoy!

Cover –
Bethlehem is covered in Chapter 8. David as priest is covered here by Dr. Ernest L. Martin (World Wide Church of G-d): http://askelm.com/doctrine/d090201.htm The interpretation of the king going away for the war is mine, based on a quote from author Sam Harris in his debates (Lk 19:27), Philo and a note from somewhere about king Agrippa. The quote from a million dead and 100,000 Jewish slaves in Corinth and 20,000 building the coliseum at Rome comes from: According to Josephus, up to one million five hundred thousand men (1,500,000), women and children perished or were enslaved as a result of the rebellion. P180, First Century Judaism in Crisis, Jacob Neusner 1975

For Paul as Herodian, please check Afterword: Was Paul Herodian? There are chapters on Paul fleeing Antioch. And my first principle of the Bible: Removing the authority of the temple, is the foundation of Paul's writings. Second principle: Justifying the destruction of Sadducean temple zealots. Bethlehem was probably the spiritual principle underlying zealot xenophobia.

Joseph and Alphaeus are nick-names for Clopas, the husband of Mary, wife of Jesus. Alphaeus means "the first" by my interpretation the first to bring back the theology of eternal life from Egypt. Joseph is given several names including Clopas and Alphaeus p845 James, the Brother of Jesus, Robert Eisenman 1997.

For a timeline you should probably check Ch 5 Understanding the Bible, Ray Shortell 2013. The standard concerns are that Jesus has two potential birthdates, one before 4 BCE when Herod the Terrible dies. Per Matthew the family fled Herod the Terrible, while the census of Quirinius of Syria was 6-7 CE, a span of about ten years. And then there are the two genealogies of Jesus between Luke and Matthew which since the first centuries have been discussed as potentially those of Joseph and Mary although apparently splitting even before a common ancestor through which the two distinct lines pass. Irenaeus 200 CE suggests that Jesus was crucified at the age of fifty (Against Heresies 2015 p160). My feeling based upon Paul's being a busy man and unlikely to sit still after the crucifixion very long is that the crucifixion happened in 40 when, as per Luke 3:1, Lysanias was tetrarch of Abilene (Understanding the Bible Ch 5).

    37 John beheaded – p106, James, the Brother of Jesus, Robert Eisenman 1997
      --Jesus picks up Nathaniel and Philip, John's disciples, as his own – Jn 1:35-51
        --p406, Understanding the Bible, Stephen L. Harris 2011
    40 Crucifixion – Ch 5 Dating the Bible – Understanding the Bible, Ray Shortell 2013
    46-48 The Famine – p564, James, the Brother of Jesus, Robert Eisenman 1997
      --Queen Helen/Paul buying grain from Egypt p920 ibid
    62 Death of Jacob (James) – xxxii ibid
    64 the fire of Rome & death of Poppea – p791 ibid
    66 Beit Horon – p885 ibid; tax revolt – p828 ibid
    70 burning of the Temple, 11 Preface, Josephus, the War of the Jews,

--Ch 1 The Power of Rome, Understanding the Bible, Ray Shortell, 2011
--Ch 32, Vespasian Burns Jerusalem, Bethlehem, the War of Jesus, Ray Shortell 2018
73 Massada falls p88 James, the Brother of Jesus, Robert Eisenman 1997
79 Vesuvius erupts killing Drusilla – p477, Acts, A New Vision of the People of G-d, Gerald L. Stevens 2016

Architectural education in Rome – If Paul was Herodian my assumption is he went to school in Rome. Herodians would have sent their children to school in Rome (Wars 1.22.2 & 1.23.1) like Agrippa: Wars 1.8.5 shows Herodian captives in Rome, Wars 2.9.5-6 shows Herodians "imprisoned" in Rome yet throwing feasts, Antiquities 18.2.4 has a Parthian noble educated in Rome, Explaining that Herod sent some of his children to college in Rome, Jospehus Antiquities 16.2.1, 16.8.3 also Wars 2.9 where Agrippa is imprisoned in Rome for a bit for being too loud for what seems to me to be with a college buddy. Antiquities 19.8.2 shows Herod Agrippa appearing in a presumed amphitheater in an outfit shining of silver and gold. Assuming Caesarea was built by Herodians (Ch 3) using gold from the tomb of David (Ch 2)…

Throughout the first century until the very eve of the war in 66, thousands of workmen busied themselves on … Herod's great project of beautifying and rebuilding the temple. pg22 First Century Judaism in Crisis, Jacob Neusner 1975

Discontent in Jerusalem … was intensified by the widespread unemployment caused by the completion of the Herodian Temple, which threw 18,000 men out of work. P137 First Century Judaism in Crisis, Jacob Neusner 1975

Paul visits Damascus for three years (Sources Ch 2) while seeking the return of Phaesalis and discovering the power of Parthia.

Cassius of Antioch – Please review sources for Prelude
Widows of Antioch – Dedication; Ch 13
Quarrying stone in Corinth – Prof Gerald L. Stephens reinterprets the word "tent-maker" on pg 388 in Acts a New Vision of the People of … 2016 and then has pictures of Roman Amphitheaters throughout the Mediterranean. Nathan Wolford of Sidelines, Woodstock, GA 2018 tells me Romans shipped stone from Corinth across the Mediterranean. Caesar ordered Jews out of Rome several times p360 ibid which led Paul to meet Aquilla and Priscilla p386 ibid who make "stage properties"… to me, "amphitheaters", at Caesar's summer home Pg 561 The New Testament Code, Robert Eisenman 2006 bringing donations (Ch 18). Rome Ch 25. Jerusalem Ch 26 Rome and Ch 27 death of Paul.

Deaths – mostly in chapters with their names, Burning of the Libraries – Prelude, Mafia – Ch 26 Sources.
Rome builds Yavneh for Pharisees – Epilogue: Editing the Talmud
I am the bread of life come down from heaven (Jn 6:51).
Three taverns – Ch 5 – Understanding the Bible, Ray Shortell 2013
Destruction of Tarichaea – 3.10 Wars, Josephus
Brood of Vipers – Chapter 2

After the Jewish rebellion of 66, the Romans destroyed the temple deliberately, to cripple the religion." The evidence on the burning of the temple is equivocal. The Romans through Josephus denied responsibility and attempted to represent it as either an accident of war or the acts of the Jews themselves. Pg 152 First Century Judaism in Crisis, Jacob Neusner 1975

Prelude – Bethlehem: the War of Jesus, Paul's Plan for Peace

1) Saggy sacks – Foreward: Understanding the Bible, Sin, Sacrifice, Heaven & Hell Ray Shortell 2017 (follow-up and previous paragraph)
2) Lying wind-bags, spiritually empty, old wine-skins (fore-skins), full of the wrath of G-d like cups of blood or wine – Understanding the Bible, Chapter XXII – The Cup of Blood, Ray Shortell 2013
3) Cups of blood or wine – Cantankerous Sadducees charged Herodians with sleeping with their wives during their periods (p458 James, The Brother of Jesus, Robert Eisenman 1998). Also see chapter 2 – "Damascus" meaning cup of wrath and blood.
4) If it turns out that our contention that Paul was a 'Herodian' can be proved, it is this line going back to Costobarus and Herod's sister Salome to which he belonged. p502 James, the Brother of Jesus, Robert Eisenman 1997

   "The case for Paul as Herodian-Hasmonean" – Chapter 7 Paul of Tarsus, Herodian Messiah, Joseph Raymond 2010

   "this imagery relates to both the `Herodian` family itself and the Establishment they sponsored, not to mention to a certain extent, `the Liar'. If the latter is Paul, he probably also carries `Herodian` blood even if Paul is not identical with the `Saulos` in Josephus – which we think he is." Pg 758 The New Testament Code, Robert Eisenman 2006

   Jesus may also be Herodian: As Jacob's (James') brother who had Ps 110:4 applied to his actions. Herod the Terrible had killed or married all of the Maccabeans. Robert Eisenman notes James having the Maccabean Ps 110:4 applied to his actions: A priest forever in the order of Melchizedek p313 James the Brother of Jesus – 1998

   ---Finding the governor of Antioch a friend of Herods and then changing to a Cassian around the time Paul was forced to leave pretty much did it for me.
5) Hermeneutic means theo-logical (Biblical logic) – The root word of hermeneutic is Hermes, the Latin or Roman G-d of thought, logic and healing. Hermes is a reference to the name of the planet Mercury in Greek/Egyptian Astrology, like the mercurial twins of Gemini found on the prow of Paul's ship (Acts 28:11). Eschatology means study of the end times, the end of days and how its apocalypse (unveiling) speaks to how we should currently behave. For more hard words that are tough to understand, read Paul, the Apostle by J Christiaan Beker 1980 until you figure out that most of his eschatological, apocalyptic, hermeneutic is devoted to decrying those opposed to his denomination.
6) Paul sought community and harmony between Herodians and Jews – p550 James, the Brother of Jesus, Robert Eisenman 1997

Longinus Pierced - Pg 373 The Other Bible, Edited by Willis Barnstone, 1984
    3a) Blood and water - 19:34 Jn
Longinus governor of Syria (Antioch) 45 – 49: https://www.revolvy.com/page/Gaius-Cassius-Longinus-%28consul-AD-30%29 (cites Tacitus Annales XIV 42.45 for some portion of the article).

In my opinion Paul's apocalypse only reveals the present: That which Paul claims to be revealing about eschatology always points back to the present and how believers should behave now. Paul's cosmopolitan focus is only on community.

"This left the apocalyptic time of the end open for a more constructive proposal, the imagining of a time when the Christian mission would reach its completion in the glorious reunion of Jews and gentiles in the one kingdom of G-d" p142 Who Wrote the New Testament, Burton L. Mack 1995

Nero summered in Corinth where Jewish slaves would dig at the canal – Pg 561 The New Testament Code, Robert Eisenman 2006

Dedication – Although many make much of Jacob (James) the Greater, biblically indecipherable from Jacob the Less (Mk 15:4) or Jacob, the brother of John, these fishermen, sons of thunder, boanerges (Mk 3:17, Lk 5:10) or Jacob, who is put to the sword by king Herod in Acts 12:2, Dr. Eisenman makes the point that the Jacob of the Jerusalem council (Acts 15:13) receives no introduction as though we should already know who he is although the apostle Jacob, the brother of John had already been killed in Acts 12:2. (pg xviii, 51 James, the Brother of Jesus, Robert Eisenman 1997). As per Dr. Eisenman's books, to me there is but one Jacob (Part IV – James v Paul – Understanding the Bible, Ray Shortell 2011), the leader of the Essenes and therefore rightly called the leader of Judah or Israel.

Chapter 1 – Beit Horon 40 CE The Road to Jerusalem

In my opinion all understanding of the Bible must start with the power of Rome. Part I- Understanding the Bible, Ray Shortell 2013

Therefore Bethlehem: The War of Jesus starts smack dab in the middle of the Roman army which rode horses 50 miles a day without stirrups. Beit Horon is the pass through which Rome must pass from the coast to reach Jerusalem. Beit Horon is where the two grandsons of Queen Helen of Adiabene (Chapters 10 - 12 on Queen Helen) from Iraq who were not born Jewish but later converted, would die defending Israel as per the dedication of Robert Eisenman's book, James the Brother of Jesus 1997:

For Monobazus and Kenedaeos, the grandsons of the `Ethiopian Queen`, Freedom Fighters and Converts who gave their lives at the Pass of Beit Horon.

Chapter one attempts to capture the frustration Rome must have felt at being forced to reconquer Israel multiple times sending soldiers generation after generation from 40 BCE – 70 CE. The Jew in this chapter is a Rechabite, a priest sworn to live in booths owning no property, only the clothes on his back, but with a skill, a craft, much like Joseph, the carpenter, Jesus' dad in the Bible. My feeling is that these were dedicated to providing nothing to support Rome much like some Amish will live below the poverty line so that income taxes are not required, conscientiously living in a way which does not support federal taxes for wars they personally oppose.

The priest is in a tent rather than in a booth as would Rechabites. This intentionally alludes to Paul's having been a tentmaker (or amphitheater as per pgs 388/535 Acts, a New Vision of the People of G-d, Gerald L. Stevens 2016). Also the pottery references our creator from the multiple scriptural references having dominion and as per Calvinists making some pots for destruction like the Egyptian Pharaoh, the gourd plant which shaded Jonah or the fig tree cursed by Jesus (yet created by him). The soldier meeting the potter is an allusion to free-will and fate/predestination suggesting that perhaps both sides have a point. The potter has mainly gourds with a few shattered pots all with striking artwork notably not violating the second commandment with people, animals or stars which might be worshiped as idols. He has no money, but still references the thirty pieces of silver thrown into the temple for the price of Jesus (Zech 11:12-13) because it was spent on the potter's field (Mt 27:7,10). Bethlehem: The War of Jesus hangs on this metaphor where the West, the Roman Army, meets the East in a priest who might understand the design of the Universe, purposefully co-creating the design of the Universe as in Abraham's discussion with G-d on whether the city might be saved for only ten good men (Gen 18:16-33, by which Jews believe we are co-creators). Or he may only be living as best he can while observing passions roiling about his peaceful center. Some have carried Calvin's potter pre-destination all the way back to Adam and Eve being pre-destined to sin. All of these allusions are included by referencing The Pass at Beit Horon.

Finally regarding the languages referenced: There is a professor who studied writing in ancient Israel concluding that at the time of Jesus the population was illiterate. My contention is that at the time of Jesus, Israel stood in the middle of three continents with multiple languages with no one knowing what language to write anything for the public, not to mention locals probably tearing down Roman signs at the most inopportune times for the Roman army and vice-versa, much like the English tearing down road signs to prevent the Nazi invasion. In addition to Hebrew, Aramaic, Greek and Latin plus whatever language the Ethiopian treasurer brought who spoke with Philip there were many languages. As the Bible itself puts it in Acts 2:1-11: And when the day of Pentecost was fully come, they were all of one accord in one place. And suddenly there came a sound from heaven as of a rushing might wind, and it filled the house in which they were sitting. And there appeared unto them cloven tongues like as of fire, and it sat upon each of them. And they were filled with the Holy Ghost, and began to speak with other tongues as the Spirit gave them utterance. And there were dwelling in Jerusalem Jews, devout men, out of every nation under heaven. Now when this was noised abroad, the multitude came together, and were confounded, because that every man heard them in his own language. And they were all amazed and marveled, saying one to another, Behold, are not all these which speak Galileans? And how hear we every man in our own tongue, wherein we were born? Parthians and Medes, and Elamites, and the dwellers in Mesopotamia, and in Judea, and Cappadocia, in Pontus and Asia, Phrygia and Pamphylia, in Egypt and the parts of Libya about Cyrene, and strangers of Rome, Jews and proselytes, Cretes and Arabians. We do hear them speak in our tongues…

(1) Thucydides (~400 BCE): "…the weak accept what they have to accept… We know that you or anybody else with the same power as ours would be acting precisely the same way." pg110 The Ancient Historians, Michael Grant 1970 - Note: Thucydides wrote in Greek. I think I read the line differently someplace else. If not, I'm translating meaning rather than words.
(2) Romeo/Juliette were a retelling of Mark Anthony / Cleopatra love affair… in my opinion.
(3) The End of Israel (Salt of the Earth), Sin, Sacrifice, Heaven & Hell, Ray Shortell 2017
(4) pg 286 101 Myths of the Bible, Gary Greenberg 2000 – Israel split with Solomon due to human slavery 900 BCE. Per me, Assyria invaded in 722 BCE resettling the ten northern tribes closer to India or in my opinion as Celts of Scotland, Whales & Ireland.
(5) 40,000 scrolls burned, more confiscated by Seneca, Burned Library at Alexandria – Seneca – On Tranquility of Mind – http://www.straightdope.com/columns/read/2233/what-happened-to-the-great-library-of-alexandria
(6) Jeremiah/Ezekiel – chapter 11 Queen Helen's Jerusalem - Beit Horon

For the larger back-story on reference (2): Romeo and Juliette were two "star-crossed lovers" whose families hated each other (like the Claudians and Cassians). They ran away and had a secret plan to fake their deaths which got mixed up and one of them thinking the other had killed themselves, both wind up committing suicide. Cleopatra, similarly, promises to support Mark Anthony, but then runs away and when both are pursued by Rome, they kill themselves, which seems a biblical Sampson and Delilah love story to me: Delilah promises to keep Sampson's secrets, but releases them to his enemies (three times). Sampson is brought bound and blinded to the fortress's foundation pillars and given the strength to kill both himself and his enemies.

Babylon invading Egypt - please check references for chapter 11, Queen Helen's Egypt.

The Jordan valley highway runs from Egypt to Parthia along the route taken by the Kurd, Saladin, to avoid the coast (p162, 164 The Crusades Through Arab Eyes, Amin Maalouf1984). Gamala would probably have been a fortress along the road which carried, to my mind, Parthian supplies and was later used by Jewish refugees escaping to Kurdistan.

Chapter 2 Damascus 40 CE The City of Blood

Five horsemen ride, the number of grace. Two people witness, the number of witness. My gematria comes from Alvin Frame of the Church of the Nazarene in Marietta, GA. He probably got it from somewhere. Some might get hooked into gematria which is kind of my intent in hinting at the ten commandments in two sets of five and not Augustine's ten commandments as I explain in *About the Author* with Paul implying by these numbers that he alone carries the truth. However the numbers are misdirection, a blind to my real point here, forcing readers to dwell upon what I'm communicating, which has to do with what happens to the horses. Where are the stables? Cavalry was very important to the Roman military. Roads were built for horses across Greece and Turkey which Paul used. Thousands of cavalry are mentioned in Josephus with cities named in Greek "loves horses" (Philippi), but horses are not mentioned in the Gospels. Why?

This term, "innovation" figures heavily in Josephus (Antiquities 18.5.1). Those of the Way refused to call any man Lord holding all men equal (Understanding the Bible, Shortell 2013 Part I – The Power of Rome) (the fourth sect refusing to call any Lord – Josephus Antiquities 8.1.6) (Acts 9:2 where Paul seeks those of "the Way" in Damascus). The High Priest, Judas, Aretas, the street named Straight and advisor Ananias (whomever he was) are from Acts 9:1-12 with my intimation that the High Priests were selected by Herod (Chapter XX The Family of Paul, Understanding the Bible, Ray Shortell 2014).

Aretas is not Caesar's favorite: Caesar was upset that Aretas took the government of Arabia as it was originally designated to become Herod's – Josephus, Antiquities 10.6.9

Phasaelis – Aretas (Aeneas) daughter. – Wikipedia, Aeneas - Antiquities 16.9.4
Philip Herod – Please refer to Afterword: Was Jesus Crucified in 40?

"Herod has 70,000 Suits of Armor" - 7.2.18 Antiquities Josephus as supported by Philo noting Flaccus' "interrogation" of Jewish Alexandrians for just such a supposed crime after Herod Agrippa visits on his return trip from Rome after accepting his kingdom from Caesar – (86) XI Flaccus

"Brood of vipers" – Mt 3:7, Lk 3:7 – I'm guessing John's terminology was "brood of vipers" which was changed into "generation of vipers". The Herod's intermarried, intertwining like a brood of vipers (half-brothers marrying half-sisters or nieces). To be fair Pharaohs did the same, Cleopatra having two kids by Mark Anthony, but never marrying him due to being married to her half-brother. Abraham and Sarah were half-brother/half-sister too. Eusebius explains that the Herods were not brothers to Jews, but were Edomites p33 Eusebius, the Church Histories, Paul L. Maier 2007.

"Love Letter" – From Paul's description of his scroll it was about granting some "safe passage", although Paul says they would then face trial. If Rome had sent anyone to Damascus, in my opinion they would have gone by way of Antioch, yet Paul traveled from Jerusalem. Paul wouldn't have been sent by the High Priests of Jerusalem either as these got their orders from Herod. My guess is the scroll was from Herodias or her minion, Herod: Herodias left Philip for Herod and later goads Herod into sailing to Rome with hopes of retaking Philip's Galilee, now presided over by Caesar's friend, Herod-Agrippa, apparently a no-account Herod until his experiences in Rome. Caesar later asks Herodias to remarry someone he selects, probably Herod-Agrippa, to give Herod-Agrippa the required Jewish Hasmonian authority of the Maccabeans lineage of Herodias. Regarding Paul's trip to Damascus, perhaps Herodias was goading Herod into executing Phaesalis and perhaps Herod sent Phaesalis a letter asking her return to continue as his first wife, much as his father had multiple wives, which would have probably even been approved by Herodias (Josephus reports multitudinous intrigues (poisonings) among the households of Herods, by which I'm implying Phaesalis' life would have probably been short had she returned with Paul).

Damascus means "cup of blood" Chapter XXII The Cup of Blood, Understanding the Bible, Ray Shortell 2013. Acts has Paul's conversion/vision on the road to Damascus, confounding the Jews who lived in Damascus until they wished to kill Paul and he escaped in a basket (Acts 9:25). Damascus fell within the jurisdiction of king Aretas, Herod's ex-father-in-law of Phaesalis (Wikipedia – weak sources since Phaesalis was also the name of one of the Herod sons). Aretas' army fought Herod and won, Jews claiming this as divine retribution (Josephus Antiquities 18.5.2) as Philip Herod's army became turncoat (1.4.3.5 Wars, Josephus). In my opinion Josephus is hiding something as he says: Historians extol the Romans and diminish the Jews (1.3 Preface Wars, Josephus). Josephus hid as Jotapata fell, double-crossing his Jewish suicide pact due to getting a mission in a dream or vision from G-d (3.8.3 Wars, Josephus, William Whiston).

I don't trust Acts/Gospels believing these to be more literature than history. I trust Galatians. Galatians 3:13-19 describes Paul's conversion and going to Damascus for three years. To me this was spring of 40 until winter of 42: After witnessing Jesus' crucifixion in 40. Paul stayed 2.25 years, but rounds up calling it three calendar years. I next trust Corinthians and Philemon. 2 Cor 11:32 has Paul escaping Damascus for fear of king Aretas whose daughter escaped Herod via Macheros where Herod soon had John beheaded. Mt 14:18 has John chastising Herod's marrying his brother's wife and Herod beheading John to keep a birthday promise to Salome, Herodias' daughter (18.5.4 Antiquities, Josephus). Josephus notes Herodias, Philip and Herod as all half-brothers/sisters (ibid) and Herod beheading John fearing "innovation" (all men brothers needing no king) (18.4.3 Antiquities, Josephus) (5.1, 5.2 Wars, Josephus) which of course Aretas and Philip Herod did innovate according to the wrath of Caesar who, and I'm making this up, may have sent Paul as Herod's emissary, Vitellus following with an army (Josephus Antiquities 18.5.3).

I have John the Baptist beheaded in 37 (Timeline, Sin, Sacrifice, Heaven & Hell, Ray Shortell 2017, Chapter 5 Timeline, Understanding the Bible, Ray Shortell 2013). Josephus shows dissimulation in 18.5.1 Ant where he notes the brother of Herod as Herod from whom Herodias was first divorced (Philip Herod - Mt. 14:3). Herod loses to Aretas because the "treachery of fugitives" serving as soldiers for the tetrarchy of Philip. In this passage Josephus neglects to mention Philip as Herodias' first husband, immediately going into Tiberius castigating Aretas and arguably distracting us from the men of Herodias' ex-husband killing those of her current husband!

Josephus' dissimulation follows two patterns. First, there is Josephus who tells the facts using a different name which might not be noticed: Herod and "Herod's" troops begin to fight Aretas, rather than Herod and "Philip Herod's" troops, or Herod and "Philip's" troops, by which the first husband of Herodias would be recognized. Also Josephus gives an interesting motive: For instance calling these innovators, Philip Herod's troops, "treacherous fugitives" implying there were only a few. Finally Josephus throws in a more interesting story: Fulfilling prophesy Caesar was furious with Aretas and afterwards his troops marched around holy ground.

The second Josephus dissimulation pattern occurs when subsequent authors insert or delete text. The Jesus passage, for instance, is unrelated to the story being told. Another inane section, Paulus and Mundi, seems designed to overwrite text which must have followed around the death of James (p402

James, the Brother of Jesus, Robert Eisenman 1997).

Also, I find it odd that Agrippa would denounce his uncle Herod in front of Caesar or that Herodias would not have suspected such treachery during their trip to Rome 4.3 Wars, Josephus, William Whiston. Although Agrippa was dear friends with Caesar having asked for Caesar's predecessor to die early and having done time in jail for the wish Wars 1.9.5, Josephus, William Whiston, I believe Josephus was misattributing motives or later overwritten as per the above, but that's my opinion.

Caesar's Coin - Violating the second commandment against graven images. Chapter III – Understanding the Bible, Ray Shortell 2013

Decapolis – Review of a map by "VisitJordan.com" while seeking information on Philadelphia in the Levant.

1) Lake Asphalitis – 4.8.4 Wars, Josephus, William Whiston
    Medicinal – p27 The Crusades through Arab Eyes, Amin Maalouf
2) Herod steals from King Herod's tomb: Antiquities 7.15.3, Josephus, William Whiston
3) Abgarus joins Aretas
    https://biblehub.com/library/unknown/the_decretals/iv_abgar_returns_from_the.htm
4) Aretas the Arabian is the fruition of Cleopatra's hopes for war between Herod and the Arabians: Josephus, Wars 1.18.4; 19. Rechabites, with no savings on which to rely, no corn stored up against the famine, were in dire need until Queen Helen sent aid (Josephus Antiquities 20.2) cementing their relationship. Aretas joins the Jews in besieging the temple (High Priests) (Josephus Antiquities 14.2.1).

Two soldiers wait – the number of witness (Alvin Frame of the Church of the Nazarene in Marietta, GA).
Three horses wait – the number of manifestation. ibid
"Rahab" – My metaphoric label. Whoever they were, they were prostituting themselves for one purpose or another, much as did Jericho's Rahab.

Explaining that Paul is of the family of Herod will be for a later chapter. Explaining that Herod sent some of his children to college in Rome, Jospehus Antiquities 16.2.1, 16.8.3 also Wars 2.9 where Agrippa is imprisoned in Rome for a bit for being too loud for what seems to me to be with a college buddy.

Gadara and Gamala both start with the letter "G" which references camels, which are the highway of the desert Rome was into roads having fortresses at both ends (Gadara and Damascus), and Caesarea Philippi was also on this road (Roman for Caesar and loves horses), but this road was too far from the reach of Rome to be controlled completely. From the grass which surrounds Gadara and the Roman aqueduct which was built, my belief is that Gadara was important for Roman horses although battle horses wouldn't come into full play until the invention of the stirrup by China a few centuries later. During the crusades circa 1200 Arabians are still using the road to skirt officialdom, the crusaders in their fortresses at Jerusalem - pg 162 The Crusades through Arabian Eyes, Amin Maalouf – John Rothschild 1984.

When the rebellion began in the spring of 66, the Romans decided that they could not fight on a Northern front against Armenia [Parthia] and on a Southern front in Judea and diverted troops to the south. pg 139 First Century Judaism in Crisis, Jacob Neusner 1975

Josephus was particularly concerned... because the Romans had hired him to write [his] book[s] partly in order to dissuade the Jews of Mesopotamia and Babylonia from trying to secure Parthian intervention in Palestine. Pg 161 ibid

Hyrcanus had been carried captive to Barzapharnes [the Partian King], when he overran Syria (1.22.1 Wars Josephus).

Paul means "tiny" or "little one" – I forget where I read this, but I'm thinking Paul was large: Paul survived riots at the temple and at Corinth claiming multiple imprisonments and beatings and is rumored to have thrown a 76 year old and 96 year old man from the temple at Jerusalem (p588-590 James, the Brother of Jesus, Robert Eisenman 1997). On his return from Corinth to Jerusalem Paul will stop at every city with a synagogue except Ephesus. For Ephesus Paul waits at a nearby city, Miletus, sending a messenger to collect the temple offering (Acts 20:16-17), yet later observes Trophimus of Ephesus in Jerusalem (Acts 21:29) who probably brought the offering of Ephesus independently (me). Paul's story on avoiding Ephesus is that he wished to haste and not stop in Asia in order to reach the temple by Pentecost (Acts 20:16-17). Perhaps this was more due to a riot caused by Demetrius the silversmith of the g-dess Diana (Acts 19:23-41). Rome took a dim view of riots (p419 Acts, A new Vision of the People of G-d, Gerald L. Stevens 2016). I Cor 15:32 – If after the manner of men I have fought with the beasts of Ephesus, what advantage it me, if the dead rise not?

Chapter 3 Gadara 42 CE Highway to Herod

1) Entombed a year. Archaeological and Biblical Research 5/2 1992 http://www.ldolphin.org/deaddead.html
   Also Prof Eisenman p598 James, the Brother of Jesus 1997 graves "whitened of themselves every year"
2) Tax-revolt – Chapter 3 – Caesar's Coin – Understanding the Bible, Ray Shortell 2013
3) For Epiphanius James reigned in Jerusalem for 'twenty-four years after the Assumption of Jesus', which if Josephus dating of James' death is correct, would place Jesus' death in 38 CE – p467 James, the Brother of Jesus, Robert Eisenman 1997
4) Lysanias reigned in 40BCE (Lk 3:1) – Chapter 5 Dating the Bible - Understanding the Bible, Ray Shortell 2013
5) ...that Sabbath day was an high day... John 19:31 ----- 40 is one of the years available per p107 Herodian Messiah, The Case for Jesus as Grandson of Herod, Joseph Raymond 2010
6) Please reference my timeline in Chapter 4, the City of Peace and Chapter 28 Herod's Gospel of Matthew
7) Herod Agrippa represents the top levels of Jewish society – p210 Acts, A New Vision of the People of G-d, Gerald L. Stevens 2016
8) ...the Romans, after two Uprisings and endless troubles over these issues, turned the tables on the Jewish extremists... Rabbis are alleged to have put a ban upon those taking Nazirite style oaths not to `eat or drink` until they had seen the Temple rebuilt... pg 762, The New Testament Code, Robert Eisenman 2006 The implication being that they will not eat meat or drink wine. p68 ibid.

Gadara is at the top of the Jordan, but six miles from the river and six miles from the Sea of Galilee. Most reference it as part of the Decapolis. One author lists it as part of Perea. Luke 8:26-39 tells the story of the Gadarene demoniac where people in apparently an hour gather on the sea-shore from Gadara. I'm not sure whether people from the lake six miles from Gadara would call themselves Gadarenes. I'm not sure the entire town could have traveled six miles in an hour to fuss over a healed demoniac. After being asked to leave, Jesus and his disciples later make their way across the Decapolis by the Sea of Galilee again without being noticed (Ch 6 The Geography – Understanding the Bible, Ray Shortell 2013, Mk 7:31). Also, Jesus' last moments on earth, to me, per John 21 (as supported by the ascension in Lk 23 eating fish and honeycomb) would have happened just north of Gadara on the Sea of Tiberias South of the Golan Heights. Here I'm intertwining metaphors from Paul (Damascus through Jerusalem apparently through back country) and Jesus based upon Geography rather than upon time. Please check my timeline in Understanding the Bible, Ray Shortell 2013. Mark and Luke has the assumption in Jerusalem or Emmaus. John says Tiberias which in my opinion would have happened across the sea in the Decapolis (Damascus to Philadelphia).

For a reference on why James is called Jacob, check chapter 5 James Tumbles

From the yearlong entombed body decomposition (1) and Prof Eisenman's focus on whitening bones I get purgatory – apparently and just from these (nothing else) originally a year of purification - as supported by my conflation of Jesus' statement with Revelations while pondering the biblical meaning: Beware he who has the power of the second death (Mt 10:28 – Fear not them which kill the body, but are not able to kill the soul: but rather fear him which is able to destroy both soul and body in hell.)(Acts 2:31 …his soul was not left in hell, neither his flesh did see corruption)(Rev 20:6 Blessed and holy is he that hath part in the first resurrection: on such the second death hath no power…). Per my grandma purgatory is a place of purification where people who are not yet good enough to get into heaven wait for the prayers of the living and those in heaven (Rev 6:10 – And they cried with a loud voice, saying, How long, O Lord, holy and true, dost thou not judge and avenge our blood on them that dwell on the earth?) although my understanding is the pope did away with purgatory some time ago.

Papal confidant claims Pope Francis has abolished hell, purgatory, heaven (Oct 2017)
   https://www.lifesitenews.com/opinion/worlds-end-update.-the-last-things-according-to-francis

Purgatory is a process not a place says pope (Jan 2011):
   https://www.ncronline.org/news/vatican/purgatory-process-not-place-pope-says

   Further references:
Eastern Region Evangelical Theological Society of the Westminster Theological Seminary PA April 5 1991 http://www.biblearchaeology.org/post/2011/03/07/The-Demoniacs-of-Gadara.aspx

Paul a large man: I believe Paul to have been Herodian. Herod the Terrible participated in the first Olympics and won three events. Perhaps some let him win, knowing their death would follow his loss, or perhaps some let him win knowing his funding for the event important. Regardless, he participated and won. Size seemed to have been of importance in declaring yourself king as Herod did and Saul, for whom Paul was originally named, was likewise head and shoulders above the rest. My assumption is that Paul is Herodian and that Herod's size probably passed through down to Paul.

Chapter 4 Jerusalem 42 CE The City of Peace
Jerusalem in Hebrew means the city of Peace (shalom = peace) which I am here using in an ironic sense: Christianity would like to call itself peaceful as does Jesus (Mt 11:30 for my yoke is easy and my burden is light) and Islam too against a history of Crusades and Jihad. Israel killed Canaanites and Philistines (Cover & About the Author, Sin, Sacrifice, Heaven & Hell, Ray Shortell 2017). At the turn of the millennia Israel lived in messianic hope of a ruler to whom all the kings of the world would bring treasure much as the gospels have Jesus accepting tribute from the wise men of the East (Mt 2).

For my brotherhood metaphor, Josephus regularly notes Roman fears of "innovation" with people deposing the king (Josephus Ant 10.7.1, 12.3.3, 15.3.1...), of people believing that all men are created equal, like the song America the Beautiful noting brotherhood from sea to shining sea. Also note in this chapter that Paul is accompanied by his Roman guard and how I'm intertwining the "hem" theme which runs through Jesus' ministry (Mt 9:20, 14:36) with clothes being thrown at the feet of Paul (Acts 7:58).

Regarding Herodian authorship of the Gospels, my contention is that Paul is Herodian (introduction to Sources), so Herodians at least contributed to the Bible. My contention, unfounded, is also that Herodians controlled the only source for documentation outside of the temple except for Alexandria which Rome also took charge of with Seneca taking 40,000 scrolls and burning what I'm assuming were their copies. Rome also controlled the temple documentation after Rome invaded and burned the temple. Herodians would have been needed at least to review the gospels put together in Rome to make sure nothing glaring was standing out that a Jewish audience would repudiate. I wonder whether such Herodians were killed afterwards or left children living in Rome, Caesarea or elsewhere? Please check chapter 28, Herod's Gospel of Matthew for further documentation (2/25/18 update Gerald L.Stevens has the reference, found the Herod I previously suspected, who was probably editing the Bible... Herod Agrippa II would have assisted Acts, A New Vision of the People of G-d, 2016).

(1) Herod authoring Matthew: Chapter 28
(2) Herod is a foreigner (Edomite) pg 33 Eusebius, The Church History, Paul L Maier 2007
(3) Mom helped her brother, Uncle Jerry, mow the lawn of the Jewish Synagogue in LaSalle, IL when they were kids, probably around 1954. Both my Mom and her brother were Roman Catholic and the Rabbi's wife took Mom into the Synagogue where Mom cleaned. The Rabbi's wife also showed Mom the replica of the temple which held the scroll behind the podium where no gentile or woman was allowed (ok, so word of mouth can be a little fuzzy, that's how my Mom told me that I remember). And of course I was an altar boy so I'm familiar with the tabernacle, a tiny representation of the Holy of Holies, where the blessed Eucharist, as the body of Christ, is kept after mass alongside the eternal flame, a candle behind a red candle-holder which my Mom says is how you can always identify a true Roman Catholic Church.
(4) Vestments kept at Herod's fortress: Chapter 20 The Family of Paul - Understanding the Bible, Ray Shortell 2011

40,000 scrolls burned, more confiscated by Seneca, Burned Library at Alexandria – Seneca – On Tranquility of Mind – http://www.straightdope.com/columns/read/2233/what-happened-to-the-great-library-of-alexandria

Untaxable: Essenes did not own 'two cloaks or a double set of sandals'. Pg 346 James, the Brother of Jesus, Robert Eisenman 1997. I'm not sure Dr. Eisenman ever made the connection. I see the two unchangeable things, death and taxes, throughout.

Sadducees temple-centered zealots (Herodian Sadducees): unlike the Pharisees, when the temple is destroyed they cease to exist.\ having completely lost their raison d'etre. p381 James, the Brother of Jesus, Robert Eisenman 1997

Note: Chapter 4 Jerusalem explains the differences between Sadducees & Pharisees. Chapter 14 Caesarea discusses similarities.

Messiah enters through the Eastern gate (Beautiful Gate Acts 3:2,10). The sun rises in the East. Josephus tells of thunderings about the Eastern gate 6.5.3 Wars, Josephus, William Whiston 1998. The

Messiah follows the mythology of the sun chapter The Son of G-d is the Sun of G-d, The Christ Conspiracy Acharya S 1999, although gainsaid in Ez 8:16-17: ...about five and twenty men, with their backs to the temple of the Lord, and their faces towards the east; and they worshipped the sun towards the east... is it a light thing to the house of Judah that they commit the abominations which they commit here?...

Chapter 5 Jerusalem 42 CE Jacob (James) Tumbles

One of my points is that Sadducees are xenophobic. Here is my source for various courtyards: http://www.bible-history.com/court-of-women/ but Dr. Eisenman first brought my attention to the temple stone landmarks warning death for foreigners in both Latin and Greek (p266 James, the Brother of Jesus Robert Eisenman 1997; 5.5.2 Wars, Josephus; And Hebrew (6.2.4 Wars Josephus). The Letter of the Law brings Death (Foreword: Understanding the Bible, Sin Sacrifice Heaven & Hell, Ray Shortell 2017). My guess is these "ancient" landmarks (Remove not the ancient landmark which thy fathers have set. - Prov 22:28) were placed before Paul's writings, based upon Paul's metaphor of Christ as the "stumblingblock" (Ro 9:33, 14:13, I Cor 1:23) (...take up the stumblingblock out of the way of my people. - Is 57:14), however not placed too long before Paul due to Latin, Greek and Hebrew being the languages carved in stone. My main point regarding "ancient" is that much like the song "Old Time Rock and Roll" which was too flashy and by my standards neither old nor Rock and Roll when it came out (it was "cheesy"), although my mind has since changed on this score, that adding the adjective "ancient" to "landmarks" was probably done at a point when such landmarks were not considered ancient, and therefore anything labeled "ancient landmarks" (bounds of our fathers) necessarily involving some degree of subjectivity. Also per Adam Hamilton's The Call pg 82, Paul uses the word "philoxenon", the opposite word, in describing how we should be (hospitable, lover of foreigners). To me Paul therefore opposes Saducean xenophobia.

Prof Eisenman makes much of Paul's two physical attacks on Jacob separated by twenty years (James the Brother of Jesus 1997 Eisenman XXXII). In my opinion the white linen robe is about resistance to Rome and purity, by having nothing further which Rome might tax, rejecting Roman rule and sex with women (plants making linen with flowers at the time apparently not known as male/female) with daily bathing for purity. Josephus Antiquities 15.10.5 notes Herod as excusing Essenes from taxes. While Dr. Eisenman on p826 of James, the Brother of Jesus 1998 associates the Essene view of the second commandment with Roman coins. In Galatians Paul says of the apostles he only saw Peter (Cephas) and James (Jacob) during this visit. I wonder if Paul considered Jude to be an apostle? The gospels don't tell us when John joined the apostles which might have been later or perhaps John just hid (he seems to have done that to me... not even naming himself in his gospel).

"polluting the temple"

Jerome contends that James (Jacob) ruled the church in Jerusalem for thirty years until the seventh year of Nero thereby dating James' (Jacob's) rule from the early 30s... p710 James, the Brother of Jesus, 1997 Eisenman

Regarding calling Herod Paul's "cousin", please see the introduction to Sources.

Regarding Paul's bow-leggedness compared to James' now broken legs, please check Sources for Chapter 15 – Escape from Caesarea.

Jacob (James) was Jacob in Hebrew. – xxvii James, the Brother of Jesus, Robert Eisenman 1998 – To me this ties into the messianic star prophesy (...there shall come a Star out of **Jacob**, and a Scepter shall rise out of Israel… - Num 24:17) and the Egyptian foundations of Chapter 8 - "Bethlehem".

Chapter 6 Jaffa 42 CE The Samaritan Woman
1) Jeremiah – Chapter IX: Moses and Prophets, Understanding the Bible, Shortell 2014
2) The temple councilor supervisor of water was an important position: First Century Judaism in Crisis, p81, Jacob Neusner 1975 – I'm guessing someone built a well on the other end of the Jewish path taken by diaspora to Jerusalem.
3) The Caesarean regiment first to be banished due to brutal unmitigated cruelty – p21, James the Brother of Jesus, Robert Eisenman 1998

Regarding Samaria running from Egypt to Syria, some may say Samaria ran along the coast only through the tribe of Joseph (Benjamin to Dan). Samaritans themselves claim to be from Northern Israel, the ten tribes that went into slavery. My previous book Understanding the Bible, Ray Shortell 2017 Postscript: Failed Messianic Prophesies notes Northern Israel as leaving due to Judah's penchant for human slavery (I Kings 12:11). When Samaritans returned they set up a temple on Mt. Gerizim or Hazor which Judah promptly destroyed, killing its supporters (2nd century BCE 1.2.7 Wars Josephus, Jer 49:33), both sides believing they hold the true Torah. My point is that Sadducees hated anyone not "Jewish enough", not a temple priest, a Sadducee, a High Priest. Sadducees are xenophobes (quote me on this). Therefore I'm using the terminology, "Samaria" as I surmise it would have been used by Sadducees rather than by Samaritans, begging pardon of any offended Samaritans for including more than Samaria. Still, perhaps an occasional Samaritan would be found far from where they were born. Notably Israel currently, in the twenty-first century, continues to use the term pejoratively referring to the Northern West Bank (Arabian (Muslim)) as "Samaria" meaning "not us". Labeling people, other than what they call themselves by using a direct quote, is ignorant. https://en.wikipedia.org/wiki/Samaria as for my exception here, I'm using the terminology purposefully, and I've explained it.

The Samaritan woman at the well comes up a couple of times in the gospels: She talks to Jesus calling him a prophet and she is called a dog by Jesus in another parable. The chapter introduces her and also introduces my opinion of Paul having limited choices regarding where to start a church.

Naked Olympics – 12.5.1; 16.5.1 Antiquities, Josephus, Forward: Understanding the Bible, Sin, Sacrifice, Heaven & Hell, Ray Shortell 2017

Chapter 7 Caesarea 42 CE Banished from Israel
1) Paul is a builder of stage properties – reference cover and chapter 3 please.
    1) Herod provided the marble street in Antioch – Acts, A New Vision of the People of G-d, Gerald L. Stevens, 2016

This chapter solidifies my opinion regarding Paul's Herodian ties. Paul gets kicked out of Israel and wonders at Herod's ruthlessness regarding Pharisees at the Caesarean synagogue who at one time were allowed to build a synagogue… Truth be told I'm only guessing there was a synagogue in Caesarea: It's awful close to Jerusalem to have been tolerated by temple Sadducees. Also, the ambiguous references to Herod's foster brother are intentional as is the text of Acts.

My belief is that Rome, through Herod, encouraged and assisted weak leaders to take control where possible, subordinating major powers which might present resistance.

"he was … vegetarian … - because animal fare was the product of sexual intercourse" Pg 320, James, the Brother of Jesus, Robert Eisenman 1997

Chapter 8 Bethlehem 42 CE The House of Bread

Dr. Eisenman says that Essenes were buried with their feet pointing to the North Star (p329 James, the Brother of Jesus, Robert Eisenman 1997). My study of Egyptian Theology is mostly through the television show STARGATE with Sherry Henderson, the owner of the Inner Space - 6558 Vernon Woods Drive, Sandy Springs, telling me of her experience with the Egyptian Hall of the Dead and weight of the feather from Dolores Ashcroft Nowicki's Initiation of Osiris although I've since visited the Louvres with its great Egyptian art. Dr. Eisenman in The New Testament Code, 2006 on page 424 cites Josephus noting Vespasian as tying the hands of Jewish captives thrown into the Dead Sea to see whether they would sink. I put together the metaphor of bread upon the water (Ecc 11:1), connected Bethlehem and Egypt and Daniel with the Hall of the Dead myself. The words in Daniel make no sense in the biblical context. They are an anomaly that only makes sense when connected with the Essenes and Egypt in my opinion. There was a witch at Saul's Endor, but I'm making up that witches not drowning are connected and therefore that Egyptian Astrologers telling kings to take a hike were known as witches (telling kings that all men are created equal).

My contention is that Bethlehem is where the Egyptian (he's an actual character in historical documents of the time) was supported by Jacob (the name James is a mistranslation of Jacob, much as Jesus should be pronounced "Joshua") with a reference to the star of Bethlehem which I believe was metaphorically the North Star to which Essene feet were pointed to in burial and which is pointed out by Egyptian pyramids. To me this is where the philosophy of the immortality of the soul was born, brought to Bethlehem from Egypt by the family of Joseph matching the original savior of Israel with Joseph saving his father Jacob and brothers after having been sold into slavery in Egypt and which Herod tried to stamp out, to kill, to trample like unsavory salt per the Gospels. The Bible notes Herod's killing of the babies who were his own children by Maccabean women (Herod the Terrible that would be back in 4BCE). Josephus numbers the followers of the Egyptian at 30,000 with their chosen ground the Mount of Olives. I'm guessing that as a Roman myrmidon, Josephus undercounted. I'm guessing Joseph, Jesus' Dad, was the Egyptian.

Please reference chapter 8 Heaven of Sin, Sacrifice, Heaven & Hell for further information on Egyptian Astrology (3). The Horus/Hours reference came from a clerk at the Egyptian store in Discovery Mills Mall around 2014 who I asked based upon Linda Goodman's reference to the Crab on the ceiling of the pyramid.

Josephus wrote from Rome about ex-slaves innovating by declaring all men equal. Apparently, per Josephus once you were a slave, you had no right to be human again. One might argue that Josephus was himself no longer a free man.

"innovation" (all men brothers needing no king) (18.4.3 Antiquities, Josephus) (5.1, 5.2 Wars, Josephus).

"that a slave who hath once been brought into subjection, and then runs away is rather a refractory slave than a lover of liberty" (2.16.4 Wars Josephus).

Jessean – The gift, Essene, Eternal life, Mt of Olives… I'm kind of making this up from Pierre Kjibolder's discussion of gift, Essene and Jesus in p27 & 28 Crucifixion and Turin Shroud Mysteries Solved. I've combined two or three references in a mish-mash and perhaps should have said something about Nathanael too. I mention this in the Postscript on the Foreword of Sin, Sacrifice, Heaven & Hell, Ray Shortell 2017.

Now who was that author who suggested Christianity spreading so quickly due to its ability to give Kings a standard against which to be judged?

Rechabite Mt 10:10 – Torah and prophets use the word "worthy" 14 times which is used in the Greek 52 times (the New Testament). The prophesies of Matthew were written first followed by the gospel of Mark after which someone without much of an editor (as per my job as a typesetter) reworked the gospel of Matthew into its current anti-Zionist form as opposed to its edited version of Lk 10:7 which doesn't propose "meat" as a reward, but perhaps suggests or opposes following Rechabites in staying at or moving from home to home. Rechabites were probably vegetarian at least by the time the Gospels were authored due to the temple sacrifice having stopped or even earlier due to not accepting Herod's priests, making Mt 10:10's description spiteful. I Timothy 5:17-18 shows the later Pauline position that scholars were craftsmen and owed a living against earlier references explaining more so not causing grief by taking money from the congregation (I Cor 9:9-12) following an occupation (Acts 18:3) with II Tim 2:15 suggesting studying to show oneself approved along with Jesus himself proposing a new law or sacrifice, that of studying Jesus (Mt 11:29 as per Jn 5:39).

Ezekiel's bones – Old Testament Resurrection - Chapter 8 Heaven, Sin, Sacrifice, Heaven & Hell, Ray Shortell 2017

We hold these truths to be self-evident: That all men are created equal. Declaration of Independence, Thomas Jefferson 1776
No one is better than you. Mom ~1978
Why do we allow a Queen? Mom ~1981
Dogs – Chapter 7 – Sin, Sacrifice, Heaven & Hell, Ray Shortell 2017

Chapter 9 Antioch 42 CE Paul's Roman Amphitheaters (Architecting the Tent)
7) Vespasian sacrifices on Mt Carmel; Bassilades reads the entrails (prognostication) – Complete Works of Tacitus, Moses Hadas, 1942
8) Paul as Herod's foster brother - pg 99 James, The Brother of Jesus, Robert Eisenman 1997
9) Paul builds Roman Amphitheaters for a living. This is my conclusion. My evidence may be found in pgs 388 & 535 Acts, a New Vision of the People of G-d, Gerald L. Stevens 2016
   Paul probably also quarried stones from the Corinthian canal. This is my conclusion. My evidence notes Jewish slaves from the war digging and dying there much later in pg 561 of The New Testament Code, Robert Eisenman 2006
10) Longinus Pierced - Pg 373 The Other Bible, Edited by Willis Barnstone, 1984
    3a) Blood and water - 19:34 Jn

Biblical scholars have long noted Christianity as starting in cities. This is because Paul's amphitheater business was city-based (check out the amphitheater of Caesarea!). There is no call for amphitheaters where there are not enough people. Prof Stevens in Acts, A New Vision of the People of G-d, 2016 has pictures of tons of Roman amphitheaters, but only says that tent-maker would be an improper term relating something about "maker of stage properties" noting Paul's profession as unclear. Acts 18:3 says Paul is a tent-maker. Whether this is intended as speculative or operational (actual or metaphoric) remains a question in my mind. Continuing as per II Thes 3 written by Paul's students (pgs 19-22 Forged! Bart D Ehrman 2011) missionaries should support themselves as does Paul. However Paul in I Cor 9:9 gainsays this claiming others should support the work he does in planting the seeds of theology.

Finding the ruler of Antioch to have changed from Claudian of the family of Mark Anthony to a Cassian when Paul can no longer stay was a turning point for me. I found it in a Roman rulers of Antioch timeline. Plus there will eventually be widows of Paul's Antioch Greeks who were massacred in Jerusalem trying to preach in the temple in my opinion. I'm making up this number (four, representing the ends of the earth, maybe Paul was looking to make such a statement) based on the ways various Pauline evangelists died (one ran away leaving his cloak or was this from Jesus' grave, one had his guts spilled out after they rotted or was this a ruler for whom was named the field of blood?, one hung himself off a bridge or was this the apocryphal Judas?, and Lazarus was in the grave a few days) (in any case there were the widows of Antioch, so there were probably more than one evangelist). And then there were the four for whom Paul paid their vows when confronted with James (Acts 21:23). Acts notes the fuss over "table service" for widows in Acts 6:1. Around March 2018 I figured out "deacon" to probably mean: Bringing Greeks and Kosher Jews together in communion, table service, eating together.

Queen Helen, of course, gets contacted out of Antioch and this chapter introduces the annual pilgrimage Jews across the Mediterranean would take to Jerusalem, why they would do so, and how as per p3 Sin, Sacrifice, Heaven and Hell, Ray Shortell 2017. Peter may have started a church in Corinth without ever having visited. p11 Crucifixion and Turin Shroud Mysteries Solved, Pierre Krijbolder 1999 notes these pilgrimages.

Regarding deacons, my focus is on the deacons of Antioch. I forget where I'd heard deacon means "table servant", but considering Peter and Paul's concerns around "separation" (Gal 2:11-14)… my guess is that the deacons in Antioch who cared for widows were aimed at table servants, communion, doctrine regarding perhaps what was later to be found in the book of Romans. In Gerald L. Stevens' book, Acts, A New Vision of the People of G-d, 2016 the "table sensitivity" conclusion is made frequently (p336) without supporting arguments.

Note, Dr. Eisenman in James, the Brother of Jesus 1997 suggests Edessa as the place of the church of Antioch, a bit closer to Queen Helen. I'm putting my Antioch as the third largest city of the Empire (Rome, Alexandria, Antioch – Josephus Wars 3.2.4 William Whiston 1998) where Paul would have had Roman building projects.

Chapter 10 Adiabene 43-48 CE Queen Helen
(1) Helen was taught non-circumcision p548 James, the Brother of Jesus, Robert Eisenman 1997
(2) In 120 CE the grandchildren of Jude present themselves to Rome requesting the Antioch bishopric as rightfully theirs (For a Quick Review of My Previous Book - Sin, Sacrifice, Heaven & Hell 2017).

Per Dr. Eisenman there is much ado about Queen Helen in the Talmud (I've only read two chapters of the Talmud and got tired of trying to figure out whether it was a sin to have someone throw bread to you under the eaves but outside of the house during the days of unleavened bread) p897 James, the Brother of Jesus, Robert Eisenman 1997. Her grandsons die in the war fighting for Jerusalem at Beit Horon (ibid p885). Paul apparently convinces her she may be Jewish without circumcision, but Eleazar, a priest from Jerusalem accompanying her sons back to Adiabene later convinces her sons otherwise (ibid p895). Queen Helen and her sons Izates and Monobazus are buried in pyramidal tombs in Jerusalem (Antiquities 20.4.3, Josephus, William Whiston).

Dr. Eisenman noted his not understanding a story where a rich woman's feet have mud on them during the siege. I'm making up that rich women had leather sandals she had boiled and eaten or sold.

Regarding the four brothers of Jesus (Jacob, Joses, Cephas and Jude), please review chapter 19, The Family of James, Understanding the Bible, Ray Shortell 2014.

Taxes were applied to men, houses, animals, sales, imports and exports. P29 First Century Judaism in Crisis, Jacob Neusner 1975

Chapter 11 Beit Horon 48 CE Queen Helen's Israel

Queen Helen puts herself in a tough spot. Perhaps her husband put her up to it hoping to incite war with Rome, while he kept his armies out of fighting with Israel (pg 945 James, the Brother of Jesus, Robert Eisenman 1998). This chapter also covers Moses and the Prophets questioning whether alternate motives might have created Israel other than Providence.

Location of Jerusalem: Check a map.
Abraham coming from Babylon: Gen 11:31 – Chaldees were the astrologers of Babylon.
Nearly sacrificing his son: Gen 22:2 … the tale is that Mt Ebal is in Moriah.
Promised Canaan: Gen 12:5-7
Setting a stone: Gen 12:8, Ex 20:25
Burying a wife: Gen 23:19
Return from Egypt: Exodus
David promised to spare a man he has posthumously killed by Solomon: I Kings 2 8-9, 36-46
Canaanite women killed: Deu 20:16-18, Ezra 10:11-12
Benjamin killed: Judges 19-21
City of Judah killed for failing to participate in the war: Judges 21

1) Mt Moriah is variously located. Jews would have it be the temple mount. Christians note its foreshadowing of the Crucifixion suggesting Mt Moriah also being the temple mount. Samaritans propose its being Mt Gerizim where the blessings of Moses were recited upon the return from Egypt. To me it makes sense that Abraham's sacrifice was offered where Moses returned, laying claim to the promise and the land bought by Abraham which fell within the land of the tribe of Joseph who led Israel into Egypt.

2) Whether the king of Babylon set his throne in Egypt is tough to answer. His Babylonian armies did reign in Jerusalem obviously which is not far from Egypt, but the conquerage of the Egyptian army apparently happened two generations later by a Babylonian king who had abdicated his Babylonian throne and been reinstalled over the armies of Syria by Persia. Were Jeremiah/Ezekiel interested in the Babylonian king, they should have been prophesying Media/Persia conquering Babylon rather than Babylon conquering Egypt.

Jeremiah prophesies successful Babylonian invasion of Egypt: Jer 46:13
--- Isaiah successfully prophesies Cyrus the Persian destroying nations Is 45:1
Ezekiel prophesies successful Babylonian invasion of Egypt Eze 29:19
Chapter 11 Moses and Prophets, Understanding the Bible, Ray Shortell 2011 covers Jeremiah in detail.

Cambyses, grandson of Cyrus, invades Egypt 525 – pg 23 The Ancient Historians, Michael Grant 1970

Second temple in Alexandria: Chapter 1, The Power of Rome, Understanding the Bible, Ray Shortell 2011

In the First Century there were really no discernible `Benjamites` left among Jews - p765, The New Testament Code, Robert Eisenman 2006

Chapter 12 Antioch 45 CE Cephas visits

Herod selects the High Priest - 15.11.5 Antiquities Josephus

1) Stumbling stone in two languages (Please check references for chapter 5) p266, James, the Brother of Jesus, Robert Eisenman 1997
Stumbling stone in Greek and in your own letters – 6.2.4 Wars, Josephus
2) Abgarus and Aretas in league. Abgar returns from the East; He gives help to Aretas in a war against Herod the Tetrarch: https://biblehub.com/library/unknown/the_decretals/iv_abgar_returns_from_the.htm
3) Pharisees shout to Agrippa Herod: You are our brother! P74 First Century Judaism in Crisis, Jacob Neusner 1975
4) Sadducees shout at Agrippa: We will be reconciled to you in death! 1.4.4 Wars, Josephus
5) Rabbi's shout at Agrippa: You are our brother! Pg625, James, the Brother of Jesus, Robert Eisenman 1997

The Decretals — Unknown

When Abgar had returned from the East, he learnt that the Romans suspected him of having gone there to raise troops. He therefore made the Roman commissioners acquainted with the reasons of his journey to Persia, as well as the treaty concluded between Ardachès and his brothers; but no credence was given to his statement: for he was accused by his enemies Pilate, Herod the tetrarch, Lysanias and Philip. Abgar having returned to his city Edessa leagued himself with Aretas, king of Petra, and gave him some auxiliary troops under the command of Khosran Ardzrouni, to make war upon Herod. Herod had in the first instance married the daughter of Aretas, then had repudiated her, and thereupon taken Herodias, even in her husband's lifetime, a circumstance in connection with which he had had John the Baptist put to death. Consequently there was war between Herod and Aretas on account of the wrong done the daughter of Aretas. Being sharply attacked, Herod's troops were defeated, thanks to the help of the brave Armenians; as if, by divine providence, vengeance was taken for the death of John the Baptist.

Footnotes:

[3295] Chapter xxix.

Antioch has Cephas (Peter, Gal 2:11) and Jude (Chapter 33) although per the gospels Judas killed himself (Mt 27:5). Joses (Barnabas) was, in my opinion, Jesus' brother too. Jacob (James) knees were probably too bad to travel. Antioch is the third largest city of Rome (3.2.4 Wars, Josephus). In 120 CE the grandchildren of Jude present themselves to Rome requesting the Antioch bishopric as rightfully theirs (Sin, Sacrifice, Heaven & Hell, For a Quick Review of my Previous Book).

Cephas's visit tears apart Paul's world. Some from Jacob come down and Cephas and Joses leave Paul. Teasing apart what happened takes some reading between Paul's lines of dissimulation. Paul will eventually note that everyone in the Eastern Roman Empire hates him (all `Christians`): II Tim 4:16 –

At my first answer no man stood with me, but all men forsook me…

Pharisee documentation is compromised (Epilogue: Editing the Talmud).

Zadock/Zealot/Sadducee: Paul argues in the temple that he is Pharisaic, believing in eternal life (Acts 23:6). School marms explain to Christians as a mnemonic that Saducees don't believe in the resurrection of the dead: They were "sad you see". In my opinion this is incorrect: Pharisees are Rabbinic and city/synagogue based whereas Sadducees are temple worshipers. Dr. Eisenman fully explains the Zadock/Sadducee/Temple Zealot circle of language in p146 The New Testament Code, 2006.

the rejection of gifts and sacrifices on behalf of foreigners in the Temple, the issue that finally started the War against Rome. pg 457 James, the Brother of Jesus, Robert Eisenman 1997

Corinth is Caesar's summer home (See references chapter 17 – Corinth)

Chapter 13 Jerusalem 48 CE The Four Evangelists
(1) Famine 46-48, pg 548 James, the Brother of Jesus, Robert Eisenman 1997

Paul responds to Cephas' visit (Peter's visit) by having his church visit Jerusalem. Paul does not accompany this mission. This allows Paul's "presence" in Jerusalem without actually visiting. The sicarii kill the missionaries horribly which gets recounted as different deaths in the Bible: Paul, and I'm conjecturing, refers only to taking care of widows in Antioch. The Gospels, and I'm making this up, list this as "Jerusalem killing all her prophets". Paul must flee these widows along with the new Cassian governor of Antioch. Pierre Kjibolder notes the annual pilgrimage on p97 of The Turin Shroud Revealed 1997 as putting "Peter" (Cephas) in Rome without his ever visiting. I just reversed this to put Paul's "presence" in Jerusalem without his actually visiting, much as my men's team requires your "presence" even when absent, which makes Galatians' 14 year absence from Jerusalem good. I trust Galatians rather than Acts. Chapter 9 documents why I think Paul sent four evangelists.

Barnabas is Joses as "twin" – (Thomas Didymus means "twin twin"). Jesus' fourth brother was named the same as Jesus except for vowels which weren't written in Hebrew at the time. In the Acts of Thomas people have Joses confused with Jesus by sight (The Other Bible, Willis Barnstone 1984). My guess is that Barnabas is Joses, Jesus' fourth brother. Cephas visited (Gal 2:11). Jude's grandchildren were at Antioch, the third greatest city of the Romans after Rome and Alexandria (Josephus Wars 3.2.4), around 120 CE requesting the bishopric as its rightful heirs (Sin, Sacrifice, Heaven & Hell, 0a For a Quick Review of my Previous Book first paragraph). Why not Joses, another brother of Jesus, too? Perhaps "son of consolation" references Joses' twinship with Jesus who died on the cross.

Sarah as Abraham's half-sister: Gen 12:13, 20:12.

I forget where I read that Jewish priests referred to diaspora as "Benjamin". I'm making up that it was a term of derision as per chapter 11 – Beit Horon.

Joseph Raymond in p132 Herodian Messiah 2010 proposes Paul as Maccabean. On page 232 ibid he proposes Costobarus as Herodian. Dr. Eisenman in James, the Brother of Jesus 1997 Appendix The Herodians proposes Paul as the brother of Costobarus. I doubt there is any other way Cephas (Peter) would have dined with Paul even before "some from James" arrive in Antioch.

Herod killed the Sanhedrin - 14.9.4 Antiquities, Josephus, William Barnstone AM 1970

Any crimes in a foreign country were to be welcomed with joy, and that the seeds of strive ought to be actually sewn – 12.48 Annals, Tacitus

Ever since the times of the Divine Augustus Roman knights have ruled Egypt as kings, and the forces by which it has to be kept in subjection. It has been thought expedient thus to keep under home control a province so difficult of access, so productive of corn, ever distracted, excitable and restless through the superstition and licentiousness of its inhabitants, knowing nothing of laws and unused to civil rule. – 1.11 History, Tacitus

There is nothing of which barbarians are so ignorant as military engines and the skillful management of sieges, while that is a branch of military science which we especially understand. –12.45 Annals, Tacitus

He then … awaited the chief men of Parthia and of Acbarus (???Agabus Acts 21:10), king of the Arabs… The advice was disregarded through the perfidy of Acbarus… - 12.12 Annals, Tacitus

Chapter 14 Caesarea 48 CE Banished again

This chapter solidifies Paul's Herodian connections, explains Paul's peace plan for temple inclusion and explains why Paul is not allowed to visit Jerusalem for another fourteen years (Gal 2:1).

"if Paul … was tutored in Rome by Seneca" pg 235 Herodian Messiah, Joseph Raymond 2010
Herodians educated in Rome. 1.32.2 Wars, Josephus, William Whiston 1998
Seneca and Epaphroditus are linked as per the sources for chapter 31 – Seneca & Poppea
Epaphroditus, Josephus and Paul are linked as per sources for chapter 33 – The War is Finished
Josephus was Hasmonean – Life 1
Herodias was Hasmonean – The Herodians – James, the Brother of Jesus, Robert Eisenman 1997
Paul was Herodian. Please review references for the Cover of Bethlehem: The War of Jesus
Therefore Paul was probably at least kin by marriage to Josephus.

John the Essene leads Jewish rioters against soldiers. 3.2 Wars, Josephus, William Whiston 1998

Jews of the temple kill the High Priest (probably because he is a collaborator). 2.17.9 ibid

Samaritans and when they see the Jews in prosperity, they pretend they are changed, and allied to them, and call them kinsmen… - 9.14.3 Antiquities, Josephus -

Perhaps Paul's Maccabean soul rages against its Roman/Herodian heritage while hating its Idumean/Edomite ancestry – Not mere words, myself the product of a mixed marriage continually seeking peace between me and myself – In my Mom's hometown of LaSalle, IL, her Irish Catholic church is two blocks away from the German Catholic church. One buries their dead on the north side of the cemetery, the other on the south. Mom is Irish and German. And on the other side, my Dad's family is German and Protestant. My Dad is management and my Mom is craft – Mom would go on strike against Dad and Dad would try to walk into the other side of the office from where she was on the picket line. My Mom is Democrat, giggling to me on the phone while Dad sits cursing in front of the television; And on other years my Republican Dad gleefully calls to say Mom is watching the returns very quietly. Before voting they each go get a friend, my Dad's friend Republican and my Mom's friend Democrat, cancelling each other's votes and then sitting down to watch the returns. Paul family needed, above all else, acceptance from the temple and Rome. Paul's Plan for Peace eventually failing, Herod spent his last years in Spain. Drusilla died in the eruption of Vesuvius with her son with rumors she had a daughter who went on to live a long and private life.

Chapter 15 Philippi 48 CE Escape from Caesarea

Paul had some infirmity (II Cor 12:7-10). I'm guessing it's bowed legs from riding horses too much. Jacob (James) was reported to have had knees with hide as tough as a camel from praying in the temple. I'm guessing it was actually from when Paul miscalculated and Jacob fell from the temple breaking his legs before Paul left Jacob for dead. Paul wants common ground. Jacob probably doesn't find bad legs "common ground".

Herod was the judge who condemned Jesus and Jewish… Gospel of Peter - It's sixty verses. Read it.

Roman saddles had no stirrups. Both Philippi of Thrace and Philippi of the Decapolis meant "loves horses".

I wonder why our gospels don't mention horses much. My grandpa raised horses. The farm kids like my Dad rode them to school in Ohio, Illinois. The farmers would take turns: Each farmer had a day they had to bring the hay.

Sarah was Abraham's half-sister: Gen 20:12

Pharisee presence in the Sanhedrin was imperative to be able to gain popular support for high court decisions. Pg 205 Acts, a New Vision of the People of G-d. Gerald L. Stevens 2016

Bernice & Drusilla – Per Dr. Eisenman these divorced and married up therefore being held in derision by the Sadducees. Pg 105 James, the Brother of Jesus, 1997 I can't imagine their second husbands, if not ruling over Jews, having re-married them or anyone not ruling over Jews having been worthy of their divorcing their previous husbands. Pg 486 of Acts a New Vision of the People of G-d, Gerald L Stevens has Bernice (a Herodian) going to Rome as the mistress of Titus.

Horses/bow-legged Paul - I've recently been struck by the number of "loves horses" cities along with the Roman road which ran from Tarsus through Ephesus or thereabouts and then from Philippi to the coast of the Adriatic near Italy. My Mom, long ago, had always said: All roads lead to Rome. I forget which reference mentioned a Roman road from Antioch to Tarsus. I googled the Roman road from Philippi to the Adriatic or watched a video of Mark Anthony (Marcus Antonius) marching his troops over the road. Long ago I decided Paul was bow-legged. Dr. Eisenman says he might have been the brother of Costobarus. Saulus and Costobarus fought in the temple environs (physically, they abused people per Josephus). Therefore Paul is a big man with bowed legs to me with a name that means "small".

Could Paul's vision have been impaired ("thorn in the flesh" 2 Cor 12:7)? Paul did use others to write his letters, and assuredly, edit them (Ro 16:22). Gal 4:13-15 suggests that Paul first preached because of an infirmity for which Galatians would have plucked out their own eyes, which I take to be he first preached with his infirmity rather than doing so because of it and they eye plucking thing to be a metaphor. Paul later has trouble identifying the High Priest calling him a "whitewashed wall" Acts 23:3-5 which I take as referring to him sarcastically as dead (purgatory Chapter 3); purifying the bones; cleaning the tombs.

Manean may have been Saulos: Pg 99 James, the Brother of Jesus, Robert Eisenman 1997
Saulos and Costobarus abuse the people, p487 ibid
Paul might have been related to Costobarus in the Herodian genealogies: p527 ibid

Costobarus also, and Saulos, did themselves get together a multitude of wicked wretches, and this because they were of the royal family; and so they obtained favor among them, because of their kindred to Agrippa: but still they used violence with the people, and were ready to plunder those that were weaker than themselves. And from that time it principally came to pass, that our city was greatly disordered, and that all things grew worse and worse among us. Pg 646 20.9.4 Antiquities, Josephus, William Whiston AM 1998

Barnabas returns to Cyprus. pg 340, Acts a New Vision of the People of G-d, Gerald L Stevens, 2016
Jude stays in Antioch. How else could his grandchildren get there? Please see references for chapter 33 – The War is Finished.

Chapter 16 Philippi 48 CE The Philippi of Mark Anthony

This is mainly a chapter on Roman history and how the families of Herod and Mark Anthony (Marcus Antonius) intertwine. Cleopatra abandons Mark Anthony multiple times. Mark Anthony kills and confiscates the property of the 300 richest of Rome. I don't know why our history books say that Cleopatra and Mark Anthony killed themselves, leaving out that they were being pursued and that Agrippa, while on his way to invade Egypt and kill Mark Anthony and Cleopatra, was resupplied by Herod. Perhaps the Cassians were not the driving force behind Roman xenophobia, but Paul ran away from the Antioch of Cassians, Claudius hid his Mark Anthony (Marcus Antonius) ancestry and the spearman of our crucified Jesus was named Cassius too (Gospel of Peter).

Josephus perceived Julius Caesar as evil: …For since Julius Caesar took it into his head to dissolve our democracy, and by overbearing the regular system of our laws, to bring disorders into our administration, and to get above right and justice, and to be a slave to his own inclinations, there is no kind of misery but what hath tended to the subversion of our city; while all those that have succeeded him have striven one with another to overthrow the ancient laws of their country, and have left it destitute of such citizens as were of generous principles… - 19.2.2 Antiquities, Josephus

Chapter 17 – Corinth 50 Castaway

This chapter is mainly interlude. The excitement of Jerusalem is over. Gallio has Sosthenes, as the temple authority, beaten (Acts 18:12-17) and Paul works on the book of Hebrews here with Caesar's secretary for eight years until Jacob (James), in my opinion, figures out where Paul is and sends a letter requesting the temple authority return to Jerusalem for discussion not knowing that Paul is the synagogue authority.

Caesar's summer home: Chapter II Caesar's coin, Understanding the Bible, Ray Shortell 2013, 3.10.10 Wars, Josephus, William Whiston 1998

Four evangelists – I'm making this up based on Antioch "widows" and the death of Stephen. I needed to kill a few in different ways in Jerusalem to match the various deaths of our martyrs and it seems a nice round number. Alvin Frame, my Bible study teacher from the Church of the Nazarene in Marietta, told me four is the number of the (four corners of the, four winds of the) world and these are Paul's evangelists sending Paul's message to the world.

Peter's church in Corinth. I'm guessing there is one. It may not date from 50. Then again, perhaps just noting Peter's "presence" in churches around the world is enough to make the point that Peter's visit to Rome may have been merely retrospective interpolation.

"penultimate" - I jest. Dr. Eisenman equates the words Sicarii and Christian, which in the absence of further indications, I doubt. It's not every day you hear the word "penultimate", which Dr. Eisenman also uses. Incidentally the word "assassin" is a word from the 1100s equated with Hashish, a drug like marijuana taken by an Armenian sect before their killings, mostly on Fridays in mosques.
Pg 726 The New Testament Code, Robt Eisenman 2006

My best reference for Zoroastrianism comes from a fishing trip with Daniel Walker in 2002 when he described what he knew of the religion as described in Post-script: Contemporaneous Religions, Understanding the Bible, Ray Shortell 2011. I've also studied a few of the non-malevolent Kaballah angels.

Training Rechabites in marble: Herod trained priests in marble. I'm guessing they were Rechabites.

Chapter 18 Corinth 58 CE The Politics of Corinth

Some felt that Paul or Acts lied when saying in Galatians he was returning to Jerusalem after fourteen years (Gal 2:1) since Acts notes multiple trips to Jerusalem. This book proposes that Paul's "presence" in Jerusalem in Acts was actually his followers bringing his "presence" to Jerusalem with the annual pilgrimage, much as Pierre Kjibolder p97 in Crucifixion and Turin Shroud Mysteries Revealed 1999 proposes that Cephas (Peter) founded churches in Rome without ever having left Jerusalem. Also here I make the case that Paul's family is strewn about the Mediterranean as the Herods and link Paul into James with both having knee troubles. During this time in Corinth in my opinion Paul will rewrite the book of Hebrews yet again.

Herodion is in Rome (Ro 16:11). His mom must have been too. Pg 67 of Herodian Messiah by Joseph Raymond 2010 has a mess of Herodians in Rome. I'm guessing these would have been expelled in the multiple (as near as I can tell) Jewish expulsions: p360 & 386 Acts, A New Vision of the People of G-d, Gerald L Stevens 2016, and also the Fire of Rome & "Christian" persecutions.

I'm thinking Herodion was a hostage, as in Paul under Felix at Caesarea per Acts 24:26, and as per Josephus Antiquities 20.8.11 Poppea retained two of the ten ambassadors with herself as hostages (William Whiston AM 1998). Josephus also notes Parthians held hostage by Rome during the truce (2.16.4 Wars (279, 289).

Paul ... was tutored in Rome by Seneca. p235 Herodian Messiah, Joseph Raymond 2010 My guess is that Paul spent time in Rome under a teacher. Seneca would have probably been the best and probably would have wanted to oversee Caesar's charges in Israel. Seneca was a Stoic who tutored rulers. Some have noted similarities between Paul's writings and those of the Stoics (p547 Acts, A New Vision of the People of G-d, Gerald L. Stevens 2016).

Seneca was a close advisor to Caesar. Pg 223 Herodian Messiah, Joseph Raymond 2010
Seneca and Epaphroditus are linked as per the sources for chapter 31 – Seneca & Poppea
Epaphroditus, Josephus and Paul are linked as per sources for chapter 33 – The War is Finished

Famine (46-48), p127 James, the Brother of Jesus, Robert Eisenman 1997

I've made up that Herodias was in Rome later changing this to one of her relatives (although there are Herodians in, and getting an education at Rome 1.32.2 Wars, Josephus, William Whiston 1998). I've made up that Seneca helped Herodias or her relative and Herodion escape. I've made up that they took passage through Corinth. The relationship between Sulla, Seneca and Epaphroditus is that all were secretaries of Caesars and the relationship between Seneca and his brother Gallio is documented on p527 James, the Brother of Jesus, Robert Eisenman 1997.

Did Paul have a girl-friend? I think the following falls under the category of: Methinks the lady doth protest too much:
I Cor 7:1 …It is good for a man not to touch a woman…
I Cor 7:7-8 For I would that all men were even as I myself…. I say therefore to the unmarried and widows, it is good for them if they abide even as I.
I Cor 9:5 Have we not power to lead about a sister, a wife, as well as the other apostles, and as the brethren of the Lord, and Cephas?
Acts 17:34 Howbeit certain men clave unto him and believed: Among the which was Dionysius the Areopagite, and a woman named Damaris, and others with them.

Epaphroditus supports Josephus – Preface 2, Antiquities, Jospehus, William Whiston 1998
Josephus initiation into Essenes – Chapter 30 Seneca & Poppea

James dies in 62 p22 James, the Brother of Jesus, Robert Eisenman 1997
James dies at the age of 96 p303 ibid

Corinth is Caesar's summer home (See Chapter 17 – Corinth).

Chapter 19 Corinth 58 CE The Letter of Jacob (James)
Jacob (James) acts as Prime Minister of the various factions in Jerusalem. This chapter also explains the Egyptian North Star philosophy infused into Judaism from the land of Moses (Egypt). I'm purposefully making it seem as though Paul steals a letter intended for the Corinthian Synagogue's leadership although leaving this unstated. In a later chapter my intent is to explain that Paul either is, or takes himself as, the Corinthian Synagogue leadership. Plus Paul either is or will shortly be travelling to Jerusalem with leadership from Roman cities around the Aegean.

Dr. Eisenman makes much of "letters written in stone" and "the letter of the law brings death" and "Paul's letters written in your hearts" plus Cephas' (Peter's) writing that a letter from Jacob (James) is required for authority per PseudoClementine Recognitions 4.25 - p647-p649, James, the Brother of Jesus 1997.

How do I know the pyramids point out the pole star? The television show STARGATE? Being an engineer and seeing a picture of one of the "exits" once? Hearing a radio talk show about how the pyramids are astronomically lined up better than modern instruments would be able to accomplish? I don't remember. I just Googled it though and they say that due to the earth's precession there was actually another pole star to which the pyramids pointed. Close enough for me.

The "Egyptian" is a character in Josephus whose followers are on the Mount of Olives. 2.13.5 Wars, Josephus.

Chapter 20 Tarsus 58 CE Astrology
In my opinion Paul's sole positive biblical contribution is herein recognized as plagiarizing the

astrological mysteries of Hercules (I Cor 13) (Postscript: Astrology in the Bible, Understanding the Bible, Ray Shortell 2014). Horus from Egypt is where we get our word for "hour" and "horoscope". I asked a fortune teller once at the Egyptian store in Discovery Mall in Gwinnett, GA and am taking her word.

Also for those scholars fussing that I've conflated all of the missionary journeys and am glossing over Paul's achievements at Ephesus... No one else understands what you're talking about. You yourselves are more wrapped up in what Luke is not saying about what happened than what is written (if Paul was so great at Ephesus, why did he stop at Miletus on his return journey instead). Your gloating about how detailed Paul's final journey from Caesarea to Jerusalem is written and how well it can be traced overshadows what can be gleaned from Acts regarding Paul's fourteen year missionary journeys starting in Antioch while absent from Jerusalem (Gal 2:1). When writing this, please mention Roman army roads which Paul followed from Antioch to Ephesus through Turkey and from Philippi to Thessalonica which go onto the Adriatic while Paul therefore probably took a boat from Thessalonica to Athens and thence to Corinth. Or when writing about "missionary journeys" mention the major cities involved from Damascus by Queen Helen's son, Antioch by the church, Corinth and an implied final mission from Rome. Or divide time up by visions, the truly Pauline category: Damascus, Temple, Peter's Housetop, Troas, Shipwreck and how these visions guided Paul's missions. Or even outline, as did Luke, using Paul's two-year stays in various cities. The current methodology of discussing Paul, by the three missionary journeys is too confusing. The second and third have no obvious dividing line or character development, more especially due to everyone's focus being on what Acts fails to say. Laity wonder whether "missionary journeys" mean back and forth between wherever Paul was staying and Jerusalem.

Chapter 21 Departing Tarsus 58 CE The unknown g-d

Paul continues to gather experiences with which to author the Bible. I'm aware "the unknown g-d" has been suggested as at Athens (p375 Acts a New Vision of the People of G-d, Gerald L. Stevens 2011). I reject the proposition believing people around the Mediterranean sought the meaning of life as does everyone in our age.

"as if from the grave" - Paul's testimony seems to be of visions of Jesus. Paul was the first biblical author.

Seneca and Epaphroditus: Please see my references in chapter 33. Not really sure how soon Epaphroditus was working with Seneca though. And that Seneca was working with Paul is still conjecture, but Corinth was Caesar's summer home. (See Chapter 17)

"irregardless": it's a nonsense word. Please reference chapter 9 for further reference on deacons.

Chapter 22 Antioch 58 CE The Widows' Revenge

In my opinion Paul was responsible for the deaths of their husbands; his desire to liberalize temple zealots leading to the deaths of four evangelists from his church in Antioch. Perhaps the brothers of Jesus went to Antioch afterwards to work off the karma created by Paul. Again... we're more focused on what Acts fails to say... (where is Joses (Barnabas)?). Also in my opinion Jerusalem gains the moniker "killing all her prophets" from the evangelists of these widows.

Religion of Abraham – faith Heb 11:17-19 – By faith offered his son and received him back.
Opened to all – Heb 6:19-20 – Our forerunner Jesus entered beyond the temple curtain.
New covenant – Heb 8:13

Second son – Gal 4:28 (not written to the Hebrews, but Paul had access to this too)
Grafted olive tree – Ro 11:17 (not written to the Hebrews, but Paul understood this by "faith")
Gen 22:18 - all the nations of the earth shall be blessed (in Abraham)

Technically the blessings of the second are found in Galatians and the blessings on Gentiles are found in Romans, but the seeds of each are found in Hebrews.

Chapter 23 Jerusalem 58 CE The Book of Hebrews

Paul gathers strength to attempt once more to integrate the temple. Paul arrives with people and donations from many Greek churches. In my opinion the reason Hebrews is so unlike Paul's other writing is due to the amount of time Paul spent with groups of people reviewing/revising the text. I'm making up that Paul had a sealed scroll from Seneca.

This last bit about Herod/Herodias fighting over a Centurion's property is fiction with basis and purpose. Regarding purpose, Paul is picking up stories for Acts 5:1-10 where Ananias and Sapphira lie about selling a house for less than they sold it. Humorously I'm telling a story exactly opposite of what the gospel authors wrote, but upon which, perhaps, they based their story. Also I'm dwelling upon how Nero kicked Poppea to death. Finally, the story is about how Herod would have had good reason for wanting centurions in his life.

According to Josephus, Herodias wheedled her husband into requesting a promotion from Tiberias. Herod was rebuked for listening to a woman and retired to Spain in 39 (18.7 Antiquities, 2.9.6 Wars, Josephus, William Whiston AM 1998). They had traveled to Rome to present Herod's case for promotion. However to me Josephus was a compromised source (See sources for chapter 2 – The City of Blood). In 2.9.5 Wars, Josephus, William Whiston 1998 it is Herod Agrippa who travels with Herod/Herodias accusing them to Tiberias (review footnote 24 of 19.9.2 Antiquities ibid). Agrippa apparently unsuspected by Herod and good friends with Tiberius.

I'm a bit fuzzy on which Herod (Bernice, Drusilla, Mariamne, Agrippa) was where and when. I pulled birthdates from Wikipedia and grabbed a name here and place there. Wikipedia mostly cites Josephus, but sometimes Tacitus. The main point is that these were kin to Paul who would therefore not have been in "prison" at Caesarea with Felix, Drusilla's husband. My first writing had Herod/Herodias throughout (having missed their "retirement" in 39), but then needed an overlay for the Herods after I figured Josephus wouldn't be lying about who people were and where they were, only what they were doing or more to the point, what their purpose was and why they were doing something (i.e. the "fugitives" in Philip Herod's armies who apparently sided with Aretas against Herod due to Herodias' divorce of Philip).

I'm also dwelling on how several names were messed up making things tough for figuring out who was High Priest as per the gospels, although of course names have been transmitted to us through a couple of different languages. Chapter VIII Misquoting Jewish Scripture, Understanding the Bible, Ray Shortell 2013.

Cephas was renamed "the Rock" as an encouragement per the Bible. My guess is that he was called Cephas long before the gospels.

Regarding the Hebrew word for "spirit", please review references for the cover page.

Killing all the prophets – I'm guessing whomever authored Acts dwelt upon the widows of Antioch as much as I. Acts 6 – also reference Dedication of this book.

1) …the Romans, after two Uprisings and endless troubles over these issues, turned the tables on the Jewish extremists… Rabbis are alleged to have put a ban upon those taking Nazrite style oaths not to `eat or drink` until they had seen the Temple rebuilt… pg 762, The New Testament Code, Robert Eisenman 2006

Chapter 24 Caesarea 58 CE Paul the Writer

Paul starts working again on more books for the Bible. I'm making up that Seneca sends for Paul. Again, I am unclear on the specific familial relationships amongst Herods. Regarding Philip Herod, please refer to Afterword: Was Jesus Crucified in 40 and Chapter 2.

Chapter 25 Rome 60 CE The Egyptian

Several sources suggest that Daniel was backdated. Daniel is the first book of the Bible to reference an afterlife (Heaven, Immortality & Resurrection, Sin, Sacrifice, Heaven & Hell, Ray Shortell 2017). Its prophesies are written in the past tense. Daniel misses several of his own rulers while getting minutiae of his "prophesied" days correct (I'm assuming.. the detail is outrageous). The writing on the wall has always bugged me, because it only says that part of a hand wrote on a wall… in a foreign language needing interpretation. Plus this "weighing". Put a feather in the hand and the Egyptian Hall of the Dead where your soul is weighed against a feather and it all makes sense to me. The idea is my own.

Joseph is given several names including Clopas and Alphaeus p845 James, the Brother of Jesus, Robert Eisenman 1997. In my opinion he was "The Egyptian" of Josephus' Antiquities 20.8.6. Josephus, as always flattering the Romans while neglecting things like the Pella flight from Jerusalem which took James' followers North to Iraq (James, the Brother of Jesus 1997 pXVIII Robert Eisenman). Dr. Eisenman notes Jesus/Joshua (the names are the same in Hebrew) as the son of Joseph while noting that the dad of Jesus may not have been actually named Joseph (p841 James, the Brother of Jesus 1997). The Egyptian would have brought the Bread of Life from Egypt as when Jesus' family fled to Egypt to escape Herod Mt 2:13. Bread comes from Pierre Kjibolder as does Eternal life which Kjibolder ties into "Nathanael" p27 Crucifixion & Turin Shroud Mysteries Solved 1999. Tying "the Bread of Life" into the Egyptian, Daniel, witches floating (Ch 8)… is mine (Foreward, Postscript, Sin, Sacrifice, Heaven & Hell, Ray Shortell 2017)

In Josephus the Egyptian flees into the desert with several deceived followers. In my opinion that's the way Josephus would have recorded Jacob's Pella escape. Josephus couldn't record Rome's failures or he would have faced death as did Paul upon the failure of Paul's Plan for Peace. 20.8.6 Antiquities, Josephus

Three Nets of Belial – p6 Sin, Sacrifice, Heaven & Hell, Ray Shortell 2017

The Egyptian per Josephus hangs out on the Mount of Olives as did Jesus and his companions. And there are many such overlaps. pXXIV James, the Brother of Jesus, Robt Eisenman 1997

Chapter 26 Rome 62 CE The Kiss of Death

James is murdered. The Egyptian, Joseph, in my opinion, escapes taking 4000, like the crowd Jesus feeds, North to Antioch or Kurdistan or Southern Iraq. Josephus underestimates the size of the crowd, in my opinion, to please his Roman overlords.

Regarding my reference to the Mafia cleaner, it comes from the movie Pulp Fiction 1994

James is a translation of Jacob:
"Actually three common English names come out of this: James, Jacob and Jack."
https://probe.org/why-did-the-book-of-jacob-get-changed-to-the-book-of-james/

"The Jewish High Priest, Ananus, instigated the death of the highly respected James the Just of Jerusalem, the brother of Jesus, about AD 66." Pg 22 Acts, A New Vision of the People of G-d, Gerald L. Stevens 2016

"Between the death of the procurator Festus and before his replacement, Albinius could arrive on the scene, Ananias seized opportunity to have James, the Brother of Jesus killed." Pg 462 Acts, A New Vision of the People of G-d, Gerald L Stevens 2016

Albinius served over Judea 62 – 64 Wikipedia

As for James, it is said that he was martyred in the year 62 CE also during the buildup of hostilities that precipitated the outbreak of the Roman-Jewish war in 66 CE. pg 69 Who Wrote The New Testament? Burton L. Mack 1995

James died in 62 – XXV James, the Brother of Jesus, Robert Eisenman 1997

Chapter 27 Caesarea 63 CE The Gospel of Herod

I'm killing Paul in this chapter although he may have still been alive in 66 ratting out Jerusalem to Caesar's secretary in Corinth, Seneca. Jacob (James) dies in 62 and neither he nor Paul seem to have written afterwards to me. An alternate ending might have Peter and Paul debate in the Roman synagogue which burns in 64 where perhaps both meet their fate. Gallio retires to Spain (in 62?) and his brother Seneca is forced to commit suicide in 65 by Nero (Nero committed or was forced to commit suicide in 68). Poppea was kicked to death by Nero in 64 (Wikipedia). Paul might have died at any of these. My point in killing Paul in Caesarea is tying together the deaths of Paul and Jacob. I'm making up that the cleaner was from Rome and named Longinus (Gaius Cassius Longinus, Gov of Paul's Syria in the fifties, with his namesake killed by Mark Anthony in 42 BCE check cover sources). For most of these, please also reference p527-529 of James, the Brother of Jesus, Robert Eisenman 1997.

Eusebius notes "Matthew" as providing these prophesies for the outline of the gospel. p14 Crucifixion and Turin Shroud Mysteries Solved, Pierre Krijbolder 1999

I can't imagine Rome was happy about Herod's remodeling the temple and then Rome's having to destroy it again (after the Babylonians had destroyed it the first time). 15.11 Antiquities Josephus, William Whiston AM 1998

I'm pretty sure there are a couple of Messianic prophesies we've not heard. Rome did their best to prevent uprisings. It probably has something to do with the mass suicides with Josephus (please check references on Chapter 31) and at Massada, although Roman commanders seem to kill themselves frequently too for some reason.

The Cassians of Rome dispute which Romans should be considered more than barbarians (32.233, 34.256 Gaius, Philo, 1.9 Histories, Tacitus).

Josephus will later declare of Jerusalem, "You are the only people who think it a disgrace to be servants to those to whom all the world hath submitted. You are not freedom fighters, but recalcitrant slaves (Wars 2.16.4)."

Sadducees describe Rome as Egypt (the land of sin) or Babylon where Judah was exiled from the temple (Rev 14:8).

Herodian brood of snakes (Ch 2).

Not sure where I'd read of the robbers, but the two crucified with Jesus were also called robbers (Mt 27:38). Josephus calls anyone he doesn't like who plunders "robbers", but never uses the derogatory term against Romans following their commander from what I can find 2.4.2 Wars, Josephus, William Whiston 1998

From Josephus I'm guessing Matthias was translated as Matthew.

Chapter 28 Rome 63 CE The Temple Wall Affair

The Temple Wall Affair - pg530 The New Testament Code, Robert Eisenman 2006

In my opinion there was no "Temple Wall Affair" (Josephus, Antiquities 20.8.11 William Whiston 1998). In my opinion men don't go to war over a fart. In my opinion the embassage went to Rome to fuss about the Herodian (Saulos/Paul) death of Jacob (James) and the pursuit of his dad, Joseph the Egyptian. In my opinion The Temple Wall Affair is a red herring like the dance of Herodias' daughter (Mt 14:6) detracting readers from the real story (the death of James and war of Herod against King Aretas). Twenty years later Josephus writes of the causes of his coming to Rome ("priests in bonds of a trifling nature" meaning, to me, the death of Jacob, 2 Life, Josephus, William Whiston AM 1998), but either he or later Roman editors come up with this stupid story about a fart causing a war, to unlink Josephus from James and Rome from responsibility. That's my opinion. Poppea adores Josephus and this strange foreign religion, probably because of the flattery of the book of Esther. Nero is eventually forced to kill her because she blabs everything and probably keeps hanging around the synagogue in Rome, probably secretly converts, and probably spends time with Cephas, for which Nero will eventually burn the Jewish quarter, although none of our history books describe the Fire of Rome in 64 as against the Jews. It must have been a small Jewish quarter and synagogue. Rome had already kicked the Jews out several times over the years.

Paul retires to Spain: According to Tacitus, Caesar's would "retire" various political opponents and then later often tire of the monthly stipend, sending someone to execute the "retirees". Herod and Herodias were "retired" to Spain (Ch 23) as was Gallio. Seneca would be executed before he could make his planned retirement there. Romans 15 mentions Paul's desire to preach in Spain and Clement notes that Paul did preach in the West, although whether this meant Rome or Spain, I cannot say.

Esther: Understanding the Bible, Steven L. Harris 2011 p241-243 Gives strong indications of being produced by Diaspora. Greek and Hebrew versions differ.

Wikipedia: Esther is not found among Qumran documents. Esther might be Ishtar, Mordechai might be Marduk.

Zecharia Sitchin, The Tenth Planet: Marduk was the planet between Mars and Jupiter blown to smithereens during a nuclear war and becoming our asteroid belt. I think I saw this on an ancient mysteries special once.

Mayan Calendar: Showing ten planets with the planet between Mars and Jupiter having the right periodicity for Marduk. I think I checked this out once around Dec 2012 when the Mayan calendar ended and folks were expecting the end of the world.

Me: Esther was written to convince Poppea to side with Josephus. Perhaps Poppea was secretly Jewish. Esther also shows Roman authorship in that the hero is a woman. Finally Esther shows Roman Stoic authorship explaining the violence of Jews to an audience that would shortly be murdering Jews across the Mediterranean (Chapter 1 - We are only doing to you what you would do in our place were our positions reversed) forcefully encouraging Romans to pillage and plunder Jews around the Mediterranean as documented by Josephus. Esther possibly also relies on gentile supposition regarding how much Jews want their children to become lawyers writing laws to gain acceptance into pharisaic synagogues.

The "brothers" of Jesus are the brothers of Jesus (XIX The Family of James, Understanding the Bible, Ray Shortell 2014). My belief is that the story of Esther is intertwined with the overwriting of the family of James "literarily" p903 James, the Brother of Jesus, Robert Eisenman 1997. My further belief is that Dr. Eisenman's proper naming of "The Temple Wall Affair" will go down as a major contribution in the history of Bible commentaries p489 The New Testament Code Robert Eisenman, 2006

Poppea requests Nero's first wife's head on a platter. Pg274 ibid.

The charge against the Establishment of `sleeping with women during their menstrual flow`. Pg 226,458 James, the Brother of Jesus, Robert Eisenman 1997

The charge of "polluting the temple" with graven images by foreigners - p826 James, the Brother of Jesus, Robert Eisenman 1998

The death of Jacob (James) overwritten by the stoning of Stephen (Acts 7), Ch 14 ibid.

Please check my story of how Rome supported the Pharisees for how Esther was incorporated into the cannon (Epilogue: Editing the Talmud).

Chapter 29 Rome 64 CE Rome burns

Disloyal Romans are "cleaned" (Ch 26). My conjecture is that the fire of Rome was intended to destroy evidence and that Nero built on it afterwards to prevent its return as opposed to the popular proposition that Nero burned Rome so that he could build. As for where I heard Nero's fiddle was actually a zither, I'm guessing it was an NPR host one afternoon listening to the radio. My guess is that a transgression of secrecy is what killed Seneca and Poppea along with Cephas and Paul - reference Chapter 30 and also The Destruction of Israel (Salt of the Earth), Preface, Sin, Sacrifice, Heaven and Hell, Ray Shortell 2017

Burned books – Acts 19:19 (Quoted in the Dedication)

40,000 scrolls burned by Julius Caesar, more confiscated by Sulla, Burned Library at Alexandria – Seneca supports the destruction of private libraries – On Tranquility of Mind – http://www.straightdope.com/columns/read/2233/what-happened-to-the-great-library-of-alexandria

Refractory slaves - 2.16.4 Wars Josephus

Josephus had more records – p77 footnote unrelated to the text Josephus, the Complete Works William Whiston 1998

Part of the booty is a treasure of books from the library of the temple and the Sanhedrin which Josephus takes with them to Rome. Pg 51, Crucifixion and Turin Shroud Mysteries Solved, Pierre Kjibolder 1989

The missing part of the sixteenth book, and the two books which follow, must have dealt with the further casualties from Nero's increasing savagery. Pg 275 Tacitus, The Ancient Historians, Michael Grant 1970

…there were very few survivors who were in a position to contradict anything he [Josephus] said. Ibid Pg 265

Josephus overwritten by more "juicy" detail. Pg 64-65 & 402 <conflated>, James, the Brother of Jesus, Robert Eisenman, 1997

I'm speculating that the Gospel of Thomas was written by Rome. I've documented my opinion in Chapter 28 that Esther was written by Rome and in Chapter 27 that the prophesies of Matthew which provide the outline of Matthew were provided by Herods. Eusebius notes "Matthew" as providing these prophesies (p14 Crucifixion and Turin Shroud Mysteries Solved, Pierre Krijbolder 1999 which also notes "Peter" as dying in 58).

Peaceful: My yoke is easy and my burden light (Mt 11:30)
Render unto Caesar what is Caesars (Mt 22:21) & Caesar's Coin, Understanding the Bible, Ray Shortell 2011
Smoking reed – Oh, I massacred this one – (Mt 12:20, Is 42:3)
Lamb cross – Deu 21:23, Gal 3:13, Jer 11:19, Acts 8:32

Ephesians and Colossians were written by the Pauline School. Pg 214 J. Christian Beker, Paul the Apostle.

Chapter 30 Rome 65 CE Seneca & Poppea

"perfidious" – Josephus' men committed suicide and yet not Josephus. Josephus named Vespasian the Messiah. Josephus says he did all three sects: Sadducee, Pharisee and Essene. In 2 Life, Josephus notes three years of apparently Essene training p1 Josephus The Complete Works, William Whiston AM 1998. I can't figure out what the fuss is about in the footnote, but it has something to do with timing for three initiations in a shortened number of years and Josephus Wars 2.8.10 relates that after three years the community was divided into four sections where the seniors had to wash after touching a junior. I take this to mean Josephus' induction was incomplete. Regardless Queen Helen did three sets of seven years penance p239 James, the Brother of Jesus, Robert Eisenman 1997 much as did Jacob for his wives. I can't imagine initiation into Essenes for less than one set of these. And intending on joining for the purpose of learning only, might make one untrustworthy… unless, at his position in the Sadducees, Josephus was able to simultaneously continue as an Essene. Dr. Eisenman from the PseudoClementines and Dead Sea Scrolls notes Peter and James' "initiation of Moses" which lasted seven years, but we had already guessed that. Finally per paragraph 3 of Life Josephus goes to Rome at the age of 26 (in the year 62) befriending Poppea… later to surrender to Romans. Perfidious!

"perfidious" – Seneca burned the library at Alexandria, Rome Burns - Chapter 29. As a scientist I'm immediately prejudiced.

Gaillio visits Corinth before retiring to Spain. Gallio was the Roman judge before whom Paul appeared in 50-52 in Corinth and brother ot Seneca. I'm making up that Gallio retired around 60 and visited Corinth one last time before retiring to Spain. Gallio was Seneca's brother. Refer to chapter eighteen, the politics of Corinth, for details.

Poppea… this is big and involved in everything. She supported Josephus' embassage 3 Life, Josephus, William Whiston 1998. She died for having too big of a mouth (my opinion), kicked to death by Nero, but perhaps instigated by a mystery group intent on destroying Israel, and overwriting Judaism… unless Nero was the mystery group.

The Cleaner – See The Kiss of Death Chapter 26

"the Poor" Chapter 10 Taxes - Sin, Sacrifice, Heaven & Hell, Ray Shortell 2017

Sadducees stop accepting Roman donations/sacrifice: Chapter III Caesar's Coin, Understanding the Bible, Ray Shortell 2014

Nero poisoned by lead: I'm making this up. I'd heard somewhere that folks thought tomatoes were poison back then because people who ate them went crazy. The folks who ate tomatoes left them on pewter dishes (lead). Myself I left an aluminum pot of tomatoes in the sink one night leaving Denny's at my job as a bus boy. The cooks fussed at me the next morning showing me how the pot's bottom had been dissolved and fell off. That would have been the summer of 86 I'd guess. That Denny's on 23rd Ave in Moline, Illinois has long since closed.

The book of Esther – See Chapter 28

Sporus – Was the man Nero had castrated and called "Poppaea". This would be from Suetonius who authored essentially "romance" novels as a Roman historian.

Chapter 31 Rome 66 CE The Surrender of Josephus
Nazareth probably doesn't exist – Chapter 6, The Geography, Understanding the Bible, Ray Shortell 2011
Saul is tall – I Samuel 9:2
Josephus is big - survives a big fight – 3.8.6 Wars, Josephus, William Whiston AM 1998
Josephus dedicates Antiquities to Epaphroditus. 76 Life, Josephus, William Whiston 1998
Epaphroditus was involved in the death of Nero p800 James, the Brother of Jesus, Robert Eisenman 1997
Seneca was a tutor of Nero p800 ibid
Josephus was a Hasmonean as was Mariamne, a wife of Herod p48 Crucifixion and Turin Shroud Mysteries Solved, Pierre Krijbolder, 1999
Josephus consults Herod Agrippa II who also consults with Festus on Paul, Acts A New Vision of the People of G-d, Gerald L. Stevens 2016
Josephus had access to the library of the temple (Jerusalem), Roman imperial archives and the library of Epaphroditus p51 ibid
Epaphroditus was a friend of Paul (Phil 2:25) p220 Herodian Messiah, Joseph Raymond, 2010
Seneca was the younger brother of Gallio ibid p140

Gallio allowed the beating of, the synagogue ruler of Corinth Acts 18:12-17
Paul claims that Sosthenes supports Paul, I Cor 1:1
Paul was tutored by Seneca in Rome p235 Herodian Messiah, Joseph Raymond 2010

Seneca was Caesar's secretary. Epaphroditus was the next secretary of Caesar. To me they had a relationship. Epaphroditus supports the writings of Paul and Josephus. Seneca tutors Paul. To me, while uncertain as to the details of the relationship between Seneca and Epaphroditus, it is big.

Chapter 32 Jerusalem 70 CE Vespasian burns Jerusalem

The temple is a `fortified isolated enclave` - prof Eisenman's books, but durned if I can find it again.
Failing to worship Caesar as G-d – Philo of Alexandria
Failing to worship Caesar as Savior – John Crossan in one of his debates
Joshua, Yeshua, Jesus are the same word - Scholars
Rome pulled armies from France and Germany… I think this reference was from Wikipedia on Vespasian. Makes sense to me. Rome invested a lot against Jerusalem. Preface 2 Wars, Josephus
Titus leads a legion from Alexandria, Egypt – Josephus?
Josephus praises Vespasian as Messiah. 3.8.9 Wars Josephus
Caesarea holds the bloodiest of legions. Scholars
Rejoice in evil. 12.48 Anals, Tacitus, referring to someone in Alexandria. I'm guessing Caesarea too.

Vespasian waits, declared Messiah. Josephus chains smashed & golden chains. Josephus

Josephus is chief negotiator – Josephus (generally)
Vespasian the merciful stalls – Josephus
Gadarene aqueducts – pictures & historians
Gadarene aqueducts water grass for horses – me.
Vespasian receives surrendering refugees – Josephus
Sadducees destroy their support. They rob people. – Josephus
Sadducees store grain in the temple – me - from it burning in the Talmud which I refuse to read
Factions fight with each other – Josephus
The Jewish temple infighting follows the Roman model - me

Vespasian builds a wall – Josephus
Refractory slaves – 2.16.4 Wars, Josephus
Woe to Jerusalem! 6.5.3 Wars Josephus
Josephus knocked out –

Mud on her feet – Chapter 7
Rabbi Yohannon ben Zakkai escapes Jerusalem in a coffin and starts the Pharisee school with Rome's blessing as per the Talmud <Wikipedia>. Talmud: I refuse to read this. It's a long section of library. The one book I pulled discussed whether you had sinned for catching a loaf of bread under your eaves, but outside of the house that someone had thrown to you during the days of unleavened bread. Sorry. No offense intended.
Messiah saves coming in through the Eastern gate like the Sun (Masonic references).

Rome burns the walls. Josephus
Soldiers plunder – 3.19 Histories Tacitus
Vespasian becomes Caesar – Tacitus
"the year of four Caesars" – Wikipedia

Nero dies. Praetorian guard defends Rome against Roman armies. I'm guessing based on Tacitus.

Starving Jewish soldiers plunder Jerusalem – Josephus
Eating babies – 6.3.4 Wars Josephus
Esther – Chapter 28 The Temple Wall Affair

"Herod spends money from David's tomb rebuilding the temple" – Chapter 2 and 18,000 out of work, pg 137 First Century Judaism in Crisis, Jacob Neusnser 1975

"The temple at Jerusalem served as… the center of a Jewish banking network" p149 Who Wrote the New Testament, Burton L. Mack 1995

Temple gold melted into the walls between the stones which were pried apart stone by stone (Mt 24:2, Mk 13:2, Lk 21:6). Chapter I, The Power of Rome, Understanding the Bible, Ray Shortell 2011

Priests trained as masons – they wouldn't let anyone inside. Not sure where I heard this. My belief is that Paul did the training or received his training here.

No idea where I found that zealots burned the temple food or tried to destroy it with water and mud. It's mentioned in several sources, but no place in Josephus that I can find. The food stores were burned by Rome and zealots would have used water or dirt to try to put out the fire and save the granary. My god-father, Doug Johnson, was killed storming a granary in an oxygen mask when the fumes got under his beard in Ohio, Illinois in the eighties. My grass pile burned for days after I put it out soaking the area with a garden hose… the embers and heat eventually dried out the grass enough for it to continue burning and it was smoking two days later charring more than expected.

Genealogical records are burned: Genealogy (of the Priests et al), Chapter II, Christianity, Removing Jewish Authority, Understanding the Bible, Ray Shortell 2011

Simon rises from the temple rubble… sort of… – 7.2.2 Wars Josephus

Josephus takes temple records and books: Please see references for chapter 29 Rome Burns.

Vespasian enslaves 100,000: p22 Acts, A New Vision of the People of G-d, Gerald L Stevens 2016
Tribute is required – 4.74 Histories, Tacitus

Book of Esther Please see chapter 30, Seneca & Poppea.

The second temple in Alexandria: Please see chapter 11, Beit Horon.
Vespasian or his son Titus burned the second temple at Alexandria 7:421 Wars Josephus

According to Josephus, up to one million five hundred thousand men (1,500,000), women and children perished or were enslaved as a result of the rebellion. P180, First Century Judaism in Crisis, Jacob Neusner 1975

Jews leave by the thousands following the Egyptian – 2.13.5 Wars, Josephus

Masada – Pretty much straight forward history, but some are unaware.

"Bathtists escape to Kurdistan" – as near as I can tell what Dr. Eisenman is communicating. My focus is more as a Roman Catholic on Paul. Pg 4-5 The New Testament Code, Robert Eisenman 2006. Dr. Eisenman gets much more detailed with "daily bathers" retreating to Southern Iraq as Manicheans and winding up in the Koran. The same page points out a specific Antioch which I've taken as the Antioch mentioned in Josephus as the third largest city of Romans from where Cassius sought legions and Mark Anthony (Marcus Antonius) ruled and from where the grandchildren of Jude are taken back to Rome (Chapter 33 – The War is Finished). So some fled from Israel to Antioch which was the gateway to Iraq. To me, that Kurds don't have their own country, that multiple countries fight against this possibility, might be explained that they have a different tradition than that of Turkey, Iran and Iraq although I'm unfamiliar. Dr. Eisenman follows the Jacobians (Jamesians) through their traditions in the Koran – p3, James, the Brother of Jesus, Robert Eisenman 1997

Chapter 33 Rome 125 CE The War is Finished
Was Paul Herodian? Chapter 20 Understanding the Bible, Ray Shortell 2013
Herod grafting his family onto a Maccabean root… this metaphor is mine (me), I think.

Context justifying genocide… me.

Pluto/Mars – Astrology. Please see About the Author or chapter 20 Astrology.

Stephen preaching. Chapter 9 Jewish History per Stephen (Paul's Authority), Understanding the Bible, Ray Shortell 2013

Jesus weeps (Jn 11:35). Hell-fire (Mt 11:21-24). Combining these two is metaphoric by me.

Wine sounds like Greek in Hebrew. Chapter 22 Understanding the Bible, Ray Shortell 2013

1) And Nathanael said unto him, Can there anything good come out of Nazareth?... Jn 1:46
Solomon granted Hiram king of Tyre certain cities of Galilee which Hiram went to and viewed, but did not like the gift. Afterwards the cities were named Cabul which means in Phoenecian "that which does not please" (Josephus, Antiquities 8.5.3).

The KJV rendition of this, I Kings 9:13, does not explain the terminology of "Cabul" as Phoenician or clearly "unpleasing". To me then the Gospel of John was probably not based off of what one might read in I Kings 9:13, but an indication that the Gospel of John was based upon Josephus or whatever his extra-biblical sources were on King Solomon, although how clear I Kings 9:13 might have been about this in Greek or Hebrew remains unclear to me.

Pierre Kjibolder makes the point that perhaps the gift (Nathanael) was insight into the nature of eternal life p27 Crucifixion and Turin Shroud Mysteries Solved and therefore Nathanael was probably implying that the savior was not worthy of discussion.

Early copies of the Corinthian writings reside at the Vatican… I'm guessing. However see chapter 30 Rome Burns for notes on Josephus pulling documentation from the temple.

Epaphroditus wrote the gospels… or led its authors. Where did I hear that Epaphroditus was the student of Seneca and possibly the same Epaphroditus mentioned by Paul? Seneca was the brother of Gallio who beat Sosthenes in Corinth. I'm making up that it was Epaphroditus who wrote the gospels. Herod was Matthew in my opinion. See Chapter 27 – The Gospel of Herod

Epaphroditus involvement in the death of Nero... Apion was a known historian at the Museum of Alexandria, who invented the ritual murder accusation against the Jews. His successor, ... like Seneca, was also a tutor of Nero... both had falsifications that sent even Josephus into paroxysms of indignation. Pg 800 James, the Brother of Jesus, Robert Eisenman 1997

Epaphroditus, who had also been Nero's secretary previously and someone with whom Paul appears to have been intimate... encouraged Josephus. pg 35 James, the Brother of Jesus, Robert Eisenman 1997

Josephus and Herod Agrippa II will also assist in creating the gospels. My guess is that Josephus wasn't telling the whole story. If Epaphroditus authored the Gospels, and both died around '96 as per pg 35 ibid, ... Herod Agrippa II comes from... please see Chapter 27, Herod's Gospel of Matthew.

Herodian divorcees, Bernice & Drusilla reference Chapter 15 Escape from Caesarea (Acts 24-26)

Invalids not allowed in Jerusalem (Lev 21:18). This is mine based upon Dr. Eisenman's James, the Brother of Jesus: The Conversion of Queen Helen and the Ethiopian Queen's Eunuch p883-922, 1997 although 2.24 Apion, Josephus notes homosexuals as not allowed.

Eusebius raves about heresies. P109 Eusebius, the Church Histories, Paul Maier 2007

Grandchildren of Jude hauled before Domitian, Foreword – Sin, Sacrifice, Heaven and Hell, The Meaning of Christianity, Ray Shortell 2017, p800 James, the Brother of Jesus, Robert Eisenman 1997 And executed a decade later under Trajan. p684 ibid. And crucified. p530 ibid

Epilogue – America
The battle continues
1) Herod had the previous Sanhedrin executed p484 James, the Brother of Jesus 1997, Robert Eisenman
Epaphroditus authors/edits the gospels – reference sources for Chapter 31 The Surrender of Josephus

Epilogue – Editing the Talmud
Christians shall not Judaize by resting on the Sabbath, but shall work on that day resting on Sunday instead.
Council of Laodicea 363

Afterword
Death of John – 36-37/Josephus – p501 The New Testament Code, Robt Eisenman 2006
Philip Herod was the husband of Salome, Herodias' daughter; ibid
The Philip in the Bible was actually just named Herod (Herod Herod); ibid
Resulting Pella flight to Northern Syria (Gadara-Gamala-Caesarea Philippi-Damascus-Kurdistan) of followers of John the Baptist – 37/38 p523 ibid

Thesis
Prophesies where we've lost the key. "Oracle" and footnote. Josephus 4.6.3, William Whiston, 1998

BIBLIOGRAPHY

James, the Brother of Jesus – Robert Eisenman 1997
Crucifixion and Turin Shroud Mysteries Solved – Pierre Krijbolder 1999
Understanding the Bible – Ray Shortell 2011
Sin, Sacrifice, Heaven & Hell – Ray Shortell 2014
The New Testament Code – Robert Eisenman 2006
Understanding the Bible – Stephen L. Harris 2011
Josephus – William Whiston AM 1998
101 Myths of the Bible – Gary Greenberg 2000
Paul, the Apostle – J. Christian Beker 1980
Acts, A New Vision of the People of G-d – Gerald L. Stevens 2016
Herodian Messiah – Joseph Raymond 2008
The Ancient Historians – Michael Grant 1970
The Christ Conspiracy – S. Arachya 1999
Sherry Henderson (Initiation of Osiris, Delores Ashcroft-Nowicki), The Inner Space, Roswell GA ~2011
Forged – Bart D Ehrman 2011
The Gospel of Peter – Bernhard Pick (no date)
The Other Bible – Willis Barnstone 1984
The Fifth Gospel, The Gospel of Thomas Comes of Age – Patterson, Robinson, Bethge 1998
The Age of Reason – Thomas Payne 1796 (Gramercy 1993)
The Lost Books of the Bible and the Forgotten Books of Eden, Meridian 1926
Who Wrote the New Testament – Burton L Mack 1995
Complete Works of Tacitus – Modern Library 1942
Linda Goodman's Love Signs – Linda Goodman 1978
Alvin Frame, Bible Study teacher (gematria) ~1993 at Church of the Nazarene in Marietta, GA
On First Principles – Origen 300 (Geist 2013)
The Gospel of Mary Magdalene – LeLoup 2002
The Gospel of Judas – Kasser, Meyer, Wurst 2006
Eusebius - The Church History – Paul L Maier 2007
The Crusades through Arab Eyes – Amin Maalouf 1984
First Century Judaism in Crisis - Jacob Neusner 1975
Who Was Philo Judaeus of Alexandria? Dr. Henry Abramson Oct 10, 2013
   https://www.youtube.com/watch?v=U6zvpUK7Gi8
The Decretals – Agbar returns from the East; He gives help to Aretas in a war against Herod the Tetrarch
   https://biblehub.com/library/unknown/the_decretals/iv_abgar_returns_from_the.htm
Eastern Region Evangelical Theological Society of the Westminster Theological Seminary PA April 5 1991
   Purgatory - http://www.biblearchaeology.org/post/2011/03/07/The-Demoniacs-of-Gadara.aspx
The Dead Sea Scrolls and the First Christians – Robert Eisenman 2004
The Call, The Life and Message of The Apostle Paul – Adam Hamilton 2015
Understanding the Bible – John R.W. Stott 1999

ABOUT THE AUTHOR

Ray Shortell was raised in the Quad Cities, Illinois where most had trouble understanding his quiet and metaphorical speech. After attending Roman Catholic Church regularly and becoming an altar boy, Ray Shortell went away to College at the University of Illinois earning a degree from the College of Engineering in Computer Science while reading the Bible. For non-Catholics, please be aware that the Roman Catholic Church instructs laity (that's us non-priests) that we're not allowed to read the Bible except under the guidance of a priest. After joining the University of Illinois non-Denominational chapter of Intervarsity with the Baptist Student Union, Mom sent me Catholic tractates explaining that non-Denominational meant they weren't Catholic, while Aunt Elaine told me stories of the bishop in residence at St. John's which was itself emblazoned with the Biblical metaphor: In Spirit and Truth.

Afterwards in an office prayer group in Atlanta Diane Brophy drilled me on I Cor 13 and asked why I didn't know the Ten Commandments and their five by two structure (Augustine's Ten, used by Roman Catholics, skip the second against graven images and split the tenth into two). Then there was a Bible study at 5am on Mondays at the Church of the Nazarene in Marietta by Alvin Frame. Then there was the Catholic Bible at St. Andrew's Catholic in Roswell (there are seven more books to the cannon, Protestant people) and Denver Bible study at St. Michael's Catholic in Woodstock on the five authors of the books of Moses (JEPDR) where Fr. Mike circa 2005 proposed that the Catholic church demands humility and obedience along with claiming that to argue with the church you must first learn five languages. This is untrue. Even after learning the five proposed languages the church will still follow Paul's counsel: Him that is weak in the faith receive ye, but not to doubtful disputations (Ro 14:1). Incidentally I've had exposure to the five languages (Copts just told me their Bible is the same). I've also read or listened to books on tape of biblical critics like Karen Armstrong (A History of G-d), David Greenberg (101 Myths of the Bible) and Robert Eisenman (James, the Brother of Jesus).

For my writing there was a psychology book explaining that people are judgers based upon rightness, fairness, logicalness or a rational combination of the three which worked into Jungian Astrology. After attending the Inner Space Course in Kaballah (Sandy Springs, GA) and reading S. Acharya's (The Christ Conspiracy) and Linda Goodman's (Love Signs) I published my astrological take on I Cor 13 in The Oracle magazine and included it in my first book, Understanding the Bible where I found the purpose of the Bible to be removing all authority from the Sadducean temple authorities. Pierre Krijbolder's (Crucifixion and Turin Shroud Mysteries Solved) found my language of metaphor to be the primary biblical methodology, after which my study focused on finding literal cross-references supporting my understanding of Biblical metaphor. Sam Harris in his debates found the lynchpin of Lk 19:27 for me, and my second book, Sin, Sacrifice, Heaven and Hell was published concluding that Rome created Christianity, authoring the gospels to seek the permanent destruction of Israel.

This current book is designed to tease apart the motives of Herodian Paul and the Claudian and Cassian families of Rome. Paul wanted to remove the authority of the temple leadership to create one church. Claudians, like Caesar's Mark Anthony (Marcus Antonius), wanted to support Herodians like Paul to ensure peace and taxes. Mark Anthony killed Cassius whose family, remaining in power in Rome and later in Paul's Antioch, had love for neither Herodians nor non-Romans. Herod attempted to befriend the Cassians, but his attempt eventually failed (source: me) with the destruction of Israel and deaths of a million and enslavement of 20,000 Jews building the Roman coliseum (p22 Acts A New Vision of the People of G-d, Gerald L. Stevens 2017).

My belief as a gnostic catholic is that our creator stirs passions of love and hate from age to age creating that which excites us most until we find peace. Ray Shortell takes his motto from the Bible: You shall know the truth, and the truth shall make you free (Jn 8:32).

Made in the USA
Monee, IL
03 February 2020